Also by Patricia Angadi

THE GOVERNESS
THE DONE THING
THE HIGHLY-FLAVOURED LADIES
SINS OF THE MOTHERS
PLAYING FOR REAL

and published by Black Swan

Turning the Turtle

Patricia Angadi

BLACK SWAN

Originally published in Great Britain by
Victor Gollancz Ltd

PRINTING HISTORY
Gollancz edition published 1991
Black Swan edition published 1992

Set in 11/12pt Linotype Melior by
County Typesetters, Margate, Kent

Black Swan Books are published by Transworld Publishers Ltd,
61–63 Uxbridge Road, Ealing, London W5 5SA, in Australia
by Transworld Publishers (Australia) Pty Ltd, 15–23 Helles Avenue,
Moorebank, NSW 2170, and in New Zealand by Transworld
Publishers (NZ) Ltd, 3 William Pickering Drive, Albany, Auckland.

Made and printed in Great Britain by
Cox & Wyman Ltd, Reading, Berks.

For the prototype of Tom Turtle – with love.

1

The marriage of Thomas Turtle and his wife, Harriet, finally split up over an unimportant argument about his parents. Not really a very logical turn of events, because Tom was not, by that time, sufficiently concerned about his background or his parents to care, actively, what others might think of them.

'I think,' Harriet said one very fine April morning, 'that I shall redo the sitting-room. I can't stand the squalor of it as it is. We need a bit of architectural cleanliness and some Conran curtains. And I can no longer put up with that ghastly old chair that you and the cat have wrecked.'

Tom laughed: 'But I don't sharpen my claws on it; how do I wreck it?'

'You crash into it.'

Tom pictured himself crashing into it and rather liked the description. 'I like the ghastly old chair and the boring old curtains; they make me feel safe.'

Harriet's expression of venom would have silenced many an adversary. 'Safe to sloom about and turn everywhere into a shambles you mean.'

Tom smiled. 'I can think of much better ways to spend all that lovely money of yours,' he said.

'Actually, I was considering having the sitting-room refurbished at the magazine's expense, and then have it photographed and written up. I think they'd wear it.'

She was the interior design editor of an expensive glossy with a salary far in excess of Tom's university lectureship.

Tom snorted his disgust. 'What a bloody waste,' he said, sliding further down in the ghastly old chair and biting into his late breakfast toast and marmalade. 'Money to the rich from the richer; it's obscene; shouldn't be allowed. Now if you really wanted to do some good to somebody, you should get your horrible glossy to pop over to Wembley and do up my poor old mum's . . .' he paused fractionally to denote inverted commas, '. . . "lounge" and photograph that.' He laughed out loud at the idea of Harriet's bosses' reactions to the idea.

Harriet stood rigidly beside the table that was still cluttered with the remains of breakfast. She was steely with anger. 'I scarcely think,' she said, 'that all that wrought iron, gold taps and the plate collection on the wall would appeal to the readership.'

Although she had echoed his own thoughts, Tom felt an irrational prickle of irritation.

'It wouldn't appeal because your lot have been busy telling them what should or should not appeal; instructing them on what is and what is not good taste, whatever that may mean. You're such a bloody cultural snob; one minute brimming over with classi-cal swags and Osborne and Little curtains, and the next, stark with pillared post-modernist rubbish.'

'If I'm a bloody cultural snob,' Harriet's voice had risen to a strident shout – the conceit of the man, he was impossible, with his smug intellectual logic and the condescendingly patient tone of voice, 'you are a pretentious prick, pretending you don't abominate your parents' appalling taste as much as I do, pretend-ing you don't come from the sort of background that you do . . .'

'Ah,' Tom interrupted her, smugly. 'Now what exactly do you mean by pretentious? The gaps in your expensive education are showing, my dear – you don't, of course, mean pretentious, you mean *hypocritical* which, anyway, doesn't describe me because I adore flaunting my working-class background. Take your parents' mansion in Monken Hadley – now that *is* pretentious.'

Harriet found her self-control on the verge of abandoning her completely. She shook with rage. 'You are perfectly willing, I note,' she screamed, 'to live off these pretentious snobs for the whole of your married life . . .'

Tom raised his hands in defence. 'Well then, in case your bosses won't do up our place free of charge, let's save some of the family money and leave the sitting-room as it is.'

He smiled a warm, conciliatory smile and was actually very surprised when a plate hit him on the head. Apart from the fact that the plate broke on impact and caused him considerable pain, he had never known Harriet to lose control of her temper to this extent before. He sank even lower into the chair and shielded his head with his arms as more china and other objects flew across the room until Harriet finally stood, panting with the exertion, and shouted, 'That's it! I've finished with you, you bastard. I'm leaving for good and this time I shan't be back.'

Tom heard the banging and crashing of drawers pulled on to the floor and cupboard doors slamming, and a deep sense of melancholy settled over him as he dabbed at the blood on his forehead with a tea towel that he'd been able to reach without moving from the chair. Why? he wondered unhappily; how many times must this sort of scene repeat itself when things had started out so well?

Harriet filled a small case with anything that was to hand, not bothering with little things like toothbrushes

9

and knickers. This was it. There was no going back. She just needed to escape the mess and misery of the present situation.

She stormed downstairs, the case banging against the banisters. Usually, it was about now that she began to think, is all this upset worth it? Do I really want to start over again? But this time was different. It had never been quite like this before. It was make your mind up time; time to take the plunge and go, once and for all. She slung her coat and bag over her shoulder and made for the garage remembering with slight panic that recently she had had to get Tom out to help her with the up and over garage door. It had taken to sticking half-way, and needed two to manhandle it upwards. That could spell disaster.

Full of determination and with teeth gritted, she made a fierce upward onslaught on the door and, to her delighted amazement, it positively leaped up and over without a trace of let or hindrance. She was as free as a bird to fly straight out of the old life into the new. What a miracle. Fate was assuredly on her side. Her spirits soared, along with the garage door, and she drove the VW Golf out through the gates of Laurel Lodge, Friern Lane, Whetstone. It was all so simple; why had she delayed so long? Pick up the children from school at four and drive straight over to mother. Could stay there for as long as it took to sort things out, and then have the freedom to do exactly what she liked. Much happier for everyone.

For Tom, the situation was rather different. It wasn't that he was unduly upset by the departure of Harriet. She was always departing and returning some time later to try the marriage out yet again, but the plate throwing was something rather different and he was

10

left with an unpleasant sense of failure which soured everything.

It *should* have worked out satisfactorily, this marriage. They had discussed it endlessly, in an atmosphere of calm, good-natured analysis. One could have called it philosophical enquiry; something they were passionately involved with at the time, both having read PPE at Oxford, which was where and how they met. He had liked Harriet because she was so absurdly sure of herself. He was amused by her snappish petulance; it had appealed to him from the moment they first met.

It was at Oxford that he felt he had finally left his childhood and adolescence behind, along with the long hard climb to university. He had moved on to a different plain altogether; Wembley to Oxford was a considerable transposition. Harriet saw his background as a comically humble one from which he had crawled with relief, while he looked back on it with affection and some respect. On her side, it was her grandfather who had made the money and her father who had been elevated to the House of Lords so, as Tom often pointed out, she'd had two generations to adjust.

'A clash of cultures,' Harriet said.

'Nothing of the sort,' said Tom.

The feeling of dejection and let-down after Harriet walked out continued to overwhelm him as he sat on at the uncleared breakfast table in the sunny, well-ordered house.

This gave way to a great rage at the downright bloody stupidity of the whole thing. Selfish bitch – forever wanting to sweep away the present with some new, mad scheme that took her fancy. Forever demanding change without considering whether the change would profit anyone else. He thought of the children with a new wave of despair: she would sweep them

11

along with her without the slightest difficulty. The dynamism and self-assurance that had attracted him to her in the first place worked equally well on whoever she met. Off with the old and on with the new.

He didn't stand a chance with the children: a boring old college lecturer wedded to his profession, so that, much as he loved them, time taken up by family meant time stolen from work. Whereas Harriet would sail out of the marriage in an aura of courageous and effervescent excitement which all would admire and applaud – including the children. She would inform everyone how boring and how impossible Tom was, and they would believe her. She was, after all, such fun! Exhilarating to be with! Her enthusiasm and animation were infectious!

Tom got up with a suddenness that made the cat bolt for the cat flap in terror. He collected all the unbroken china on the table and threw it mightily against the wall. The din was stupendous. At least he felt even on that score: he had smashed more crockery more noisily than she had, even if it had been too late to break anything over her head.

2

Harriet drove fast and rather recklessly, her heart beating unnaturally quickly and her mouth feeling dry. She felt euphoric, as though she had just achieved an outstanding victory – which of course she had. It was mind-blowing; too much to contain on her own; must share the triumph. Couldn't take a step like this as though it was just a thing one did every day. Should go straight to the office, of course, but there was no way she could deal with work at the moment; ring up and tell them she was ill; the assistant could cope, do her good to take on a bit of the pressure for a change.

At the same time she was bursting to share the sense of release with someone. So who to visit until school came out? Mother was out of the question; had to work out how to break it to her in a way that wouldn't have her screaming vengeance at Tom so that she would find herself having to defend him. Laura was the obvious choice; celebrate with Laura, that was the answer.

The old school chum: odd how one or two stayed with you through your life; Laura was unfailingly around and the same, no matter how long the intervals in between meetings. She had married Alan Summerson, a successful designer of smart furniture and, although she and Harriet were opposites in practically every respect, Harriet sometimes found Laura's family-orientated ordinariness restful.

'I've finally done it,' she said as Laura opened the door to her. 'Left the bugger, and for good this time. No going back.'

She slumped down in one of the more comfortable chairs that Alan had designed, and took in, with a sense of rising distaste, the air of easy, untidy domesticity in which Laura's place always seemed to bask. She could certainly never live in such a slovenly atmosphere. That was one of the bones of contention with Tom; something she was now free of for ever, thank God.

'Oh God—' Laura looked genuinely distressed. '*Really?* What happened? Tell me all. I'll put the coffee on.'

Harriet leaned her head back on the Habitat cushion and made a conscious effort to remember the various stages of relaxation she had picked up at yoga classes,

13

but it was far too much of an effort, and she brought her head back up with a jerk of irritation.

'Just one of the regular style bust-ups about nothing in particular, but it went very sour and I suddenly decided I'd had enough and threw a whole lot of china at him.'

Laura let out a gust of laughter, and then looked anxious. 'You didn't? Is he all right? I mean, did you hit him?'

'Yes, but he didn't drop to the floor unconscious so I suppose he's all right.'

Laura cleared newspapers and toys from a small table and replaced them with a packet of biscuits. 'Oh dear, poor Tom. And how awful for you; you must be feeling ghastly if you're serious about the whole thing. Sure it isn't just another blow-out that can be repaired?'

Harriet's euphoria changed into irritation. 'Laura dear, you must be mad. I feel positively exultant – brimming over with good cheer. I have finally managed to get myself out of an impossible situation, and I'm *free*, don't you see? Free to live my own life without the constant drag of rows, irritation and despair. What bliss.'

Laura stopped herself from saying what about the children, because that would sound like a criticism. Sound as though she was saying, well, *I* wouldn't want to wreck the children's lives so *I* wouldn't walk out, no matter what. Because you couldn't tell what you'd do in that sort of situation. So difficult to understand other people's crises.

But her thoughts obviously showed through.

'I suppose you consider me a shit for breaking up the happy home,' Harriet said. 'But I haven't got your stamina, and anyway you like Alan far more than I like Tom. He's much nicer than Tom.' As she said this she realized that she did not actually think it: Alan was in many ways worse than Tom, even more smug if that were possible. 'Anyway, I've decided to start a new life before it's too late, and then everyone will be better off, especially the children.'

They drank coffee together and Harriet smoked while Laura ate chocolate biscuits.

'I feel as though a ton weight's been lifted off me.' Harriet sprang out of her chair and pirouetted round the room. '"I feel happy,"' she sang, '"Oh, so happy, it's amazing how happy I feel." From this moment on, Laura, my life will take on new meaning; I shall achieve miracles.'

'You haven't done too badly as it is,' Laura said, unable to resist being slightly swept up in Harriet's exuberance. That was the thing with Harriet, *nobody* could resist becoming involved in her enthusiasms.

Laura brought her mind back to Tom and the children. She had always been very fond of Tom, thought of him as the kind, gentle, humorous type. The two children were both rather withdrawn and seemed always to be under Harriet's spell. Would they walk out with her?

'It's not that I haven't tried,' Harriet said, 'as you well know. I haven't given up without a struggle – nineteen bloody years of it – but I can't take this ghastly assumption that he's never wrong and I always am. Even when he doesn't say it – though he usually does – you know damn well that he's thinking it; you can tell by the odious smug smile he puts on.'

'But you were always such equals I thought,' said Laura. 'Both so clever and so well suited, on a par with each other; I always thought of you like that.' What a great shame that two of her favourite people could not stay jelled together the way they should. 'What will you do? We could put you up here if you need somewhere.'

As she said it, she froze with anxiety at the idea of Harriet and her children trying to slum it with Alan and her and their four. It would be a claustrophobic disaster. She smiled encouragingly and tried to look as though this thought had not occurred to her. Poor things, they would need comfort and sympathy and company.

Harriet veiled the horror that might have shown in her expression at the thought of sharing life with Laura and Alan for even a short time; they had never dared to go on holiday together. 'Oh angel, thank you, isn't that just like you.' And it was of course; always ready with help and sympathy and love. She was a fantastic friend. 'But I wouldn't dream of it; we'd probably be at each other's throats in seconds, with me in this over-the-top triumphant mood. No, I shall descend upon Mother; her house is plenty big enough to absorb us without even noticing it. We can occupy the servants' quarters without making the slightest dent on her life style. She might even enjoy it for a little while, you never know.'

Emma Turtle waited impatiently at the school gates for her mother to pick her up. She stamped from one foot to the other, and wondered if Adam would ring before she got home. Just her luck if he did, and then be put off by Pa's superior way of answering the phone so that he wouldn't dare to ring again. She'd got his number but didn't want to appear keen. But if he *had* rung, then it could look as though she was just returning his call. Not as good as having him ring her, though. She kicked at the gravel angrily; typical of Ma to be late and then airily to dismiss it because she had something important to finish. Just as though nobody else's activities mattered.

The car drew up ten minutes later. Adam was bound

to have telephoned by now. Oh sugar. And why was Ben in the car? Ben always went home by himself, he hated being picked up.

'I've been waiting hours,' she said, getting into the back with furious slamming movements. She resented riding in the back; Ben had not actually quite reached the age when he was allowed to sit in the front, so she could have insisted, but that would waste even more time. 'Why are you here?' she said to Ben. 'You ill or something?'

Ben didn't answer and Emma suddenly noticed that he looked stricken. What was different about him would have been hard to describe: he just looked taut and red-eyed as though he'd been crying. She felt a small seizure of fear: something was wrong.

'Slight readjustment and alteration of plans,' Harriet said briskly, and Emma watched the hard, tight smile in the car mirror and realized no-one was dead or anything. 'We're going to Grandma's for a few days.'

'Why? Is she ill?'

'No no, she's fine, it's me, I need a rest and I thought you'd be better looked after at Grandma's place with me.'

'Oh God, you've walked out again.'

'We had a bit of a row.'

Emma's rage overflowed. 'So you had a row, so you're forever having rows. Why the hell should I have to move to Grandma's because you and Pa have had a row? I don't want to go to Grandma's, I want to go home. I'm not just a piece of your property that you move around with you like your word processor in case Pa gets his hands on it.'

Harriet checked the desire to point out that she had not brought the word processor. 'Don't *talk* to me like that, Emma!' The insufferable rudeness of the child was beyond belief. If she hadn't been driving the car she felt she might easily have hit her. 'Your grandmother has asked us, me and you two children, to stay with her for a few days, and I have decided it would be good for all of us, your grandmother included, if we did just that. If you want to refuse Grandma's invitation, then you can tell her yourself when we get there.'

'Invitation, my foot,' said Emma.

Once they got there and disappeared upstairs to their rooms, she discussed the situation with Ben, who was embarrassed and distressed by turns.

'What happened? Did she tell you?'

Ben turned his back on her in the bedroom he was usually apportioned in their grandmother's large and rather stately Georgian house in Monken Hadley. He never liked to be confronted when his emotions were as unstable as they felt at that moment. 'She was outside when I came out of school and said to get in the car because we were coming here. I didn't ask anything because I saw she was freaked out. I don't know why she's taken us along with her this time, unless she thinks it's final.'

'Oh, final shminal; wish to God it was, at least we'd know where we were then.'

Ben's eyes filled with tears yet again and he started to shake. 'But suppose she pushes Pa out of the house? I wouldn't want to live there without him to sort of keep the balance.'

'Well, you could go and live with him.'

'But being with him without her would be just as bad and she mightn't give him enough to buy a decent house with and living with Pa in a bed-sit would be impossible, wouldn't it?'

'Quite horrific. They'll probably have to sell the house and buy two poky flats.'

Ben lost the wavering control he was exercising and

burst into tears. 'I don't want them to do that. I don't want to move away from the house and live in a flat, and who would have Hamlet and Gertrude? Cats never settle if you move them and Hamlet needs Ma to feed him and Pa to take him for walks when I'm not there.'

Emma hugged her brother. 'Don't talk nonsense,' she said. 'Dogs and cats get over things in the same way that we get over things. It's not the end of the world.'

'It is,' sobbed Ben. 'Whatever you say, it *is* the end of the world, or at least my bit of it.'

3

Tom did not sit long among the breakfast clutter; so many things had to be got on with no matter what bombshell might have exploded – if indeed it had exploded at all. It was possible that she could walk back into the house this evening, or phone to say that she'd be late, or just be late without phoning; she'd done that often enough. And he had been left on his own before when she had taken the children to her mother's for the night, or gone off with them somewhere for a day or two. He had always relished the wonderful sense of freedom he had experienced, having the house all to himself, at those times. So he could be wrong to suppose that, this time, one part of his life had just shut down and a new chapter was about to begin. And would it be so very different anyway? It was important to stop brooding about the whole thing in any case, so he got up from his chair, letting the *Independent* slide to the floor and spread its pages in a heap, and moved to the telephone.

'Lexi? It's me, did you manage to get that article done?'

He hated typing, and Lexi, who attended his college seminars, just loved obliging which left him free to get on with something else. 'No, no, it doesn't matter if you haven't done it yet, really, it doesn't matter at all. Tomorrow? That'll be splendid. Most grateful, really. I've got plenty to get on with. Tomorrow lunch time? OK – well if you could, bread and cheese would do and I'll supply the beer. Good. Wonderful, see you then.'

The day slipped into its normal routine and the sense of failure that he'd felt earlier began to lift. He wondered if he would go into Harriet's room and use the word processor. She was adamant that it was hers and she didn't like him to touch it, even when he had made her see how selfish and unreasonable that attitude was. Of course, Harriet being Harriet, realizing the logic of the argument only meant that she held to her own view with even more obstinacy than before. If she was leaving for good, the WP would be the first thing she'd take, so he had better make the most of it while the going was good.

He went into her room, switched on the machine and found the disc he always used. Typing was boring but word processing was something else: he found endless pleasure in working out layouts and statistics and pictorial charts for his students. There was one he'd started the other day when Harriet was in Leicester.

Hunger overtook him at about three o'clock, and he was startled to see the time. Hamlet was lying beside him, occasionally lifting his head and emitting a growling whine to remind him that, while he had become adept at controlling the bladder, there were limits; his tail thumped whenever he received a glance.

'You're right, Ham, there are more important things to attend to.' He had to eat, in spite of the faculty lecture to prepare and essays to comment upon before the next tutorials. He would have to put his mind to all that later. He'd got behind through helping Lexi choose paint for her kitchen and then helping her to paint it, but you had to return a favour with a favour, and it was pleasantly relaxing to DIY in somebody else's flat.

Anxiety returned when he found there was very little in the fridge he could eat. Why hadn't Harriet said, for God's sake? He could have done the shopping himself if only she'd said. But then this was all part of the stratagem to show up how his inadequacies made her well-ordered life unnecessarily difficult. She actually enjoyed slamming a piece of cold ham and a tomato in front of them all and saying, 'Sorry, afraid I just didn't get the time to get to the shops today, had to clean up everyone's mess in the house on top of the council meeting and phoning the gas people about the cooker which took the best part of the morning in itself.'

Sure way of making everybody feel guilty. Tom had always used barbed banter to restore his own self-esteem: 'Today's harrassed and put-upon career woman making herself felt. Why don't we make a list of all the things you'd like us to do and then we'd do them; it would seem a logical answer.'

Harriet had looked as though she would have liked to run him through with the knife she was using on the cheese. 'You speak as though I could rely on things getting done if we used that method.'

'Why not try us?'

'I should really like to do the shopping if I had a list,' Ben said.

'You can't do the shopping if you can't drive the car.'

'I could do the shopping,' Tom said, 'if you made a list.'

'Make a list, make a list. Why should I have to make a list for you? Why can't you make a list for yourself?'

'I wouldn't know what you'd want to cook.'

'Taking it for granted that I'm going to cook, of course. You could buy something to cook yourself, or even get a takeaway.'

There had been a silence. Harriet was known for her cooking and for the pride she took in it. She scorned help in the kitchen as being clumsy and time-consuming. She ridiculed all attempts by any of them to produce edible food. Even the children, bringing back school-cooked treasures, had been bruised by her smiling, 'That's *lovely*, darling, what is it?' No-one could cook like Harriet and everyone was aware of it.

Tom found a large potato and put it in the micro-wave. Disgusting when not done in the proper oven, but quick. He thought with pleasure of buying things that he alone wanted to eat and being able to eat them exactly when and how he wanted to. What joy. Might even go now – he looked at his watch, remembered that she'd got the car and swore aloud. Gertrude was winding herself in and out of his legs and appealing for food with an almost soundless mew. And if there was no cat and dog food, he'd have to go now, car or no car. He felt in his pocket and remembered he hadn't taken out any money yesterday.

So, no Whiskas, no Chum, no money, bank shut and the nearest cash dispenser must be at least a mile away. A few moments of intense and seething frustration, then the facing up to the new challenge, bringing with it the question of how to deal with the situation in the most efficient way possible. If he took the bicycle, that would mean looking for the pump and probably not finding it, added to which, taking the bicycle would mean he would have to go out again to take Hamlet for his walk. Hamlet was too good mannered to shit in the garden. An exemplary environmentally conscious dog – the gutter or nowhere for him. So, a brisk walk, with Hamlet in tow, to the cash dispenser, then a modified shopping expedition at the local stores on the way back. Shouldn't take more than half an hour, so he could spend the rest of the evening on university work. With the house to himself, he'd be able to whizz through the essays in no time at all: finish them by tonight. Then an hour or so revising previous faculty lectures he'd given to bring them up to date and add a few new jokes to keep the students awake. He became enthused with the idea as he considered it. Satisfactory thinking.

He found the pvc shopping bag with Harrods printed on it, called to Hamlet and opened the front door just as the telephone rang. Answer or leave it to the answerphone? Might be important: 'Hallo?' he said. It was Adam, Emma's latest, and Tom found himself unreasonably irritated.

'She's not here.'

Silence, then, 'Oh . . . do you know where she is?'

Stupid question. 'No, I don't. You could try her grandmother.'

Silence again, then, 'Have you got the number?'

Tom was incensed with himself for making the suggestion when this was the obvious follow-up. He could never remember the bloody number and why the hell should he bother anyway? It would, though, be slightly crass to admit that he didn't know his mother-in-law's number, or at least keep it by the phone.

'Wait a minute.' He put down the shopping bag and searched on the table for Harriet's phone book. Naturally, it wasn't there; not in the drawer either.

'Haven't got it on me; you can look it up: Cheevers, Lady Leonie, living in Monken Hadley. Directory enquiries will tell you.'

He replaced the phone feeling guilty: he knew perfectly well she was ex-directory, but there was no reason why he should make it easier for some oafish boy to contact his daughter. Let him do his own chores.

The shopping operation took the best part of two hours, during which time it had started to rain heavily and Tom and Hamlet arrived back drenched and exhausted.

Tom had bought more than he had meant to: might as well do it properly while he was at it, even if you did pay twice as much at these small local stay-open-night-and-day shops; it was worth it in order to save precious time. He'd bought plenty of tins and packs of canned beer, and these, together with bread and lavatory paper just in case, had over-filled the pvc Harrods bag and been packed into flimsy plastic carriers. The handles of the carriers cut through his fingers and stretched further and further as the journey proceeded, before finally tearing and sending tins clattering into the gutter. It was a miserable turn of events and Tom's spirits were, accountably, at a low ebb as he crawled back into the kitchen with locked fingers, sodden feet and a dripping Hamlet who shook himself liberally in the hall. The whole episode seemed, at the time, to be something of a major disaster.

He decided that the only thing that might revive his spirits would be to relax in a bath for a long, long time. Hot water, strong-smelling, male-orientated bath oil – a Christmas present from Harriet's mother, so expens-ive and rather decadent – would restore his physical comfort and soothe his withered morale. Descending cautiously into the too hot water, he had the sensation of every trouble he had ever experienced being blissfully soaked away and he sank into tranquil oblivion.

The front doorbell, later, jerked him into a violent waking spasm, and he was out of the bath before becoming noticeably conscious. Might be something important: proofs by messenger; Ben, perhaps, not wanting to go to his grandmother, poor wretched boy; why should he be forcibly transferred somewhere else at his mother's sudden whim? Might even be Emma.

Hamlet was in an ecstasy of defensive barking, and the bell went again, far too soon after the first time. 'All right, I'm coming,' Tom shouted, looking for his bath robe and finally winding the towel round his waist. He ran down the stairs, leaving damp footmarks all the way. His wet hair dripped down his face but the towel was not big enough to allow any mopping up. The bell went again, making him jump with the stridency of it.

'All *right*, I'm there,' he yelled above Hamlet's deafening aggression, and he flung open the door to find a small dark girl standing there.

She eyed Hamlet with a look of dread but he was already visible smiling, with teeth bared, and full of wriggling joy at the opportunity of welcoming a new friend.

'I'm so sorry to have rung twice.' Three times, damn it: Tom suppressed the desire to retaliate. 'But I thought you wouldn't hear with the dog barking like that.'

Totally illogical remark: the bell rang before the dog barked.

'Could I talk to Emma?'

'Emma's not here.'

'Oh, isn't she back yet? I wanted to ask her something about the maths homework.'

'No, she's not back.'

25

He suddenly wondered why this person had shown no surprise or embarrassment to be confronting a half-naked stranger like this. Not so much as a sorry-have-I-disturbed-you remark. He flicked his dripping hair out of his eyes and wiped the water off his face with his hand, and began to feel cold and distressingly exposed.

'Do you know when she'll be back?'

Of course he didn't know when she'd be back. How could he possibly know when his daughter would be back? Even if her mother hadn't just wrenched her out of the family home he wouldn't have known when she'd be back.

'No idea,' he said, trying to make the towel more secure round his waist.

'It's rather important; do you know where she might be?'

He remembered that he had already got himself into difficulties about answering this question. 'No, terribly sorry, can't tell you.'

The girl looked distressed, but he kept a hard heart and head. Please go away, little girl, and let me get back into my nice warm bath, even if it is six o'clock in the evening and I shouldn't really be wallowing in a bath at that time of day.

'Well,' said the girl, who was not really so little and had to be all of sixteen, Tom reckoned, 'when she comes back, will you please tell her that Rajini called to find out about the maths homework; perhaps she'd come over and see me. I live down the road, you know.' Tom didn't know, but she smiled at him, including him as one of her friendly neighbours. The situation was bizarre, he kept thinking; why didn't she *go*?

'If you'll excuse me,' he said, making a small movement to shut the door, 'I'm getting a bit cold.'

'Oh *sorry*,' she said. 'I thought you were sun-bathing.' And she backed off the step, waved to him and walked down the path, stopping at the gate to wave again and smile radiantly.

Tom stared in amazement. The rain had only recently stopped; true, there was a faint gleam of damp sunlight, but *sunbathing*? In April?

There was an air of unreality about this whole disastrous day.

4

Alan and Laura Summerson had married in the same year as Harriet and Tom, and they had all met fairly frequently since then, mainly through Laura's conscientious insistence-on-keeping-in-touch tactics. Friends were, to Laura, friends, and as such should not be neglected, forgotten or allowed to drift away. She had admired Harriet greatly at school as being the sort of person she, herself, could never aspire to be: extraordinarily good-looking and brilliant at everything she attempted. An obvious head girl who was admired by pupils and teachers alike. Laura found it difficult to understand why they should have become friends in the first place, but supposed that she had had sufficient character of her own to be a supportive rather than a slavish admirer. She felt that perhaps she'd had a slightly restraining influence over Harriet's more ruthless tendencies.

Harriet was a welcome contrast from the gentle conformity with which Laura, whose father had only recently been promoted to bishop, was surrounded at home, since Laura occasionally found it difficult to live up to all the smiling benevolence of her large, dominantly clerical family.

Harriet might have been content just to remember Laura and Alan in moments of stress, need or anniversaries – she did invite them to the occasional dinner, usually when other guests dropped out at the last minute.

Laura reciprocated eagerly, in a rather flustered manner. She could never hope to do small, intimate dinners – where she often felt rather out of place – as efficiently as Harriet did. Tom, also seemed rather out of place at his own dinner parties. He usually started some intensely intellectual argument to the annoyance of Harriet and her other guests.

Laura's dinners for Harriet and Tom were never a success because both Harriet and Tom were so obviously bored by the other guests and Harriet was not good at hiding her amused contempt for Laura's attempts at entertainment. Tom had a propensity for sitting in a corner on his own at these dos, reading any newspaper or magazine he could lay his hands on. When Laura took the trouble to hide these beforehand, he often fell asleep over the liqueurs.

They might have drifted apart later, when the children arrived, because Harriet and Tom stopped at the regulation two – one boy, one girl – while Laura and Alan went on to have four – two girls and two boys, thus putting themselves into the category of middle-class family couple rather than middle-class career couple.

Alan earned enough as a designer in a firm of furniture makers to make it possible for Laura to stay at home with the children. All very desirable and satisfactory for everyone concerned: nobody was complaining and, in spite of small differences, Laura and

Harriet remained close enough for Laura to be the first to receive Harriet's news of the split.

'I really think she means it this time,' she told Alan when he got in from work. 'Such a shame, I'm sure she could have avoided it with a little tact and tolerance – at least until the kids were a bit older.'

Alan said: 'I can't imagine how she's put up with him for as long as she has. Harriet doesn't like to compromise.' Alan and Tom had little in common, although they enjoyed leisure times together. 'Fond as I may be of the old layabout, living with him must be hell.'

'Living with Harriet can't be much easier. Funny, they seemed to complement each other so perfectly when they started off, I thought.' Laura felt inexplicably sad, as though someone or something was dead.

'I think it's a miracle they've stayed together so long,' said Alan. 'Non-compromisers, those two.'

'So you said before.' Laura was nettled by the slick summing up, more so because she found herself agreeing with it on logical grounds. 'I suppose that's why you and I are still together, because I'm a good compromiser.'

Alan caught her round the waist and sat her on his knee. 'So am I a good compromiser.' He kissed her affectionately then eased her off his knee and ambled out of the room, obviously thinking of something else.

Laura felt annoyed that he didn't share her concern and desire to talk about it. She continued to turn over the various aspects of the situation in her mind all the evening and into the early hours of the night.

When Alan rolled out of bed to have a pee, her active thoughts became vocal: 'I'm very upset by Harriet and Tom breaking up,' she said, resentful that Alan should be able to fall into bed and sleep when she couldn't.

'Huh?' said Alan, fumbling his way back into bed.

'I don't like marriages breaking up,' said Laura, 'because it usually means it's the beginning of a long sequence of unhappiness for a lot of people.'

Alan had perfected the technique of managing the journey from bed to lavatory and back without waking up, so did not answer, and Laura finally fell rather miserably asleep.

'Poor Tom,' she said the next morning, because her mind refused to let the matter drop. 'Hat makes herself so un-do-withoutable that he must be left in a total vacuum.'

'For God's sake,' Alan countered sharply, 'he's surely old enough to fend for himself. I presume Harriet's just had enough of doing everything for him and wants a life of her own. It's not such a disaster, happens every day. Could you be a love and turn on the shower, I'm a bit late.'

'I just find it sad that people can't put up with each other even when they find out their partners don't happen to be what they thought they were to begin with.'

Alan's patience began to wear thin, and he stepped into the shower, hoping to discourage further conversation. 'Tom,' he shouted, 'is a big boy now, and you shouldn't consider him as poor Tom who is about to become one more lost lamb to tuck under your motherly wing.'

Laura smiled a little and shook up the pillows on the bed.

'Oh here we go, criticizing my way of life again,' she said, beginning to laugh. 'All right, I'll continue to wait on you hand and foot and not pity poor Tom if you promise not to mind when I want some time to myself.'

Alan smiled back at her out of the shower without hearing much, but when he left for work after breakfast he put his arms round her and gave her a squeeze.

'I adore your way of life, my dear, as long as it concentrates entirely on me and the children. Can't have you wasting your talents on any lame dogs, that's all. And you can count your blessings that you married a genius who can manage his life competently, however absent-minded and disorganized his wife is.'

'You manage to say the nastiest things in the nicest way,' said Laura watching him brush her cheerfully out of his mind in order to concentrate on the early appointment he had at work that day. 'Bring back some of that nice cheese you found in Soho, I want to do something special for the weekend.'

She walked slowly back into the kitchen. One down and four to go. Taking a saucepan and a wooden spoon, she moved to the bottom of the stairs and beat a tattoo. 'Up everyone, up I say. Breakfast ready, last one down fills the dishwasher.' There was total silence in the house broken only by the sizzle and spit as she laid bacon in the pan. She had a slight stab of guilt at the idea of the heart disease she might be laying in store for them, but she had at least compromised by only allowing them a fried breakfast twice a week.

That word again; was her life truly one long compromise? And did it matter anyway?

Daisy came bouncing down the stairs and straight on to a chair, waiting to be served. 'It's Jewish assembly today,' she said. 'Reuben is going to talk in Hebrew and I'm going to sing "Shalom, Shalom".'

'That'll be nice,' Laura said. 'Remember it's music this evening, so put out your pieces so that we can go straight on when I pick you up.'

'Oh shit,' said Daisy. 'Louella asked me to tea.'

'Please, Daisy, don't use that word. I don't like it.'

'But Max says it all the time.'

'I know, and I wish he didn't, but at least he's five years older than you. When somebody of seven says it,

31

it just sounds silly. Max only says it to show off.'

'I expect that's why I say it. I think it's a nice word: shit, flit, wit, bit, nit, tit; they're all nice words.'

Louise, who was ten, sauntered in and sat down in silence, followed shortly by Max.

'Shit,' said Max, breaking the lace on one of his trainers.

'For goodness sake,' said Laura. 'Can't anybody say anything without using that word?'

'Mummy said you are showing off when you say shit,' Daisy told him.

'So?'

Daisy was silenced, and there was no further conversation until eldest brother, Hamish, emerged: 'Did I hear,' he said, 'that the Tom Turtles have split up again?'

'Harriet and the children are certainly staying with her mother for the time being,' Laura said. 'But I expect it will all blow over before too long.'

'Glad we aren't pushed about like Ben and Emma,' said Louise, with her mouth very full of cereal. 'I like knowing where I'm coming back to each afternoon.'

'But it must be quite nice to have changes like that,' Daisy said. 'I mean if Daddy pushed us off to stay with Gran and Grandpa one week and Mummy took us to see the other ones in the country the next week, it'd be pretty ace, wouldn't it?'

'No, no,' Hamish shook his head. 'It would be a disaster; we would all become psychopaths because we'd have no roots. No matter how awful one's parents are, it's better to have them around because of the security.'

Laura smacked his head. 'At sixteen, you're just about old enough to be tipped out of the nest,' she said, 'so watch it.'

5

Rajini Bhairavi sauntered back from confronting Tom in his bath towel towards her own home. The flowering trees were in full riotous bloom and gave the street a Mikadoesque prettiness that Rajini found rather irritating ever since she'd had the job of making tissue paper blossom for last year's school Gilbert and Sullivan production.

'I'm one of the chorus and detailed to help with the scenery,' she'd told her family despondently. 'I did think I'd get one of the three little maids, even if it wasn't Pitti Sing.'

'Couldn't have a black Pitti Sing,' her brother reminded her.

'Can't see why not,' said Rajini. 'Our English teacher's dead keen on blacks, I would have thought she'd have given me the part just *because*.'

'Rajini, please,' their mother joined in the conversation. 'I don't want to hear this talk about blacks. We are *Indian*, please remember. Your father would be extremely annoyed if he heard you.'

'So what else is new?' Rajini muttered under her breath.

'What did you say?'

'I said I must go to the loo.'

Monisha Bhairavi clicked her tongue with irritation. So important to get Rajini back to India for some long period, otherwise it would be too late. She had picked up such bad habits, seemed to have no notion at all of Indian ways. What man would want a graceless girl like this as a wife? Must get her back without fail, and quickly. Ashoka was behaving unrealistically in his insistence on his children getting this English education. What did education matter if Rajini became an unacceptably vulgar and uncouth person? She had so much to learn of the Indian qualities of grace and charm and humility; she seemed to have picked up nothing, nothing at all of these virtues, in spite of her having got a scholarship to the best north London girls' school; the manners of English girls left so much to be desired.

If only Ashoka had allowed a return to India for the birth of Rajini, she was sure that this fact alone would have been sufficient to instil into her daughter some of those gentle senses. But, because he was a doctor, of course, he had to insist on the importance of western medical advances, so that both Rajini and Ravi were born under the bright, hard lights and sterile conditions of a London hospital, with none of the family around – not even Monisha's own mother. Not a very happy experience with anaesthetic and instruments because of complications. There would have been no complications if her mother had been there to take charge. None of her sisters had had complications and Mother had been there at each one of the births. Ashoka could call it superstitious nonsense if he liked, but there was more to it than that.

Ravi was a little better behaved than Rajini, but then he was two years younger, also at a top boys' school, and with boys it was not so essential that they should be born in an atmosphere of gentle calm, because, of course, their lives would of necessity have to be far more aggressive. It was difficult not to be complaining a little, though in many ways she was better off than many others. She had to accede to that. A beautiful house, a successful husband, expensive furniture and

34

many ornaments and pictures that were the envy of the relations who came from India to visit them. They did, after all, command great respect and she was considered to have achieved a prosperous and comfortable life for herself. She had no real reason to complain, but there were drawbacks, and she had never been able to overcome completely her nostalgia for India and her family. If only Rajini could share a few of her own pleasures and be more respectful to her parents. If only she felt love and respect for her country and her own culture. It was a shame.

Rajini approached Emma the next day at school. 'Your dad's really dishy, isn't he?'

'What?' Emma stared blankly.

'Your dad – I went round to your place yesterday to ask about the maths homework, didn't he tell you?'

'No, I didn't see him. What *do* you mean, dishy?'

'I thought he was gorgeous, so tall and distinguished looking with his hair just going grey like that. He must have just got out of the swimming pool, he was all dripping wet.'

Emma laughed. 'You must be mad, we don't have a swimming pool, and I can't believe you're talking about my father, he's gruesome. We've just left him as a matter of fact.'

'What do you mean? Left him?'

'Well Ma is fed up, spaced out and cheesed off with him, so she's left him.'

'But you? Have you left him too?'

Emma shrugged, feeling suddenly sick and ill at ease. 'Ma took us with her; I suppose they'll have to sort something out.'

They queued up together in the dining-hall canteen. Rajini felt embarrassed and unsure. Did Emma really mind so little? Her father must be shattered.

'Poor thing,' she said. 'It must be awful to have your family just take off and leave you.' She wanted to ask what sort of thing he had done that would merit such treatment but was afraid of intruding.

'He brought it on himself,' Emma said, and remembered her mother was for ever saying just that. 'He's so maddening; insists on being right all the time. That's what drives Ma round the bend, because she's actually more intelligent than he is, but he can always prove she's wrong.'

'My father is like that; you can never argue with him, but of course my mother never tries. She just says you must do what your father tells you, and then does exactly the opposite herself, pretending she didn't understand what he said.'

'Ma could never do that, she screams at him and hits him round the head.'

'Really?' The idea that Emma's mother, whom she had met once and often seen at school functions, would actually be capable of beating her husband seemed remote in the extreme. She appeared to be a very frightening, domineering lady, always in a hurry, immaculately got up, and with a loud voice, but still — beat him round the head? She became further sympathetically inclined towards this sexy, down-trodden man she had encountered yesterday, who had stood at his door with rivulets of water running down him. Her heart went out to him.

'You see he's so *hopeless*,' Emma went on, 'even though he's so clever. Can't organize things properly, like remembering birthdays or keeping appointments or being on time for anything. And Ma is just the opposite. She's amazingly organized and good at everything she takes on; fantastic like that she is, and she's so smart and does everything efficiently and at tremendous speed; everyone thinks she's prodigious.'

'Do you think she is?'

'Yes, of course I do; she's terrific. But I do get on with Pa quite well on the whole when Ma isn't there. I shan't stay at Gran's for long, but my little brother's a bit upset, so I shall have to hang around for a bit till something's sorted out.'

'But he's not so little, is he?'

'Twelve; young enough to be torn apart.'

'But you're not?'

Sudden embarrassing tears surged into Emma's eyes and coursed down her cheeks. Rajini noticed, but didn't like to show that she had and cursed herself for being tactless. Of course she minded; anyone would. She tried to imagine herself in the same postion but found it quite impossible because it would never happen in her case.

There was quite a long silence while Emma gained control of her voice again. 'I do mind of course, because it's upset our lives fairly drastically. It's sort of like a bomb falling on the house and destroying it. But it happens all the time now, doesn't it? I mean hundreds of families split up every day; it's not the end of the world. If people don't get on, they can't be expected to go on living together.'

Rajini almost laughed, but checked herself. 'They can if they're Indian,' she said.

Emma went back home to Whetstone directly after school without informing anyone. Tom opened the door to her and looked overjoyed, while Hamlet went into paroxysms of demented pleasure, squealing, licking her face when she bent down to greet him and finally skittering round the hall to fetch a bone or a stick or a ball – anything at all to present to this beloved person, lost for all of two days. Emma was pleased to dissipate her own emotions by hugging and kissing him rather than her father.

'Just came to collect some things,' she said.

She saw Lexi hovering in the background with a sheaf of papers and was instantly furious. What was *she* doing here, the oily skunk? Always hanging round Pa as though he was God almighty and she was the ministering angel. What a slithy tove she was.

'We're just going to have tea,' said Tom. 'Want some?'

'Don't have time.' Silly, because she was starving, and there was no need to get back straight away; Ma wouldn't even notice she wasn't there. Probably wouldn't be there herself come to that.

Tom put his arm round her shoulders. 'Come on, I've got some hot cross buns.'

'But it isn't Good Friday.'

'I know that, but it doesn't stop me eating hot cross buns.'

Lexi looked incensed: she had bought four buns – two each.

'Make the tea, Lexi, would you?'

Tom and Emma went into the sitting-room together, with Hamlet still pretending he was young enough to play with a slipper he'd found under the sofa. Emma looked round with a sense of shock: after such a short time at the elegant Cheevers' household, she actually noticed the untidiness all round her. Nothing at all seemed to be in the place that it should be in: some books were in the bookcase, but many more were on the floor and they shared space there with cushions, mugs, plates, shoes and various articles of clothing. Tom also seemed to be mending the big station clock he had brought back from one of his lecture tours, on the floor; bits were scattered everywhere.

'God, Pa, the place is a tip. How do you get it into this sort of mess so quickly?'

'It isn't easy,' Tom said, tipping a pile of jumbled

essays off a chair to join the shambles on the floor. 'Needs a great deal of practice.'

Emma remembered hearing her mother telling Grandma Cheevers that their Mrs Stark, who cleaned up for them twice a week and did the ironing, would probably now be coming to Grandma's while they were there. She suddenly gave Tom a hug before slumping on to the sofa. 'There isn't a thing out of place at Grandma's,' she said, and they smiled together.

Lexi hovered, sullenly. 'Shall I do further copies of the lecture on the processor?' she asked. She had put all four hot cross buns out for them without taking any for herself.

Emma laughed. 'Use it while you can. Ma said this morning that she was going to fetch it tomorrow.'

Tom curbed the 'mean old bitch' that nearly escaped; he was not going to resort to vilifying the enemy – that was her ploy. He looked over at Lexi. 'So we'd better do just that: copies galore while we've got the chance.'

'It *is* hers,' Emma said, rather sharply.

'Of course it's hers, so is practically everything else in the place.'

There was silence while they buttered their buns, then, 'Are you staying?' he asked.

'Er – Ma's expecting me back to supper.'

'Ah, then of course you must go.'

The recent air of cosy sympathy they had shared waned a little as Emma went up to her room to collect a few more things. She wondered what to take and what to leave: a week's supply of clothes? A month's? A lifetime's? She packed her alarm clock, her teddy bear, her photograph of Tom and Harriet on a beach in Greece, six pairs of knickers, three shirts and a few bottles of body lotion, shampoo and pimple cream.

'Bye,' she shouted as she swept through the hall on

39

her way out, giving Tom no time to react other than to look up from mending the clock.

Back at the alternative home, she made her way round the side of the house into the extensive garden where her grandmother was snipping at obtrusive undergrowth.

'You're very late,' said Grandma, peering through the greenery. 'Ben has been in for some time. If I had known you weren't going to be in for tea I wouldn't have asked Mrs Mann to make a cake.'

'Sorry; I had to collect some things.'

'Collect some things?' Leonie Cheevers looked as though this statement was quite beyond her comprehension. 'Well I don't know where your mother has got to. She never tells me anything of course; makes it very difficult to know how many to cater for. Dinner will be at half-past seven, so please don't be late. Mrs Mann is doing one of her cheese soufflés and she would be most upset if you kept her waiting. Soufflés collapse if they aren't served immediately, you know.'

Irritating to be surrounded by such precision, but Mrs Mann's soufflés were even better than Ma's. And anyway Ma hadn't had the time to make so many of her specialities lately. Emma thought of her father, ensconced in squalor and eating hot cross buns and things out of tins, and she remembered how pleasant that had been. Both life styles had their different merits; so did you trade in your father for super soufflés, satin cushions, Persian rugs and silver candelabra? Did you have to make the choice?

Later that evening, as they sat up to the elegant table full of sparkling silver and glass, relishing the perfect cheese soufflé, Emma's mind continued to dwell on the contrasts in her life.

'You are absolutely right to leave him, dear,' Leonie said to Harriet. 'I realize that the whole thing will be a

40

ghastly upheaval for you, but you really can't go on in this unsatisfactory way, it's making you ill. I knew from the start it would never work. Your backgrounds were too incompatible. It tells in the end. The money went to his head; just let him see what it's like to have to earn it.'

'Don't be absurd, Mother.' Harriet was exasperated by her mother's stupidity, having had a particularly trying day. 'We've been together for nineteen years after all. Tom earns good money, he's just not practical about it, that's all.'

'Exactly!' Leonie sounded triumphant, as though Harriet had proved her correct. 'Not practical! His sort of upbringing only prepared him to deal with small sums.'

Ben and Emma giggled and Leonie swung her gaze round to them with an air of wounded outrage. 'You may laugh,' she said, 'but you don't realize what distress your poor mother has had to endure. You are far too young to understand such things. If it hadn't been for your dear mother, you wouldn't be in the privileged position you are now.'

'If it hadn't been for dear Pa we wouldn't have been here at all,' said Emma.

Harriet joined in the laughter. 'Behave yourself, Emma,' she said.

6

The word processor had gone; mysteriously spirited away one afternoon when he was at work. So Lexi brought her own typewriter and Tom continued writing in his own, unreadable scrawl. Much preferred to get things down like that, in rough first, so that there were no inhibitions about crossing out and making a mess of something that was a mess already. He hated correcting a typescript; a sin to spoil something so neat and tidy as typing with scribbles and scrawls or, in the last resort, thick, gooey, revolting Tippex.

Lexi was very boring but very useful, and managed to keep her devotion to Tom just below the cloying level. It wasn't that she was unintelligent, just tremendously eager to learn, a characteristic which Tom found difficult to resist: logical discussion and the imparting of reasoned argument was an essential part of his being. It also gave him the sense of doing something useful – it was his vocation. Something that Harriet had found unforgivably tedious.

The fact that Lexi found him attractive and was not averse to showing it was also gratifying. Sex with Harriet had become something that had invariably made relations worse rather than better. Though Tom had enjoyed it because the fantasies he called up when making love no longer involved Harriet; they generally wound themselves round Diana Rigg, though occasionally it was Whitney Houston if things had been going particularly well with his work and he felt invigorated.

Harriet made it fairly clear that the whole thing had become a duty which, while she found it quite enjoyable, took far too long where Tom was concerned. She lost interest after the first ten minutes whereas Tom liked the long voluptuous build up with his eyes shut – something she found slightly humiliating, almost as though he was thinking of something else.

The tension between Lexi and Harriet had always been obvious. Lexi could not abide Harriet who ignored her and probably didn't register her as a presence. Just one of Tom's numerous students, she would think. Odious woman, thought Lexi. She doesn't deserve someone as gentle and as brilliant as Tom. She obviously has no soul and thinks only of herself. It was easy to see, though, how she had trapped Tom in the first place: adept at laying herself out to seduce and then cling to someone she thought desirable. Lexi had seen it whenever there was an attractive man in the offing; she'd seen it when their friends, Laura and Alan Summerson came round; she was all over those two, especially him.

'I've got to be a dutiful son,' Tom told her after he had been on his own for a week. 'My father is ill, and I've got to go and look after both parents for a day or two.'

He had begun to feel trapped. Lexi found a daily reason to call round, sometimes without even phoning beforehand, so that his mother's call to tell him that his father was ill opened up the possibility of escape from the mess of the house, the inadequate and boring meals and Lexi. It was also an opportunity to assuage the guilt of not having found the time to visit his parents lately. They were so undemanding, that there were times when he forgot them for long periods; and they never complained, which made him feel worse.

The idea of going back to his roots for a few days actually horrified him, but he suddenly decided that he needed the catharsis of switching off from the present edgy atmosphere and plunging himself into the alien lifestyle of an aged couple living in Wembley, who happened to be his parents. It was a drastic move, but a real challenge – like immersing himself in a cold bath.

He took the underground. He had always resisted Harriet's suggestion that they should have a second car. 'Unnecessary and extravagant,' he had said, 'as well as being anti-social. It's a great pity the rest of you don't use your bicycles; it keeps you healthy and cuts down pollution.' He enjoyed the eccentricity of cycling in to work as well as the long, uninterrupted periods of contemplation it afforded him. But now that there was no car to fall back on, there were occasions when his good intentions began to falter.

It was an impossible journey; the Northern line through eleven grim little stations to King's Cross, then change on to the Metropolitan line and Betjeman country to Wembley Park – God, the memories it brought. Hadn't done the Metropolitan bit since his youth; always visited them in the car with the children in the back, making a duty visit to Gran and Grandpa. He was pleased that neither of the kids ever made a fuss about the visits. Harriet only agreed to come on special occasions, like a birthday, but Emma and Ben responded enthusiastically, even if slightly patronizingly as they grew older, to George and Millie. 'They're so lovable,' Emma once said. 'Like cuddly bears.' 'Much nicer than scratchy old Grandma Cheevers,' Ben told Tom out of Harriet's hearing. 'Her whiskers always scratch when she kisses you. Grandma Turtle is all smooth and soft and wrinkly and she smiles all the time.'

Perfect description, Tom thought as he sat on the underground that day, travelling back to his past – hoping for what? he wondered. A salving of conscience perhaps, and a good square meal? At Christmas these same cuddly parents always came to stay for the three days, Christmas Eve, Christmas Day and Boxing Day, when they would all go to a show together. It was their yearly treat, and only allowed because the other grandmother couldn't bear the sentimentality of Christmas, insisting that they all stayed with her for the week over the New Year. Tom had invariably pleaded pressure of work in order to escape on January the first.

The district had changed a bit since the forties, when

44

George and Millie had managed to put a deposit down on the small semi-detached that was going cheap because of the war. George hadn't been called up because of his asthma and the rheumatic fever he'd had as a child, so was able to keep his job as a fishmonger and later turn the business into a fish and chip shop. He had never had a great deal of ambition, but they were able to retire in reasonable comfort. The idea of moving from Wembley, where both had been born and brought up, was never in their thoughts. 'Wouldn't feel comfortable anywhere else,' Millie said. 'All this rubbish about retiring to Clacton,' George said: 'I reckon it's a fatal mistake.' They agreed about practically everything.

Tom had been a tremendous surprise, born quite late in the marriage and the only child to survive several miscarriages. 'Don't know where he gets his brains,' Millie used to repeat over and over again, 'George says it must have been the milkman,' and they would still chuckle together at the old joke.

'So glad you could come, love,' Millie hugged him as she opened the door. 'Dad's really very poorly. The doctor says he ought to go to hospital, but he doesn't want to, and I don't want him to go. It isn't as if I don't know about nursing with what I learned in the war, and with you here it would make it that much easier.'

The old common-sense attitude, which he had heard expressed so often in his youth, hit him like a breath of fresh air. No money to pack his father off to the London Clinic with Harley Street in attendance, so she willingly put aside her life to make sure that he was happy as well as efficiently nursed.

'Mum, you're an angel, I'll stay till he's better and do all the chores for you.'

Millie smiled. 'That would be a miracle,' she said,

'with your reputation for housework. If you could spend a couple of days, though, it would be a godsend. Couldn't take you away from the family for longer, it wouldn't be right.'

'My dear Mother.' Why ever couldn't he call her darling in the inconsequential way he had become accustomed to calling the bitch-wife darling? She was his darling old mum, and all he could say was, 'My dear Mother'. 'My family don't need me at all at the moment, and you do. I shall stay for as long as you want me.'

He had tried to make the statement without any underlying venom, but she looked at him keenly. 'You've got trouble? Then you shouldn't stay at all. You must get back to sort it out; no good running away. Just pop in and see your father and then go back. I can manage perfectly well.'

He left the explanations till later and went up to see his father.

'Bloody fuss about nothing,' said George Turtle, smiling and looking rather as though he had died several days previously. 'But it's good to see you, lad.'

Tom later found himself telling his mother of the split and feeling as though he were ten years old and relating the story of his unfair treatment at a football match.

'She did a lot for you in the early days though,' said Millie. 'Made you feel at home in the sort of set you moved into after college.' Tom guiltily felt himself wince at the reference to Balliol as 'college'. 'She was always a hard woman, I must say,' Millie went on, 'and as for that old mother of hers, well, she makes me feel as though I should apologize for living. But then, that's the way she was brought up, can't blame her really.'

'Of course you can blame her, bloody bad manners, that's all.'

'Oh no, not really, and Harriet's always been perfectly polite.'

'You're hopelessly forgiving, Mother, you should really learn a little malevolence.'

'Good manners never did anyone any harm,' Millie said rather severely, and Tom felt himself shrinking in years to a mere six or seven. It was all very restful and comforting, and the knowledge that he was needed and appreciated for the following few days was a great restorative.

Ben, on the other hand, back at Grandmother Cheevers, was suffering a crisis of anxiety. He felt suddenly, one afternoon, that he needed to see his father. The idea had never really occurred to him when they were all together. Pa, as a part of the whole system, drifted in and out of life rather vaguely and almost unnoticed. Not anyone you actually *needed* because Ma did most of the necessary stuff like cooking and reminding you about things and getting you up in the mornings. So this whole sensation of needing was quite a new one.

But when he reached home that day after school, the house looked quite dead. He had felt safe and happy as he walked down the familiar street with its large, separated houses, their attached garages and their tidy front gardens. He was at home here, recognizing curtains, knowing who lived behind them, not feeling isolated like he did in Grandma's big house that always seemed to be hiding inside its great garden at the end of its gravel drive.

It was when he came on his own house that his spirits drooped: the garden looked untidy and neglected compared to all the others; something he had never noticed before. Hamlet didn't bark when he rang the bell and no-one came to answer the door. The effect of this on Ben was fairly startling in its intensity:

47

the lower part of his body appeared to sink into the ground, leaving him to cope with a great void somewhere round his middle. He stood on the doorstep alone, abandoned and absurdly frightened that life would never be the same again. Suppose Pa had gone: just taken off because they'd all walked out on him. Suppose he never came back. Suppose he'd *died*. Of grief, of starvation – committed suicide perhaps. And where was Hamlet? Had Pa got rid of him because he couldn't cope?

He turned and walked back out of the gate, down the road and on to catch the bus back to Grandma Cheevers' place, his whole being quite paralysed with foreboding.

7

'Tom dear,' Laura said over the telephone the following week, 'we've been thinking of you so much and wondering how you're getting on. Why don't you come over and have dinner with us on Wednesday?'

Tom's mind switched into overdrive at once: *Laura* asking him to dinner? What was the catch? Alan certainly wouldn't be thinking about him and wondering how he was getting on – could it be that Laura was acting as an undercover agent for the enemy? Surely not, wasn't she one of the few genuine saints of this world, along with his mother?

'Ah, Laura, what a surprise. Thought you might have crossed me off your visiting list.'

Laura had broached the subject of Tom yet again with Alan the night before she made the call and had suggested asking Tom over to dinner.

'Ask Tom to dinner?' Alan had said. 'You must be mad. What will Harriet think? I should have thought, out of loyalty to her . . .'

'And what about loyalty to Tom? Both of them are our friends, remember.'

'Yes, *but* – I mean to say – she was the one who came to you as a friend for support.'

'Which I gave, but I really think Tom is the one who needs support more than Hattie. She did the walking out . . .'

'And can you blame her?'

'I'm trying not to blame anyone, I'm just attempting to consider them as the same sort of people they were before all this happened and to stay friends with both of them.'

Alan laughed. 'Famous last words; it never works; you'll only succeed in making two enemies instead of one.'

'Dear Tom,' she said the next morning on the phone. 'You don't stop being my friend because you don't happen to see eye to eye with Harriet at the moment.'

'Hattie might not share your view; I think she might try to murder anyone who considers me nice to know.'

'Nonsense, you exaggerate; she's not so shrewish as you make out.'

'Laura, you're too nice to be allowed, believing in people the way you do. Thank you, I'd love to come. About seven? And I'll bring the usual wine.'

Laura put the phone down, feeling better for having done something she considered right whatever Alan had said. It was surely telepathy that made Harriet ring immediately afterwards.

'Laura?' The voice was as strong and positive as ever, yet Laura had the feeling that there was

49

something a little different in the tone. 'My dear,' said Harriet, 'I must come and have an unburdening; would this Wednesday be any good? Don't bother about food, I'd come after the kids had been dealt with, say nineish and bring some of that really nice Riesling. We could have a splendidly boozy natter.'

Laura had opened her mouth several times during the conversation, but panic had stemmed any comment that came immediately to mind.

'Well – Wednesday is a bit, er—' Do you keep quiet or are you open and above-board? *Can't* keep quiet, that would be akin to treachery. 'As a matter of fact – er – Tom's coming over that evening, but if you – I mean – do come anyway.'

'TOM? That's typical. Obviously trying to worm his way into your good books so that he can tell you how badly I've treated him.'

'No, he didn't – I mean – I rang him to see how he was.'

'You rang him?' There was a silence that fairly crackled with ice, then 'Oh . . . oh, I see.'

'Don't be so dense.' Laura was angry with Harriet for proving Alan's point so immediately. 'You know perfectly well I'd love you to come too, but if you feel you can't come when he's here, well then, come another day. I can't just stop liking Tom because you and he don't want to live together any more.' Her brave front collapsed as soon as she finished speaking: oh God – had she alienated Harriet for life?

'You like him?' Harriet's voice was malevolent. 'You can have him, with my love and a pound of jam – special offer. But don't expect me to drop in; I don't have the least desire to fraternize. We've nothing to say to each other any more, so meeting would be tedious and embarrassing in the extreme.'

'But surely you've got to arrange things together.'

'Solicitors can do that.'

'What about the children?'

'They can do what they like. Of course they'll live with me but I shan't stop them seeing him whenever they want to, if they ever do; can't really think that they will. He hasn't done a thing for them in years; much too involved with his bloody students.'

Laura despaired, silently. It all seemed unnecessarily sad.

And, as Tom stood on the doorstep on that Wednesday, she began to think that perhaps the idea of contacting him so soon was a mistake; she should have left it a bit longer. A crazy sense of embarrassment hung over the welcome.

'Tom, darling,' – kiss, hug, – 'come in, come in.' Painfully over the top. It was usually 'Hi, Tom' and no physical contact; what was the matter with her? Alan was equally ill at ease; he was reminded of being a guest at a funeral of someone's aged parent where there was the awkwardness of not wanting to appear too cheerful and yet knowing that the bereaved might well be feeling a hysterial sense of release. He affected a sullen lack of interest. How could Laura have dropped them into a situation like this?

By the end of the meal, however, the atmosphere had been mellowed by the soothing effect of good food and wine.

'I'll have to watch myself,' Tom said, in a state of sozzled contentment. 'Living on my own like this, it would be easy to sink into a limbo of self-centred stagnation. I might become, to quote Thesaurus: "a good-for-nothing, a ne'er-do-well, a wastrel, a slubberdegullion" – what a wonderful word that is – Tom Turtle, the ultimate slubberdegullion of all time.'

'An ability to quote Thesaurus from memory would surely excuse you from that category,' said Alan.

'But you're not like that at all,' Laura protested. 'You're full of energy, you do more lecturing and teaching than anyone I know, you never stop.'

'Ah, but it's the other side, the sluttish side that is likely to catch up with me and overwhelm me. With no bitch-wife to nag me and drive me and feed me decent meals and clear up after me, I am most likely to become engulfed by my own detritus. Or I might become a bag lady, escape to the road and sleep rough.'

They collapsed into a fit of riotous laughter, at the end of which Tom found himself crying unrestrainedly. 'So sorry. God, so sorry. It's the drink. So sorry.'

Laura sat beside him and hugged him, quite unable to speak, while Alan looked on in deep embarrassment.

It didn't last long, and soon all three made an effort to separate themselves from each other and from the débâcle.

'I must be drunker than I thought,' Tom said, blowing his nose.

'You're not drunk, you're sad,' said Laura.

'Breaking up a marriage isn't a joke, it's either a shock or a culmination of years of misery,' said Alan. 'Either way it's a bloody emotional event.'

'Went back to my childhood last week,' Tom told them, trying to keep his voice even and bantering. 'My father "took ill" as my mother put it, so I returned to the womb. Quite a nostalgic trip. Mother gently reiterated that I should never have married above my station the way I did.'

Laura laughed. 'How sweet, did she really? I didn't think anyone actually said that any more – not out in the open as it were.'

'That generation still think it though,' Alan said, 'one way and another. My dear old Mama positively exudes

52

the phrase "so why couldn't you find a nice Jewish girl?" without even saying it out loud.'

Tom wiped his eyes and blew his nose, still feeling ashamed and humiliated. He seethed with anger at Harriet being unable to adapt in the way that Laura had adapted.

'Must have been difficult for you,' he said to Laura. 'Have you been forgiven?'

Alan put his arm round Laura. 'They do their best.'

'We did quite a lot of conciliatory work,' Laura added. 'I became Jewish so that the children could be considered true Jews; it has to go through the mother you see.'

Tom considered the oddness of having religion play a part in life; something that had never cropped up between Harriet and him.

'Did it bother you? Changing over, I mean?'

'No,' Laura smiled in a way Tom found very innocent and a little bit annoying: people shouldn't be so obviously nice as Laura was, it wasn't decent. 'Having been brought up by a father who was about to become a bishop, who was the son of a dean and a relative of numerous church dignitaries of the good old C of E,' Laura said, 'I was a bit fed up with it all and delighted to branch out in a different direction.'

'Afraid we're not very kosher,' Alan said, 'though I don't have the guts to retain my non-faith when I'm with the parents; no need to upset them more than necessary. Make the best of both worlds really, Christmas and Chanukah sort of thing: very hypocritical of course. The old people don't like it at all; they're really amazed and rather cross that our marriage has lasted so long when they all said it wouldn't. Denying your heritage, son, throwing away all the good things we taught you.' He hunched his shoulders, raised his hands and spoke in the Jewish comedian accent.

'But Summerson? Where did that name come from?'

'Ah – thereby hangs a tale. Would you believe that my great-grandfather found the name Sonnenschein rather a handicap in England in the nineteen-twenties, so what does he do? Changes it literally to the English equivalent – Sunshine. And can you imagine being Alan Sunshine all through your young school life? It became my ambition to change it as soon as I was legally able; thought Summer Sun a good compromise. Another thing my father doesn't forgive me for, even though he was quite willing to forgive his grandfather for the far more heinous sin of changing it in the first place.'

Tom's spirits lifted with amusement as he listened to Alan talk about throwing off his background in much the same way that he had. But he and Harriet were at opposite ends of the scale from these two easy-going, tolerant creatures; couldn't really be considered in the same breath; they were compromisers, both of them. Naturally they would stay together, come what may.

Laura was continuing her dissertation in a sweet, tolerant way. Tom found it maddening. 'I think,' she said, 'no one religion is absolutely better than another, so you could probably put me down as half-Christian, half-Jewish, half-Buddhist, half-agnostic and about an eighth-Hindu.'

'That makes you two and an eighth people.'

'Right.'

Tom leaned his head back and slid down in his chair. His emotions were out of control with violent swings from laughter to depression, from despair to hilarity, from sentimentality to hysteria, just as though the end of the marriage had somehow swiped away sweet reason and restraint and his mind had taken off. Tragedy had become comedy, or the other way round, and disorderly thinking had taken him over.

Altogether bizarre. He had become embarrassingly drunk without noticing.

'What an absurd collection of people we are,' he said. 'It seems we've all had to escape from our various heredities. Alan from the Synagogue, Laura from the Church of England, me from working-class Wembley.' He smiled round the room at both of them, and then added: 'Except for Harriet, of course, and she's running back into hers.' He finished the wine in his glass and poured himself another. 'Harriet's great-great-great-grandfather was a highwayman – she's reverting back and becoming a highwaywoman – robbing me of my rights as a father and a husband.'

God, he's boring, Alan thought to himself. Who cares whether we're escaping from our backgrounds or not?

Laura wondered how to stop Tom making a fool of himself and irritating Alan into the bargain.

'If you're going to drive home,' she said, removing his glass, 'we'd better replace that with black coffee.'

Tom laughed explosively. 'Drive home? Drive did you say? Ex-wifey has taken the damn car, don't forget; it's trains for Thomas from now on. Booze and buses for Thomas.' And, to Laura's distress and Alan's disgust, he started to cry again with no restraint at all.

8

During the following weeks, Harriet found no time in which either to regret or to congratulate herself on having walked out on Tom. There was far too much to do, and she was able to immerse herself in the organization of her time so that everything could be accomplished in the most efficient way; something she really enjoyed. There was great satisfaction in the act of overfilling her days with hectic but well thought out arrangements, dashing here and there with no time to stop and stare.

'You'll wear yourself out with all this activity,' her mother told her proudly. 'It's not good for you. Why not let others take the strain? People just take advantage when they see you are so capable.'

'It's a waste of time to rely on others,' Harriet said. 'It's far quicker to do it oneself. I'm seeing the solicitor on Monday to get the divorce started.'

Leonie Cheevers felt a small spasm somewhere in her chest at the word divorce. So final and somehow discreditable, however much one might approve of what it was bringing about.

'You are sure, darling? Don't want to give it a little more thought?'

Harriet looked at her mother incredulously. Was she now jibbing at something she had been angling for even before the marriage – all of nineteen years now?

'What *are* you saying, Mother? Of course I'm sure. You know damn well what I've gone through. You surely don't want me to waste what's left of my life when I've got so many things lined up?'

Leonie felt ashamed. 'Of course I don't, my darling. Just wanted to make sure it wasn't all too much for you to take on everything at once.'

'That's what solicitors are for isn't it? To take over the details so that I can at last be free of all the irritations and frustrations. To be absolutely free; what a wonderful thought.'

She left two weeks before telephoning Laura again, although she knew Laura had phoned several times when she was out. If Laura was going to side with Tom then there was no point in contacting her, but the solicitor wanted to know, unofficially, what Tom's reaction might be before they started proceedings. 'Then we can gauge, Mrs Turtle,' he said with the oiliest of smiles, Harriet observed, 'the most profitable approach for us to undertake.'

Such fools, Harriet decided; she could tell them exactly what his reactions would be: he would be delighted to be rid of her so that he could enjoy his disordered, disorganized life without her constant carping. It was obvious. But he would also take great delight in arguing out myriad small points with the solicitors which would alienate them because he would be for ever proving them wrong. This would be a good thing for her, because it would show him up as impossible. But Laura might have heard of his intentions straight from the horse's mouth and that could make it more convincing for the fool solicitors.

She had gone into the office early all this week because of having to take time off to see the solicitors; a lunch with her immediate boss had sweetened him sufficiently to allow her to absent herself now and then. She needed to sound Laura out about Tom which she could just about do in a long lunch hour.

Laura was delighted. 'Oh yes, do come over; what about now? I don't have to take the kids to anything after school and I've got some cold chicken and ham. Come now.'

She immediately started tidying up the rooms; picking books off the floor, stuffing odd socks behind cushions and pairing off shoes before lining them up in the hall. Such a relief that Harriet had got over her suspicions and pique; good for the state of the house, too; she always felt constrained to tidy up a bit before Harriet came. Though the Turtle house obviously suffered from Tom's untidiness, Harriet always managed to make it appear pristine when anyone called.

Alan often talked about the bad taste and disgusting lushness of the Turtles' expensive furniture, but Laura felt that Harriet probably said the same about their mixture of Alan's sleek designs and the few elegant Edwardian pieces she had brought from home. She wanted to be sure that everything at least looked its best when Harriet came.

Harriet swept into the house, looking outstandingly well dressed. 'I'm up to my eyes,' she said. 'Can't tell you what my week's been like: particularly difficult editorial decisions at work which took up far too much time just when I was trying to do an article for the local rag and have meetings with Emma's teachers about her attitude to school. Then the solicitors started to play up. I could really do without that when it's all perfectly plain sailing.'

'What are you actually going to do?' Laura asked cautiously, just in case Harriet would think she was prying.

Harriet looked at her sharply: had Tom's solicitors told her to sound *her* out? Probably not, she decided. For one thing, Tom would be most unlikely to have resorted to solicitors whom he considered, on the whole, as incompetent crooks, and then Laura would never agree to anything that smacked of underhand snooping.

'Well, they wanted me to go for mental cruelty—'

'Cruelty?' Laura laughed in spite of herself. 'Wouldn't that be rather difficult to prove?'

'Not really.' Harriet was huffy. 'I mean the way he just threw money away on things without having an idea where it had gone, for instance. Do you know the telephone was cut off twice and the gas once because he hadn't paid the bills? Just imagine how I felt when that happened.'

Laura remembered being helpless with laughter when Alan discovered he'd forgotten to pay the phone bill, and how furious he was with himself.

'And he does lose his temper you know, and shouts; even hits me sometimes. I really do get frightened and the children are petrified.'

I bet you do, thought Laura. It must be quite shocking for the worm to turn when you don't expect it. She couldn't imagine Tom in a rage, but she could imagine Harriet being able to push someone to the edge of distraction with her aggressive efficiency.

'Anyway,' Harriet went on, 'I told them I don't think that will be necessary. I'm sure he'll agree to anything I suggest. He must be delighted to be free of me; I don't think he'll make a fuss and then I can sell the house and give him half the proceeds so he could get a little flat somewhere. If he does make a fuss, then I shall dig my heels in and sue him for something or other, and if the children don't want to leave the house, I may have to push the mental cruelty thing so that I can keep it and them and he'll just have to go.'

'But that's monstrously unfair, Hattie. I think he would be terribly upset, I think he's already very upset.'

'So he *has* been getting at you. He can't be very upset; he's treated us for years as though we weren't there. Always completely bound up in his work, we hardly ever see him. And that Lexi who trails round after him all the time – don't tell me he doesn't sleep with her. I could get him on that fact alone.'

'Get yourself a drink,' Laura said. 'I'll bring in something for us to eat.' She had to get away into the kitchen to escape from the painful bitterness. How could behaviour change so quickly just because of a decision to change circumstances? Tom and Hattie had never been like this together. Some bickering, certainly, and plenty of complaints, in the same way that she

59

complained of Alan, but this – this was malevolence and it was hateful. Must think of some way to get off the subject, but how? Harriet had obviously come to talk of what was uppermost in her mind. There was no way they could make any other sort of conversation, no way they could gossip and giggle and discuss the disadvantages and inferiority of men in general as they usually did, because now everything they said would be aimed at Tom, and there would be no humour in the slanderous accusations and recriminations.

'Of course he might not agree to sell the house,' Harriet followed her into the kitchen. 'And it might make it a bit difficult if he refuses to move out.'

'He doesn't have anywhere to go, does he?'

'No, but he could find somewhere temporarily, like I have. I mean he's got parents too, and a job. He isn't destitute for God's sake; it isn't a case of a cardboard box after all.'

Laura decided that the solicitors must have influenced her to become as insensitive as she was now appearing to be.

'They've told me,' Harriet went on, 'that I should move back in and make life such hell for him that he would move out of his own accord, but I think I would be afraid to do that; he might murder me.' She gave a short laugh. 'Anyway, he's so bloody obstinate that he would stick it out from sheer pig-headedness and desire to prove a point.'

How could you even consider such an option? Laura thought as she arranged plates and glasses on a tray with rather shaky hands. Bloody solicitors; but how could Harriet not understand and therefore reject their advice out of hand?

'Surely you could come to some sort of agreement yourselves without bringing in all this in-fighting and nastiness,' she said.

60

'You're crazy,' said Harriet. 'Coming to an agreement with Tom means that he will argue each point in pedantic detail so that in the end you find yourself agreeing with and even putting forward ideas that are exactly the opposite to the ones that you started with. Compromise is impossible with Tom.'

Non-compromisers, those two, Alan had said. So what would I have done if Alan had walked out on me? thought Laura. The tray was rattling in her hands because of the shakes in them. Oh God, she thought, I would have compromised like mad, made a complete ass of myself. Don't think about it.

'Let's eat, drink and be comparatively merry for the next few minutes,' she said. 'I want your opinion on this cheese I got the other day.' She wondered if she would be able to talk to Harriet in the old way ever again.

9

Rajini Bhairavi was attempting to get her parents to agree to her going to Emma's party. The discussion had been going on for some time. There had always been a strict taboo on parties where boys might also be invited. 'You know quite well that it is not our custom to allow this, Rajini,' her mother insisted. 'You know this very well already. In Indian circles, yes, because we are then all together as a family; but to allow young people alone together, it is not done.'

'But Amma, this is completely different, Emma's having the party at her grandmother's house and her grandmother's incredibly strict, Emma's warned everybody; absolutely no chance of any hanky-panky, she's already warned everybody about that.'

Monisha Bhairavi raised her hands: 'You see? You see what I mean? The fact that she has to warn everyone! It is not at all a decent sort of party with very unsuitable young people going there. If we were back in India, then you would be betrothed by now, perhaps even married, so that there would be no danger of scandal or hanky-panky, as you call it. Tell her, Ashoka, tell her that she should have nothing to do with these Turtle people; we know nothing of them except that they do not have net curtains to their windows and their garden is very untidy.'

Rajini did her best to control her fury; it was no good being aggressive; just have to work away patiently, perhaps get Appa on her side; he was far more broadminded. She turned to her father. 'Appa, Emma's grandmother is a very important, very rich lady who lives in an enormous house in Monken Hadley. She is called Lady Cheevers and she's the widow of some lord or other. Emma's mother is an honourable. They're fantastically respectable and her grandmother is letting Emma have a small party in this great enormous house and garden and she's going to be there all the time because the last thing she would want is a scandal. She wouldn't *allow* a scandal. It's going to be absolutely proper. Please, please say I can go.'

Her father was visibly disturbed by his daughter's pleading. All things to do with the children he had left for Monisha to deal with, but where discipline arose, and now that both the children were of an age where it had begun to cause some problems, then naturally, as father, it was his duty to uphold it. The truth was, having been in England for the past thirty years and having become a much-respected eye surgeon with consulting rooms in Harley Street, he tended to find that the importance of Indian customs and beliefs had begun to bother him less and less. He felt guilty about this but being a very honest and gentle man it was impossible for him to be the dominant, all-powerful father he was expected to be. He often wished that he could rant and rave at his children when they became too European in their behaviour.

'Your mother and I will talk about it,' he said, giving Rajini a hidden smile, 'and we will let you know later. You have a great deal of serious study to make up you know. We want you to stand first in your exams.'

'But there are no exams now, Appa. There's *plenty* of time, really there is. I mean, I don't go gadding about every night, do I?'

'I should hope you don't.'

'Well then—'

Ashoka took his daughter's hand and smiled at her with a look of total indulgence. 'Amma and I will talk about it,' he said.

Good enough, Rajini thought to herself; he'll get round Amma, so she kissed his hand and went to telephone Emma with the news.

'It is to be expected,' Ashoka said to Monisha in his gentle, unassuming voice, a voice which won him many of the hearts of his female patients. 'They have been born and educated in England and it is to be expected that they will have assimilated the English way of life. This is our country now, we have chosen it and we should live by its laws and its customs.'

'How can you say such things? So disloyal to your real heritage.' Monisha was distraught. 'It is not that I mind paying some sort of lip-service to English ways, that is only polite, but it is when I hear of all these bad things that go on now where the young people are concerned. Do you not agree that things have gone badly wrong for the young people over here? The drugs, the violence, the promiscuity, the way they are disrespectful to their elders?'

'It's important to keep the balance: in India there is more violence, more cruelty, more corruption and chicanery and more hypocrisy than you will ever find over here.'

Monisha got up from her chair and walked to the window in an effort to control her frustration at this perfidious attitude. He seemed to be betraying everything which she held in high esteem, just sinking into lazy ways and taking the line of least resistance: no strength of character.

'Rajini must return to India immediately,' she said, with an untypical insistence brought about by her anxiety, 'otherwise all will be lost. I will go first to find the right partner for her; Mother and Father have already made the contacts as you know. If you cannot come now, I will judge which one I consider the best, then you must bring her over for the ceremony. It is already very late and we may have lost the chance of at least one of the boys as I believe he is about to be betrothed to another. I will make arrangements tomorrow. We must waste no more time.'

'Moni, Moni,' Ashoka put down his paper. 'Please be sensible. You know this is not possible. Rajini is going to university. It is impossible for you to take her to India at this time, impossible for her to have such upheaval this year. In any case, she is not ready for such a step.'

'She is seventeen and you say she is not ready? When do you think, then, that she will be ready? And what boy will be left to take her when you consider her to be ready? I tell you, she must not be allowed to waste her time in these European ways without going home to acquire at least a feeling of her own country.

She must not become just another tearaway Anglo-Indian disaster, I could not bear this.'

She realized that hers was a forlorn hope; though Ashoka would never actually forbid his wife to do something, in the way some of the Indian husbands still did, he would just do nothing about it and that would make it impossible even for the first step of her going to India to be accomplished. It was, of course, *possible* for her to book a flight to India for herself but, at the same time, it was unthinkable. She could not bring herself to disobey his wishes to such a degree. So, it seemed, Rajini was to be sacrificed. What shame and humiliation. Poor, poor Rajini.

Poor Rajini was, at that moment, sharing her satisfaction at the way things were obviously going to go with Emma on the telephone. 'It's all right, Em, I finally persuaded them, or at least my dad didn't say no which means my mum will come round in the end, it's *so* brilliant. I can't tell you how relieved I am because if Dad had thought it wasn't on, then it would have taken far longer to make him come round and I might even have had to resort to some sort of fiddle. You can't imagine how difficult it is because of them being Indian and old Indian customs and everything; totally mad but you can't really blame them, it means so much to them and everything.'

Emma laughed. 'You talk about them being Indian just as though you weren't.'

'Oh yes I know, it's pretty horrific of me I agree, but it isn't as though I'm not really pleased to be Indian and proud of it and everything, just like everyone is, but that isn't to say I can't see what's wrong with some of their ideas. Like, I mean, like you don't agree with some of the things your grandmother sticks up for. It's the generation gap as well as the culture gap, but to go back and marry some jerk they pick out for me – well, I *mean*, can't really imagine that, can you? Not now at least; maybe when I've had a good look round and can't find anyone I like myself, then maybe I wouldn't mind having a look at some of their ideas, but not now, for goodness sake. But the maddening thing is that I do feel guilty when I go against what they believe in. When you're born into something, even when you're brought up with different sorts of influences all round you, you still get this sort of guilt feeling when you don't do what they say you should.'

'Like walking under ladders,' Emma said.

'Exactly. By the way, I laid on the old English aristocracy bit to the parents like crazy because they're always impressed with that sort of thing.'

'We're not aristocracy,' said Emma, 'we're trade, according to what old Brutus told us in humanities. It was really interesting. I always thought we were aristocracy before that; Grandma always makes such a fuss about Pa being working class and us being upper-upper – can you believe they'd be so stupid?'

'I certainly can, you should hear my gran talk about the untouchables and about us being Brahmins – Lingyat actually, which is even better I believe.' They both went into peals of laughter. 'But it's so great your mum actually marrying someone who was working class; my mum would never, never have been allowed to marry an untouchable or even the next step up – can't remember what they're called – never possibly. Will your working-class dad be at the party? I fancy him like crazy you know, and I've got a great idea; I'm going to get my dad to ask him to coach me and my brother. I'm bound to have to retake my As if I want to get to Oxford or Cambridge; I made a total bish of my history mocks. Don't you think that's a brilliant idea?'

'You're crazy, you must be, though I have to say he's supposed to be ace at teaching people, gets everybody through absolutely anything; it's a question of pride with him, he has to succeed in anything he takes on. Positively obsessive he is.'

Ben, meanwhile, was worrying himself into a state of frenzy about the certainty that Hamlet would miss him so much that he would probably die from a broken heart. He was also sure that his father regularly forgot to feed him or take him for a daily walk. He realized that if this happened – especially the daily walk part – then Hamlet could quite possibly die from constipation because of his phobia about not doing anything in the garden. He did not dare to bring the subject up in front of his grandmother who hated Hamlet because he was not well-bred, and would certainly not agree to his staying in the house when everyone was out all day, but he did broach it with his mother who didn't con-sider it of much importance.

'Pa's not an idiot,' she told him, 'and he's fond of Hamlet; he wouldn't be unkind to him.' Always thought more of the damned dog than he did of her as it happened.

'But he might forget without me there to remind him.'

'Ring him up when it's feed time.'

But Ben knew his father of old; you had to go on and on reminding him; once wasn't enough. He'd just put the phone down and forget straight away because something else would happen, and you couldn't go on ringing up every few minutes the way he had to remind Pa when he wanted him to be on time to take him to games or a match or an interview with his teacher or anything. Notes were really no good either, because he lost them or didn't have time to read them properly. You had to be there to say 'Come on, hurry up,' and 'Only five minutes to go,' and 'Have you got your brief case?' every three minutes. He just *knew* his Pa; he might let Hamlet die by mistake because he forgot him. He wouldn't mean to, but he needed someone to look after him and remind him of things.

10

Having won the battle of being allowed to go to Emma's party, even to the extent of persuading her mother to make some bhajis and chapatis to mix in with Harriet's party-type eatables, Rajini turned her attention to the task of achieving a course of coaching from Tom. The obvious plan of attack was to assure them first how wise they had been to allow her to go to the party.

'It was a really great party. Everyone went spare over your bhajis, Am, they positively wolfed them up; much more popular than Mrs Turtle's stuff, and all calling for more. Mrs T was quite offended. Emma and me thought it would be nice to have a proper Indian party next time at our house with the music and everything and in saris. Great idea don't you think?'

'Well, I . . .'

'But their *house*, Amma, is really something else. Quite gigantic with positive *grounds* rather than a garden: lawns and a lake and everything, and they had lights out there so it looked absolutely palatial.' No need to enlarge on the fun they'd had in the garden; couldn't imagine a party at her house being nearly so good, but perhaps they could go on somewhere afterwards. 'The old lady was a bit like a duchess or a maharani really; fearfully regal and proper, rather unreal actually. They're a great family, you've just got to meet them sometime.' Mustn't breathe a word about Mrs Turtle walking out on her husband or bang would go all chances. 'You know Emma's father is a professor, don't you?'

Ashoka Bhairavi, who up to now hadn't been listening, heard the last sentence. 'A professor of what? Which university?' he said, without looking up from the letter he was writing.

Rajini's jaw dropped. 'Oh, I don't know what he's a professor of – history I think. And he was at Oxford – or Cambridge, but I think it was Oxford; she was there too, you know, his wife was; they're both incredibly brainy which is probably why Emma is so good at everything and Emma says he does coaching in his spare time from being a university professor. I was wondering if you thought it might be worth while me having some extra help in history from him, as I'd probably have to retake my As if I want to try for Oxford. What do you think?'

'Quite unnecessary.' Monisha spoke loudly and angrily. All this absurd craving for extra learning would only make Rajini less amenable to a quiet home life; might induce her to become one of those career-seeking girls with no thought for family and home. 'You don't need all these qualifications, Rajini. Why can't you leave that to Ravi and concentrate more on the sort of learning you will need for a happy life?'

'If she has the ability,' said Ashoka, 'then she should give full rein to it. If women can be prime ministers, then they should be given all the opportunities possible. I will talk to Mr Turtle and ascertain his qualifications.'

Perversely, Rajini felt angry with her father for his curt dismissal of her mother's objections. If the situation had been otherwise, she would have waded

69

into an argument with him, but that would have been a bit silly in this case.

'We could perhaps ask some of the neighbours over on a Sunday to have a drink with us, Moni,' he said. 'It would be a good gesture and we could then include Mr and Mrs Turtle so that we might get to know them and also discover whether he could give Rajini some little extra push. It is possible that he knows someone in Oxford who could make it easier for her to gain entrance.'

'Mrs Turtle always takes Emma and Ben to stay with their grandmother at weekends,' Rajini said quickly. 'Mr Turtle can never get away because of his work. Actually, Emma says they hardly ever go out together, him and his wife I mean, because they are both always so busy and their times of work never seem to coincide. But I expect he would like to come because of being on his own at weekends.'

Monisha showed her disapproval in her expression. 'Then you had better make a list of who you want and I will invite them,' she said to Ashoka, ignoring Rajini and jerking her sari irritably back over her shoulder.

'Please Moni, you know all their names better than I do; you know who gets on with who. Much better for you to make the list.' He smiled at her and through her and continued with his letter writing.

Tom was surprised to get the invitation. All very formal, tastelessly printed in gold: Dr and Mrs Bhairavi – at home – Sunday 7 July. 12.30 to 3.00 p.m. He considered sending it on to Harriet, decided against it and propped it on his desk to be refused politely sometime or other. He certainly would have forgotten to answer it at all or to turn up, but Rajini rang to remind him.

'Mr Turtle? This is Rajini Bhairavi – you know, Emma's friend down the road. Are you coming to my

70

parents' party? I do hope you are because my father wants to ask you if you could possibly spare the time to give me a bit of coaching in history for my A levels. He's dead keen on me getting into Oxford and I don't think my grades will be good enough, so I'd have to retake them and I do think I could improve if I had a bit of individual help. It's just that I've got a dreadful history teacher at the moment, I mean we don't get on at all, and that makes learning so difficult, don't you think?'

'Er—' said Tom.

'Oh, *do* come. I've told my parents that your wife and family are never there at weekends so they wouldn't be able to come, but I said I thought you might like to, just for a change sort of thing. You would, wouldn't you? Like to, I mean.'

Tom laughed, and remembered that he hadn't laughed for quite a time now. 'Can't see that I can refuse such a splendidly verbose invitation; will you thank your parents and say I'd love to come.' He couldn't, for the life of him, imagine why he should have changed his mind at the whim of a chatty little schoolgirl. Perhaps it was because the telephone conversation had seemed to dig him out of the unnoticed trough in which he had been wallowing.

'No, no, that wouldn't be proper; you must either write or telephone them yourself because they would want to know why I had been talking to you.'

'What wicked subterfuge. I'll write a nice little note then.'

'Brilliant – that's really cool, and will you coach me?'

'I think we'd better wait and see whether your father asks me to.'

'But he will because I suggested he should and he was really interested. Will you say yes?'

'History isn't my subject and I don't have a great deal

of time you know.' He had no intention of wasting precious time in such a way, but was unwilling to damp down the bouncy enthusiasm; it would be a shame.

'Oh please.' There was a great deal less bounce in the voice.

'We'll talk about it at the party.'

What a funny little thing she was; so unlike his laid-back, unimpassioned daughter. Could these two really be friends? Very un-Indian, he thought, Indian girls were surely shy and unassuming. He checked himself, guiltily, for harbouring such a clichéd, racist thought. 'See you then, then,' he said.

'Then, then,' said Rajini, her voice bouncing back to its original timbre. The whole thing, to her, was now satisfactorily and neatly set in motion.

'Bit of a live-wire, that young Indian friend of yours,' Tom said to Emma when she dropped in on him to take more belongings over to her grandmother's house.

'Who? Oh, you mean Rajini? Why? What's she been doing?'

'She rang to see if I'd coach her for A levels.' Better not mention the invitation; unnecessary.

'She did? What a cheek. She's got a thing about you, thinks you're sexy.' She went into a paroxysm of laughter. 'Can you imagine that? She's really weird, that girl.'

'There is nothing weird about a young girl thinking me an attractive male person,' he said, smiling. 'You're just too close to me to see it.'

'Oh Pa — you know quite well you're a hopeless old layabout, anyone less sexy I have yet to meet. I presume you're going to put her firmly in her place and tell her to get lost?'

72

'I haven't decided. I'm in need of some adoration and admiration at the moment, lacking it, as I am, from any other quarter.'

'Don't be so wet, you can't go blaming it on us; just because you're flattered by the attentions of an idiot like Rajini; it's mean. Wait till I get hold of her, I'll tell her where she gets off.'

'But I like being flattered by the attentions of absolutely anybody these days I find.'

Emma exploded with exasperation. 'Stop being so sorry for yourself. It's your own fault. You brought it all on yourself.'

Her words, coupled with her manner, were so exactly what Harriet must have passed on, that Tom gave a guffaw of laughter, in which Emma did not join.

'Well, it's true, isn't it?'

Rage blotted out the humour. The bitch-wife had got them totally indoctrinated; they believed anything she let drop, and she was usually subtle enough to let comments like this slip out in an unconcerned way during conversation. It was no laughing matter, but to remonstrate now would seem like petty protestation.

'There are two sides,' he said.

'Of course,' said Emma without looking as though she believed it. 'But for goodness sake don't lap up Rajini's songs of praise. She's inclined to fling herself at all and sundry; you might find yourself lumbered.'

It could have been bloody-mindedness that induced him to agree to the arrangement: irritation that his own daughter should be considering him with such scorn; it could have been that. Or it could have been the challenge of bringing himself down to teaching at a pre-university level – something he had never done before. It could, possibly, have been because he was flattered by her adulation, however motivated. There were all sorts of arguments as to why he found himself sitting with Dr Bhairavi, a few days later, discussing fees, methods of approach and university entrance.

'If there was some way of recommending her for entrance – you know many Oxford people I expect?'

The devious old reprobate. 'I'm afraid entrance to Oxford is on merit, not on influence.' Not exactly true, but there was no way he felt that *he* could influence anyone.

'Of course, of course, but if you were able to assess her ability, you would be able to vouch for her should she reach the required standards, this was all I was thinking.'

'This I might be able to do.' For all the difference it would make.

'I would particularly like her to make use of the education she has already had, and she seems a clever girl; stands top in most subjects I am told. Though she does not take much interest in the scientific subjects, it would seem there is much promise on the arts side which of course would give her proficiency in those subjects better suited for women.'

'Of course.' He surely had been here long enough to have imbibed a smattering of women's rights movements by this time? But no sense in arguing the point now.

'Your subject is history I believe?'

'One of them,' Tom said, coming to the conclusion he did not want to teach the daughter of this obviously bigoted man: couldn't imagine why he had even considered it.

Ashoka Bhairavi smiled. 'Only one of them? Your degree is not in history then?'

Tom became illogically incensed. 'My degree was in philosophy, politics and economics,' he said returning the smile with controlled venom, 'which means I could possibly help her with nineteenth-century sociology and economics if that was the subject of her special

74

study.' He knew that a few specialist details would probably floor a man like Bhairavi.

'Please, I don't wish to appear impolite. Perhaps you have not the time to waste on such a small task?'

Equally illogically, Tom immediately considered the extra money and the new challenge. 'I don't have much time, it's true, but as you live so near I'm sure I could manage an hour here and there when Rajini could come in for a spot of tutoring if you should wish it.'

'Come to you? That would not be so easy. I thought, perhaps, you could come here?'

Back again went the pendulum. No way was he going to wait upon them. 'Afraid I couldn't do that; have to have all my books and notes to hand. Very sorry but . . .'

'No, no, I understand perfectly. I am sure it could be managed. Let me talk with my wife and she will telephone you to find out when would be a suitable time for both of you. I am so much obliged to you, Dr Turtle.' Given him a doctorate now, it seemed.

They parted on superficially amiable terms, with Tom wondering what he had let himself in for or, more to the point, why he had let himself in for it. Well, give it a try; he could always back out of it if it didn't work.

11

As each day passed, luxury living in the Cheevers' stately home became more uncomfortable for everyone. The air was steamy and verging on an atmospheric explosion.

'You really must do something,' Leonie told her daughter. 'I can't ask Mrs Mann to cater for everyone like this for much longer, never knowing when you're going to get home late from the office: she's not up to it. It's not fair on her. You should tell the magazine that you'll only work proper office hours – nine till five like everybody else.'

It would be funny if it wasn't tragic, Harriet thought: mustn't upset the hired help, whatever else one did; that was unthinkable. If anyone had to go, it was the daughter and grandchildren, not the employee.

'So what do you want me to do, Mother? Camp in the garden? Move into a cardboard box?'

'There's no need for sarcasm, Harriet. I would have thought you would be anxious to be on your own with the children instead of planting yourself on me for an unpredictable period of time. Surely your solicitors can get him out of your house so that you can go back there. I mean, after all, you need the house because of the children.'

Was it any good trying to explain divorce proceedings to her? Harriet thought not; she was not too clear herself and immediately became enraged with the solicitors because they had not explained it lucidly, nor did they seem to have done anything at all as far as she knew. Bloody incompetence.

'Don't worry, we'll move into a hotel tomorrow until things are sorted out.'

'Don't be insulting. Of course you can't move into a hotel, you don't seem to be considering the children at all – can you imagine what they would feel? It just seems to me that Tom is getting the best of everything when he is the one to blame. Won't he do the decent thing and be found in bed with someone by a chambermaid?'

Harriet laughed in spite of herself. 'You are hopelessly

out of date, Mother, nobody minds anyone being found in bed with anyone these days.'

Not quite true, of course; you could still get a divorce for adultery, but there was no way she was going to give him the satisfaction of suggesting she was the guilty party when she wasn't, and Tom would take care that she couldn't prove her suspicions about him either.

'More's the pity,' Leonie said. 'A little old-fashioned morality wouldn't do anybody any harm.'

I can't stay here a day longer than I have to, Harriet thought, or my soul will be utterly destroyed. But where the hell shall I go?

After a particularly frustrating day at work, she rang Laura from the office the following evening, but got Alan.

'She's not in I'm afraid; out at one of her boring old evening classes – oh I don't know, yoga, art appreciation, aerobics, whatever. Can I give her a message?'

'Not really. I have to talk to someone, got to move away from Mother or I shall go mad.'

'It must be dire; why not come over and talk to me? We could drown a few sorrows together. And Laura will probably be back soon.'

Harriet accepted the idea and dialled her mother's number with foreboding to say she would be out, preparing herself for further castigation. God, what a bore it all was. The relief she felt when Emma answered was exquisite. 'Oh darling, thank God it's you. I'm going over to Laura and Alan; I might stay the night as it's Friday and I don't have to play chauffeur to you two. Will you tell Grandma for me? And keep an eye on Ben.'

Emma groaned. 'It's so unfair, making me baby-sit like this while you go out and enjoy yourself. And Grandma's bound to shout at me and give me a lecture on how impossible you are, when I tell her. I think I'll go back home and stay with Pa and get a bit of peace.'

'Don't be absurd, you know quite well you couldn't stand the chaos for five minutes.'

'Well, I can't stand this place much longer, it's so boring.'

'You're to look after Ben tonight. We'll talk about it tomorrow.'

Any more hassle and she felt she might actually cry. The whole situation had somehow got out of hand and she felt out of control and depressed. 'Please, Em, I'm about at the end of my tether.'

Emma heard the agitation in her voice and realized that she was. 'All right, just this once,' she said, a little subdued because she never remembered her mother ever being defeated by anything. It frightened her slightly.

Harriet set out at once for East Finchley, where the Summersons lived. What an area, she thought to herself. She prided herself on her ability to judge people by where they chose to live, considering her own choice of the more spacious, more countrified area of Whetstone and Totteridge to be honest and sensible. Her own house, built in the early thirties, had no side about it at all; it was big, comfortable and fairly luxurious; quite different from the Summersons' late-nineteenth-century terraced house.

As she drove through the rush-hour city traffic, she found herself considering the marked difference between the kind of houses and districts in which she and Laura had settled. East Finchley was, to Harriet, a milieu of intellectual snobbery, settled in fairly recently by those who existed, with difficulty, on middle-class incomes; those who couldn't afford to live in, and so looked down on, the smugness of

Hampstead Garden Suburb, the theatricality of Hampstead proper and the well-read prissiness of Highgate.

When she finally reached the house after a frustrating crawl, stop, crawl, stop journey, it took further considerable time to find a parking space, which convinced her of how right she was to live right away from the stress of the city. It might take longer to get there, but at least you left some of the pressures behind you.

Laura had still not returned when Harriet finally arrived on the doorstep and Alan let her in. The four children were draped over every available chair in the sitting-room, watching television. Books, clothes and other paraphernalia were everywhere, along with crisp packets, coke tins and chocolate wrappers. Harriet shuddered and wished she hadn't come; it reminded her of having to clear up after Tom. There'd be no more of that sort of squalor once she'd got him out of her house; she wondered how Alan could stand it as he'd always seemed an ordered sort of person.

He shut the sitting-room door quickly and guided her down to the studio, built out into the back garden. 'My God,' he said, 'kids are insensate sometimes – most of the time actually, at least mine are.'

'Mine likewise,' said Harriet, thinking of Tom.

'The chairs may not be so comfortable in here but—'

'But beautifully designed.'

'Thank you,' Alan smiled. 'You must have read some of my ads.'

The black and white of the room was balm to her soul. 'What glorious peace,' she said, sitting down on a black pvc chair. 'Exactly what I need especially if it's coupled with a vodka and tonic. I don't think I can put up with one more minute of mess, hassle and argument.' She studied the drawings and layouts on the clean, uncluttered architect's table. 'Promise you won't criticize me or argue with me tonight, Alan. I've had enough criticism and aggravation recently to last a lifetime.'

'I would never dare to argue with you, Harriet.'

'I don't think that's a compliment; am I such a dragon?'

'Intelligent, high-powered dragons are the salt of the earth, it's just not wise to argue with them because their fire would consume you.'

'What am I going to do, Alan?' she said, taking her drink from him. 'All I ask is that I may be allowed to rid myself of my impossible husband and get some sort of order back into my life and I'm being thwarted at every turn. Incompetent solicitors, ridiculous laws, much better if we'd stuck to the old system of guilty parties.'

'But then you'd have been the guilty party for walking out and you wouldn't have got anything – no house, no children, no nothing.'

'I wouldn't have walked out then, I should have caught him in bed with someone or other.'

'Does he?'

'Oh, I think so – all those meetings when he trots off to some obscure town for a night or two, supposedly to lecture – and then there's Lexi.'

'But do you *know*?'

'Not really; never tried to find out. I thought it might make me crosser.' She smiled. 'I haven't had the time to do much gallivanting myself; all those school committees and things . . .'

Alan slid down in his chair and crossed his legs: 'Can't think why you dash around doing all this do-gooding stuff; you're wasting your potential. You are the most fantastic business woman at heart – you could make a fortune.'

Harriet felt her spirits rising. 'But I don't need a

fortune, I've got one. And I have an extremely high-powered job, don't forget.'

'Whether you need it or not is neither here nor there, the pleasure of earning it by working for yourself rather than for idiot bosses is just the thing for dismissing depression and frustration.'

Relaxing there, in the peace and quiet of his orderly studio, he thought how perfectly Harriet blended in with his furniture, and he began to chuckle. 'I think I should hire a photographer,' he said. 'I'm sure it would help to sell my chairs if I had you draped over one in the ads.'

'Pay me enough and I'll consider it.'

Harriet was flattered. He was perfectly right: she should consider launching herself into her own business before it was too late. She had all the know-how.

Alan continued to stare at Harriet, fitting so perfectly into one of his chairs, and thought how excellently he could promote the sale of his designs in partnership with a smart, hard-headed woman like Harriet. He had long been fantasizing about making a break from the firm: getting away from the drudgery of turning out rather boring designs and watching incompetents promote them. It would be interesting to try her out and see if they could work together.

'I might wangle you a job with my firm on the sales promotion side if you were interested. I need back-up in pushing some of my ideas, the board are a bit fuddy-duddy and, once we'd become established as a team, we could set up as a business on our own.'

'Really?' His suggestion intrigued her. 'Would I have a chance of getting into your firm on the sort of salary I get now in mine?'

'I would say it's a walkover with your qualifications and my recommendation.'

Laura burst into the room in a rush of apologies,

pink and dishevelled with the exertion of aerobics and enthusiasm. 'Harriet! How lovely! So sorry I wasn't here. God, I'm absolutely whacked. Drink, drink at once, to undo all the good I've just done myself. What news?'

'Alan's reorganizing my life for me, which is exactly what I need. He thinks I'd make a good colleague in his office.'

'What a wonderful idea; could you fix it Alan?'

'Of course I can fix it; Groper's leaving and Hattie would be perfect for the job. We need new blood and Hattie's would be exactly right.'

The three of them celebrated, pleased that they could concentrate their thoughts on exciting new prospects rather than boring old problems.

'I'll find a flat for the children and me, and leave the solicitors to do all the arguing to get Tom out of the house. We'll flat-hunt together Laura. If I can start something entirely new, I won't have time to worry about the divorce. Alan, you're a genius. With trust in you and God, nothing can go wrong.'

'Not absolutely sure where God's going to come in here,' Alan said.

There was a deal of kissing and hugging all round in which Laura joined, laughingly, while thinking: but Tom and the children should at least have been consulted about this. She felt an acute sense of guilt.

'What do you *mean*,' Emma said to Rajini, 'by trying to induce my poor unsuspecting father to debase himself to your miserable academic level? He's a university lecturer, not a common teacher. He couldn't possibly agree: can't be done I tell you, just can't be done.'

'That's where you're wrong, my friend,' said Rajini. 'It has been done, so there. We're having our first session next Friday. Isn't it *great*?'

Emma was shocked and found herself rigid with anger. How dare he agree to such a request? What did he think he was doing? Couldn't he see that the silly girl was behaving like some idiot groupie? She was furious with both of them. If he was so keen to get girls into university, he surely could have started with his own family. He'd never given *her* any help. She considered a moment, remembering suggestions and discussions over certain school projects in which she had been engaged, but his suggestions had always been inane, hopelessly out of date and opposed to anything she thought herself; not to be taken seriously in fact. How could he possibly be a good teacher? His ideas on things were so boring. Could he really be taken in by Rajini's enthusiasm? Did he really think it was learning Rajini was after?

'You're an effing slag,' she shouted, startled to realize how distasteful she found the idea of considering sex between her father and anyone, while the notion of her father and Rajini froze her into an agony of disgust and horror. She recognized, at the same time, that this distaste was illogical which merely increased her rage. 'Hurling yourself at him like that. Just lay off – I warn you, just lay off.'

Rajini was a little taken aback. 'Hold on,' she shouted back. 'Stay cool for God's sake. If I was in your shoes, I'd be pleased that someone admired my dad like I admire yours.' She tried to imagine such a thing and found it impossible: only old people admired her father. What was Emma fussing about? To call her a slag like that. Her face became hot with fury. If Mr Turtle had been a pop star, lots of people would be drooling over him, even though he was old. There were old pop stars who had fans, like McCartney and Stevie Wonder. Not that she fancied any of them herself, but she could at least understand those who did and so should Emma. In any case, she didn't like Mr Turtle in that way at all, just admired his cleverness and his manner and – well, yes – she did fancy him a bit as well, she conceded, but Emma was being ridiculous.

'Well, you're not in my shoes,' said Emma, 'so mind what I say.'

Rajini tilted her head in the air. 'If you feel like that you'd better speak to your dad; there's nothing I can do about it.' And clasping her school bag to her stomach, she marched off, full of injured innocence.

12

Things were not going well for Ben at school. He found that his mind continually wandered, work seemed boring and he was under a cloud of depression that sapped energy and dulled enthusiasm. Teachers noticed and remarked on it in various ways: 'Come on Turtle, move yourself,' on the cricket pitch, or 'Wake up Turtle,' or 'Pull yourself together Turtle.' Nothing more; as yet, no-one took him aside to find out what had gone wrong. He was a rather distant and solemn boy where teachers were concerned and they found it difficult to probe or to get any sort of response.

He had never found friends very easy; living a long way from the school meant that no-one from school lived near his home. Visits entailed organization, with parents drawn in for getting back afterwards. Harriet was invariably busy and Tom only used his bicycle for getting about. It was embarrassing to have to explain all this to those who asked him to tea. Ben found it easier to avoid getting invited in the first place, which was not to say that he wouldn't have liked to continue school friendships at home; it just seemed a bit too complicated to arrange.

After the split, he went to his Whetstone home as often as he could; he found he could do so about once a week without alerting either Emma or Harriet. Tom was usually out, or so closeted in his study that he scarcely noticed the comings and goings of his son; but this was not really a disadvantage for Ben, because his inner feelings were now so mixed and unclear that he was filled with embarrassment at the idea of sharing them with anyone – especially with either of his parents. He had become what school called unco-operative, what Harriet called bloody-minded, what Leonie called ill-mannered and what Emma called weird. He only went home to make sure that Hamlet was all right. He went so that he could enjoy the tumultuous welcome and the slavering adoration Hamlet afforded him and, to a lesser extent, so that he could bask in the ecstatic purring and back-arched, ankle-weaving behaviour of Gertrude's less exuberant greeting. It was so good to be able to hug and kiss something and not be ashamed of showing how much you enjoyed physical contact. It was absolutely all right with animals, but embarrassing with humans.

So it was quite an unpleasant shock when he found Tom in the garden mending a puncture on his bicycle.

'Hallo,' Tom was delighted. A great seizure of pleasure took him over whenever he saw either of his children these days. He hugged Ben to him. 'How nice to see you. How's everything?'

Ben stiffened almost imperceptibly, but Tom noticed and felt bereft. Would he have sensed such a slight movement previously? Or if he had noticed it, would he not have made some joke about never being too old to have a cuddle? Couldn't do that now because they were on opposing sides, or might be. Ben probably agreed with Harriet that the break up was Tom's fault and could have been avoided.

'Where's Hamlet?' Ben said, yet again filled with fear in case any of his suspicions had been realized: Hamlet had finally become too much trouble so Pa had given him away; he had run away; he had been run over.

'I don't know,' Tom looked round. 'Probably attacking next door's dustbins looking for carcasses. Ham, Ham,' he called. 'Come out, come out wherever you am,' and he whistled shrilly between his teeth.

Hamlet appeared with a chicken carcass in his mouth and, on seeing Ben, brought his prize as a gift of greeting.

Tom looked on at dog greeting boy, having wasted a good hour the night before watching a programme on television about the behaviour of wolves. 'Odd to realize that all that hysteria means he's greeting you as leader of the pack in wolf language.'

'Leader of the pack nothing,' said Ben. 'He misses me like I miss him.'

Tom thought: You can't feel jealous of a *dog*, it would be ridiculous.

'Why don't you take him over to Grandma's then? She's surely got enough grounds for him to run wild in.'

'She won't let me. Anyway, Ma's getting a flat for us.'

'A flat?'

'Yes, until you – until she – er – can sell this house and get somewhere else for us to live.'

They were both silent for a moment, looking at each other. 'Do you want her to sell this house?' Tom asked.

'No. We couldn't keep Hamlet in a flat. But she says it's only temporary, until you – until she . . .'

86

'But I'm not going to agree to sell it. I don't want to go.' He wanted to add, *she* moved out so she can bloody well do the house hunting, but he didn't, because that would be making Ben come down on one side or the other.

There was another silence while both tried to think of a subject that would ignore all controversial topics.

'Do you remember to feed him?' Ben asked, realizing what a useless question that was; he would obviously say yes.

'Of course I remember to feed him. He doesn't look starved does he? Anyway, he wouldn't let me forget, would he?'

'But you're out so much. What do you do if you go away?'

'They take him in next door, and they put Gertie's food out for her. There's no problem, really there isn't.' There was, of course, but no good telling him that. He had forgotten once or twice and felt absurdly guilty about it.

The doorbell rang, and there was Rajini on the doorstep, looking like thunder, with her mother in tow. Monisha Bhairavi peered beyond Tom and saw Ben. 'I have brought Rajini for her lesson; I wasn't sure if your family were here, so I thought . . .' she stared at Ben, and glanced round him into the kitchen, without making any attempt to go.

Tom turned to Ben. 'Some of them are here and some of them are not,' he said, 'but rest assured they will not disturb the lesson. They know quite well I must not be disturbed when I have a student.' He smiled expansively at her, enjoying making the most of misinterpreting her anxiety. Stupid woman; did she think he was going to rape the girl?

Ben made himself part of the deception. 'Pa's very strict about not being disturbed when he's working,' he said, smiling and losing immediately the awkward embarrassment of moments ago; he was a team with Pa again.

'Goodbye Amma,' Rajini said. 'I shall be back in about an hour I expect.' And she walked past Tom into the sitting-room.

'My mother is impossible,' she said when the front door had closed. 'Just can't get used to being in England after twenty years or so. Thinks chaperones are all the rage.'

'Old customs die hard,' said Tom.

'You can say that again,' said Rajini, and smiled at Ben. 'I've heard about you from Emma,' she said. 'You're Will aren't you?'

'No, I'm Ben,' said Ben, blushing furiously.

Much later, Tom realized that things had started to improve from that afternoon onwards. It was as though rock bottom had been reached, and from then on he started to climb out of the pit. The lesson itself had been exhilarating, partly because he was covering new ground, tackling something he had always thought before to be beneath him but finding, instead, that Rajini's overblown enthusiasm stimulated a testy animation in himself. Teaching often gave him intense satisfaction, but he had forgotten the feeling of impatient diligence that took over when launching out into virgin soil.

But at the start, she was really such a little nincompoop: all this flattery and eye-fluttering and pert love-play was quite absurd and slightly sickening, and it roused in him the desire to teach her a lesson. She didn't have to make that sort of effort, she had enough going for her without all the histrionics. The T-shirt that clung showed all that was necessary to rouse any male who was not completely moribund, and her carefully studied movements, that carelessly brushed against him, boosted the visual effect. He felt irritated enough to want to burst that particular balloon without ceremony and at once.

'If you want to learn something that will help you to get through exams efficiently,' he said, 'then I suggest you put your mind to it for the period of the lesson, otherwise we'll get nowhere and your parents' money will be wasted.' He paused, folded his arms and leaned back in his chair. 'If, on the other hand, you want me to make love to you,' he swivelled his eyes sideways to watch her expression, 'then we should have to decide whether or not we return your parents' cheque now or when you fail to get the grades you want for the university you want.'

He saw her emotions travel quite openly across her features: shock followed by humiliation immediately replaced by fury, and he felt gratified that his remarks had had the desired effect.

Rajini, on the other hand, seethed with rage. What an arrogant bastard. Unforgivably conceited and smug with it. Her cheeks burned with mortification and she turned her back and bit her nails ferociously, wondering what to do about it. She could collect her things and just walk straight out: that was probably the easiest, but that would look like defeat in the face of the enemy. Mustn't let him feel he had won. He was obviously trying to get her off his back, and she was damned if she was going to allow him to do that. Let some self-satisfied old teacher think he'd got the better of her? Oh no, not likely. He might even be thinking that she was too young to be interesting. Fuck that. She'd show him. She was as good, if not better than all those university types he had affairs with. But there was nothing to be gained by arguing, he could surely beat her at that game. She'd have to just bide her time and bloody *show* him where he got off.

She turned, with an expression of black thunder. 'Do

we work here?' she asked, without looking at him.

Tom had been watching the struggle going on with amused but sympathetic interest. He felt like a father finding the best way to influence an unruly daughter. 'So that's settled then,' he said, putting his arm round her shoulders in a fatherly way and thinking how nice it would be if he could get into bed with her there and then; just the sort of thing he could do with in his present state, however silly and immature she was. His spirits and everything else rose at the thought, which amused him further. 'We'll work upstairs in my study. I thought we might plunge straightaway into the economic crisis in Europe between the wars in this first lesson and take it from there.'

She wriggled herself away from his protective arm and they climbed up to Tom's study at the top of the house, where he cleared a small space on the overloaded table for her.

'I can't imagine how you can teach anyone in this pigsty of a place,' said Rajini with malevolence. 'If my mother had seen this room she would have had a fit and whisked me away immediately.'

'Oh, I thought it was your morals she was worried about.'

Rajini's cheeks flamed again. 'Honestly, is that all you ever think of?'

'It wasn't me that thought of it, just that I gathered your mother was thinking of it.'

'My mother never thinks of it; she's not that sort of person.'

There was a short silence and she suddenly exploded with laughter at the absurdity of the conversation. 'Oh forget it; roll on World War One.'

'So start by not calling it World War One, it's a vulgar Americanism.'

'Is it really? So there's something I've learned today

at least. Did you know Emma is furious with me for getting you to coach me?'

Tom was shocked. 'She is? I didn't know. I haven't seen her lately.'

'She thinks I'm beneath you,' she went off into peals of laughter again. 'No, not *that* way – she just thinks you shouldn't stoop to teaching idiots. She obviously has quite a high opinion of your brain power. Why has your wife left you?'

It was Tom's turn to be indignant. 'What the hell has that got to do with you?'

'I'm just interested. Was it because you're so disorganized?'

'Before the First World War . . .'

'I don't think I could put up with anyone who lived in such a mess as this.' She got up from the table and wandered round the room, peering at the stacks of paper and picking up a sheet to read it. 'Is this someone's essay? You've scribbled all over it; I'd be furious if you scribbled all over one of my essays.'

Tom was incensed at being put on the defensive. 'It seems obvious that coaching was not in your mind when you suggested this encounter.' She looked round sharply as she felt him close behind her, but this time made no sort of resistance when he turned her round and kissed her gently, first on the neck and the ear and then more aggressively and passionately on the mouth.

She lost all the fury and aggression of a short while back in the overpowering physical excitement that caught up with her now. She was breathless with the pleasure and surprise of it all, and responded to the kiss with delight. Tom, for all his amused condescension at her naively blatant approach, found that he was rocked off balance more than he had believed possible. He remembered the thought that had occurred to him when she first appeared on the doorstep with her mother: does she think I'm going to rape the girl? It seemed quite a likely possibility at this present moment. What a pity she was so young.

Ben took Hamlet out for a walk along one of his favourite pieces of common land just off the High Road where you could suddenly sense you were almost in the country because there were unexpected fields and a big sweep of green with not many houses showing. The idea of living in a flat appalled him: no garden; no space; walls that were joined to the neighbours'; he could only think of high-rise blocks when he thought of flats. Hamlet raced off into the greenness, nosing the ground and looking for something he could chase.

That Rajini was quite a raver. He thought he might wait around for the hour that she would be with Pa and then perhaps talk to her a little. She'd been nicer to him than any of Emma's other friends; hadn't ignored him like the others did. Pity she was so old though. He thought to himself what it would be like to have someone like her as a girl friend and imagined how he would talk about her at school with his friends. They all pretended they had girl friends, but he didn't think they really did. Just a lot of talk. He felt he could make up some quite good things about Rajini. Pity she was so old.

13

Laura decided that she would dress up slightly to accompany Harriet on her Saturday flat-hunting sortie and was at once mortified by her decision. What rubbish; who was she trying to impress? The estate agents? The flat sellers? All the same, she kept on the outfit she had chosen, assuring herself it would be a stupid waste of time to change.

Harriet, naturally, looked impeccable and obviously had no idea that Laura had made any particular effort in order not to let the side down.

'I've decided to rent for the time being,' she said. 'It'll be quicker and give me more time to look for something permanent. Got three to see: Hampstead Heath, St John's Wood and Regent's Park. We'd better go right away if you're ready.'

Laura abandoned the anticipation of a relaxed chat over a cup of coffee and found her keys. 'Absolutely ready.' Was it unreasonable bias to experience a twinge of distaste at Harriet's decision to live in those particular districts? Why did she have to concentrate on the most expensive places? But it obviously *was* unreasonable on her part; why shouldn't people live where they wanted to without being thought social climbers or snobs? Bias and inverted snobbery, that's what she was guilty of. After all, Alan was for ever hankering after houses in Hampstead. And anyway, East Finchley was scarcely any less sought after these days, though perhaps slightly less smart . . . she realized that Harriet had been saying something which hadn't penetrated her thinking at all.

'. . . all that way out if I'm going to work for Alan,' said Harriet.

Laura caught 'work for Alan' and envisaged the rest of the sentence. 'It would be convenient, certainly,' she agreed.

'Of course, it's only a temporary measure until I can get that wretched man out of my house. I might even go for a furnished let.'

'Isn't that fearfully expensive?'

'Well, yes, but the solicitors say they'll be able to get

93

a vast amount of the expenses out of Tom if he goes on being so obstructive.'

Was it any use to point out that Tom was much less rich than she was? Of course it wasn't. And anyway, it wasn't as if she wanted to side with Tom against Harriet; not at all; just that certain things seemed unfair at times even if they were legally correct.

Alan and Harriet should get on tremendously well in business together, she thought, as she strapped herself into Harriet's car. She was exactly the sort of business partner Alan loved – intelligent, forthright, direct and aggressive. And an attractive woman into the bargain. Alan loved working with attractive women, especially when they didn't let him dominate them, and Harriet would never let him do that. He's always managed to dominate me, she thought, but it didn't matter when it didn't concern business. He was such a conventional male in some respects; made her smile sometimes. He loved her to be the little woman waiting at home and she really quite enjoyed playing up to the role. It was all a bit of a game they both played at.

'. . . behaves simply appallingly,' Harriet was saying. 'She's really such a selfish old woman, makes all our lives a perfect misery. Ben's really suffering; gone all silent and sulky; can't get a word out of him and Emma's pretty bad-tempered as well. It's been hell these last few weeks. All so unnecessary too.'

But of course it's been hell, thought Laura, what else would the break up of a marriage be? 'Must be ghastly,' she said.

They saw three spotless, newly converted flats with carpets fitted over every inch of the floor, draped curtains, brass taps, mahogany lavatory seats and Ikea furniture. Laura thought them dire, with their cupboard bathrooms attached to each pint-sized bedroom and their dimmer lights and their entry phones. How could Harriet incarcerate herself in a place like this with two large children? The dog and the cat would be an impossibility; they would never adjust.

'Rather a long way for the children to get to school isn't it?'

'Well yes, a bit longer than before, but they're old enough to cope. Ben's twelve, after all, and Emma will be moving on to university next year. The new job will probably take up more of my time to begin with, so I'm going to have to think of my own convenience rather than theirs from now on. They're old enough to adjust, and it's good for them to have to before they turn into boring little suburbanites who don't know how to deal with life.'

Laura wondered if Harriet thought her children were unable to deal with life. 'Yes of course,' she said. 'I think it's a wonderful idea you going into Alan's office; you're exactly the sort of person he wants. He's forever complaining about the idiots who work there at the moment.'

'It's quite a step,' Harriet said. 'I've been at the old job for so long I've become a bit of an institution.' A slight gleam of satisfaction flashed as she imagined the scramble there would be for her position when she left. She had reorganized her department at work in the first few months that she was there. This meant that those who worked with her were fiercely divided into friends and foes, all making sure no-one got the better of anyone else. She had found this atmosphere stimulating to work in until recently when she had begun to find the whole situation rather boring.

'Things tick over there so well now,' she said. 'It's really become all too easy. It will be great to plunge into something entirely new, especially where I shall be paid for making money rather than spending the firm's. I like the idea, I must say. It's a sort of coming down to earth.'

A mucking in with the common herd, she thought to herself, but realized what an unfortunate impression a remark like that might make. She recalled thinking she would be doing just that when she married Tom. She had been sure that being married to someone from the sort of background he came from would immediately instil into her a sense of belonging to the mass of society instead of hovering, along with her family and the rest of her crowd, somewhere vaguely above it.

Of course the marriage had done no such thing, because she had instead sailed into a position of superiority and responsibility over Tom.

'It will be great to work as one of a team,' she said, imagining how it would be with Alan and her and an enthusiastic group of designers all combining to produce a highly polished end product. 'I like the thought of slick organization,' she said.

'Exactly what Alan appreciates,' Laura said rather sadly. Her organization had never been at all slick, Alan never stopped reminding her of that. 'It was what I fell in love with when I first met him you know. Just couldn't believe this miracle man who could organize my life so wonderfully, and was such an Adonis into the bargain.'

Harriet laughed. 'Not so bad now, either; he's the sort that improves with age; all that greying at the temples bit, it always gets me.'

Laura warmed to the thought of Harriet admiring Alan – the thought of Harriet actually admiring anything that was hers: it was quite a new idea. Odd really that Alan's stunning good looks and aggressively smooth organizational powers were the things that now made Laura feel unsatisfactory because she couldn't live up to them. She was plain and unorganized, and would really hate to work in Alan's office with him. Harriet, though, would be in her element, and be able to stand up to him as well; it was an ideal arrangement.

'I might even try to get back into the academic world I gave up when I married him,' she said, voicing an idea she had been considering. 'If he was really happy in his work, he might not mind my taking up something.'

'*Mind you taking up something!* For God's sake, Laura,' Harriet was exasperated, 'you really are hopeless. You should never give up your own life for someone else's.'

'Oh, but I had to at the time because of all the hassle and dispute with both our families.'

'About the Jewish thing you mean?'

Laura winced at the memory of it all: the breaking out of her comfortable, clerical background and leaving university just before completing her degree. And then the final blow when she decided to become Jewish, mainly because of Alan's distraught parents; they seemed to mind about it so much more than her own mother and father, who kept saying 'Well, it's your choice, darling. If you really think it's right for you.'

'It was the right thing to do,' she said. 'I've never regretted it.'

Harriet kept silent; she couldn't imagine anything being more wrong.

'I did all the Jewish bit when I married him,' Laura went on, enthused by her new idea, 'so I've been thinking I might mug up the Christianity side as well. I had it dinned into me so continuously from birth that I sort of set my mind against it in my youth: Judaism was a blessed escape then.'

'You mean you're going to revert?'

'No, no, nothing like that – anyway you can't really: once a Jew, always a Jew. And I wouldn't want to upset the family.'

Harriet became bored with the conversation as she had her mind on other things. 'Well, I'm all for it, whatever you decide,' she said. 'You've let him and the kids depend on you for far too long, I'll do my best to keep Alan as free from frustration at work as possible.'

'That would be admirable; I'd be eternally grateful.'

Laura's spirits soared. Forty-one was a good age to launch out – everyone said so; the children were growing up so that she had more time and, if Alan became happier in his work, it would make him far less demanding and difficult. It had been that that had kept her from considering it before; trying to make a really good home life, so that he could relax. It had been quite a challenge, really.

There was no doubt at all which flat Harriet would choose. Laura knew as soon as the agent took them on the tour of inspection; something about his manner that clinched it; a sort of easy, flirtatious style that said he really didn't care whether they took it or not, because he had hundreds of other clients just waiting to snap it up. It was interesting to see Harriet respond and parry this attitude, just as though they were playing a game of bargaining and bickering together; rather like the beginning of a love affair, Laura thought. She wondered why she had been invited to take part. Was it to be an audience? She was certainly enjoying the show, but there was really no audience participation. Harriet seemed to have stepped into a new section of her life and taken on a different personality since she left Tom.

It was the most expensive flat of the three that she chose, and Laura thought it more ostentatious than the other two. It was so far removed from the disorder that Tom was now living in, that it had an air of being indecently naked.

'Such a lovely lack of clutter,' Harriet said exultantly, 'I shall just be able to sit and relish it for hours at a time. What bliss.'

There was one very large bedroom, another very small and a third which was scarcely more than a box room.

'The kids can't expect Buckingham Palace when I have to pay to keep two establishments going,' said Harriet, probably noticing Laura's look of disbelief. 'Perhaps it will make them prevail on their father to be reasonable.'

So the scene changed, with all the confusion that always accompanies scene changes. Harriet exhausted, distraught and bad-tempered; Emma, by turns excited with the change of venue and exasperated by the lack of room for her belongings, and Ben desolate in the claustrophobic cell-like isolation of the minute bedroom.

He sat on his bed which had a pale pink quilted cover, and stared morosely at the opened suitcase with his belongings jumbled inside, just as he had crammed them in before they left home. He had never really unpacked at Grandma's. Hated the idea of finding new and uncomfortable places for things like his collection of fossils and his rugger boots. They would be even more uncomfortable here; the whole thing was horrible.

He decided, there and then, to return home to Tom and blow the consequences.

14

'I really don't see,' Emma said when Ben came back late from a visit to Hamlet, 'why I should have to get your tea when you come in just whenever you like. I have mine when I come in and you ought to be there then, otherwise you'll have to do your own. And I don't see why you shouldn't, anyway. You're getting to be more and more chauvinist every day.'

Ben was unprepared for the onslaught. 'Hasn't Ma left anything for us?'

'Talk sense, does she ever?'

'Sometimes she does.' He opened the fridge. 'I'll have bacon and eggs and fried bread and tomatoes, and I'll do it myself.'

'You had that this morning. Your cholesterol will be sky high.'

'What did you have?'

'Salad and that smoked salmon Ma bought.'

'She'll kill you for eating that. She told us not to yesterday. Did you leave any for me?'

'Not likely! I was hungry and there was hardly enough for me.'

'Pig. Give me some money for a pizza then.'

'I don't have money to spend on you. You should have some pocket money left.'

'Ma borrowed mine back this morning.' He had actually spent it on tins of Chum for Hamlet.

'Do a potato in the microwave.'

'I'm fed up with baked potatoes.'

'Well if you're going to be *fussy*.'

Ben sighed and took out the bacon, eggs, tomatoes and bread. 'I'll make myself some chips,' he said.

'Well don't blame me if you die of a heart attack,' said Emma.

Ben ate his meal with relish. 'I've decided,' he said as he wiped round his plate with a piece of bread and butter, 'I can't go on living here, it's too awful and small and cramped. I'm going back to live with Pa.'

'But you can't do that. Have you asked Ma? Or Pa?'

'No, not yet. But he'd like to have me back, he's always very pleased to see me and I don't see that Ma can object; she doesn't seem to have the time any more. She'll be pleased, too.'

'Don't be silly, if you go back to Pa she might not be able to prove that he's impossible to live with.'

'But he isn't; we've lived with him all our lives.'

'Ma made it possible, don't you see? Without her there it would be unbearable. You'd starve to death and get ill because of all the dirt and mess he makes.'

'I wouldn't.'

'Well I don't expect the solicitors will let you. If you make a fuss they'll probably have you taken away by the council and put in a home.'

'They wouldn't.'

'How do you know they wouldn't? You don't know anything. Have you read up anything about divorces? They would probably say that Pa kidnapped you and they'd put him in prison.'

Ben's resolution wavered. 'They wouldn't,' he repeated, more to convince himself than Emma. 'Pa wouldn't let them. I shall go tomorrow. No-one can stop me.'

'Don't know why you think Pa will welcome you with open arms. You'll just be in the way of all his girl friends and I bet they'll be furious and get him to throw you out at once.'

'What girl friends?'

'Well, there's Lexi . . .'

'*Lexi?*' Ben gave a shout of laughter. '*Lexi* Pa's girl friend? You're crazy. Lexi's awful, she couldn't be anybody's girl friend.'

'Well, she's Pa's; and now there's Rajini as well.'

Ben rolled off his chair with amusement. 'You're plum crazy. Rajini's your age. What would she be doing with Pa? And what would Pa be doing with her? She was round there having a *lesson* from him the other day.'

Emma laughed in a way Ben didn't like: a supercilious, sarky way. 'Exactly,' she said, 'but I suppose you're too young to understand anything about adult behaviour. Do try to grow up a bit. You'd see I was right if you were older. And please shut up, I can't get any work done when you're around talking rubbish.'

'Rajini's no more adult than you are, po-faced creep.'

He would have liked to have hit her but supposed that would be considered childish. The idea of Pa thinking of Rajini as though she was grown up was just plain stupid; one didn't have to be older to realize that. He wondered if Pa did have a girl friend though, and if it was that that had made Ma leave. But Ma was much more likely to have boy friends than Pa was to have girl friends: she always kissed the men who came to their house and sort of made up to them as though she liked them more than she liked their wives, but he didn't know of any special boy friend that would have made her go off and leave them like that. Not that she'd actually left them, he supposed. But anyway, she was always too busy with her work to have time to think about having affairs or anything. What could have made her suddenly go off like that?

He felt all at once angry, outraged and utterly dejected and he slammed out of the room to pack some of his things into a bag so that he could go straight to his father after school the next day.

Rajini's coaching had been arranged for the same day each week and, as the second session approached, she found herself becoming more and more agitated and out of control. He had behaved in such an extraordinary fashion: that unexpected and mind-blowing kiss and then nothing – nothing at all. The excitement and the rising sex urge were left high and abysmally dry when he disengaged himself from her, quite without warning, and moved to the other side of the table.

'I will now demonstrate,' he had said, 'the ability of the elderly lecturer who has been hired to cram one highly sexed young woman into university.' And without any further reference to the incident, he started to discuss with her aspects of the character of Adolf Hitler in the thirties.

She made several attempts to bring back the previous atmosphere, but was thwarted every time. He ignored sultry glances and moved away from accidental-on-purpose hand on arm gestures, or the bending of the head over the book from which he read. And all the time there was the suspicion that he was laughing at her efforts – regarding them as childish. Her fury grew with each minute, but she was unable to break out of the restraint he imposed, and became tongue-tied in the face of such disassociation.

She had tried telephoning but always came up against the answerphone. Emma cut her dead at school, and she found herself floundering angrily in a distressing isolation. She was sick with anxiety as she rang the doorbell for her second session. What stand to take? She had been over and over it in her mind for the past seven days and had come up with no answer at all. She felt humiliated that her legs had gone to jelly

103

and her heartbeats were positively painful.

Tom swung open the door with a smile all over his face. It was obvious *he'd* had no sleepless nights over it, Rajini thought viciously.

'Welcome to the highlight of my week,' he said, putting an arm round her shoulders.

Rajini whirled round, dropping her armful of books and the contents of a crowded pencil case on to the floor, while floating pages of essay caught in the draught from the door. 'Stop patronizing me!' she shrieked and hit him forcefully, with the flat of her hand across the mouth.

There were several seconds of shocked silence while they surveyed each other and before they both, at the same moment, bent down to collect the fallen debris.

'I wasn't patronizing . . .'

'Yes you were; treating me like a child of ten; humiliating me, tearing strips off me. You're unspeakable and I'm not staying another moment.'

'I've bought some doughnuts for our tea.'

'I don't like doughnuts.'

'So I'll eat the doughnuts and you drink the tea.'

Rajini was crying without noticing that she was, and her face was scarlet with indignation, but she stamped upstairs to his study rather than down the steps into the street.

He brought tea and doughnuts up on a tray, having given her sufficient time to compose herself, and incidentally give himself a few minutes' recovery time as well. She had asked for it of course, but there had been no need to be quite so hard on her. It occurred to him how mortified he would have felt if anyone had treated Emma like that, however much she had asked for it, and he melted with shame.

Neither of them spoke as he poured out two cups of tea and bit into a doughnut.

'Did you do the reading?' he asked, finally, with the idea of calming down the situation.

'There is no way,' Rajini said, 'that I can talk about bloody World War Two before we have talked about us.'

Tom considered reminding her that they would be talking at her father's expense but restrained himself, leaned back in his chair and looked at her over his glasses; while cutting down on the attack, he was not prepared to extend helpful gestures.

There was a further silence, and Rajini took a doughnut. 'I've been thinking about you the whole week,' she said.

'That won't get you into university.'

'For God's sake stop it.' Her voice rose to a shout. 'If you can make love to me like an adult, then talk to me like one.'

'But I haven't made love to you like an adult, we have shared an adolescent kiss in the heat of a moment, that's all. It doesn't warrant a week's wasted thought. Behave like an adult and I'll treat you like one.'

'Behave like an adult?' Rajini yelled. 'And how does one set about that I'd like to know? Neglect oneself and one's surroundings to the extent that nobody can live with you? Or be like my father and behave like a little Hitler to his daughter? Or like my mother who lets herself be treated like a doormat? Or like your wife who drags her children away from their father and their home without ever asking what they might want or believe?'

'No-one's perfect,' Tom said, enjoying the logic of her observations, 'but I would still consider it a waste of time to contemplate the pros and cons of a single kiss for seven whole days.'

Rajini almost smiled, and the intensity and solemnity of the moment began to melt from her mind. It was difficult to retain wretchedness and despondency at such a high pitch for any length of time. 'Well, perhaps I relaxed for some of the seven days,' she said, 'but you don't seem to understand that it's completely different for you: to you I am just another idiot child needing education, whereas for me, you are the possible pathway to a bright and glorious future – and incidentally, a way to escape from my family. That's quite apart from the fact that I fancy you like crazy.'

'It certainly is different for me, idiot child, because in my case you could be the probable pathway to disgrace, ruin and bankruptcy.'

'Hardly that – I'm nearly eighteen don't forget.'

'So I'd be spared a prison sentence, but I would still be leading astray a young and tender virgin into impure ways.'

'Who said I was a virgin?'

Tom picked up a book and opened it. 'I think we touched on the state of Europe between the wars in our last lesson,' he said. 'Perhaps we could look at the essay you were supposed to start during the past week.'

It was at that moment that Ben arrived home to stay, and Lexi came to hand back the typing she had done for Tom the day before. Tom became enraged at the interruptions, and there was no way back to the conversation after the various situations had been dealt with. Lexi was paid and despatched, disappointed and resentful, and Ben settled down to his homework on the brink of tears at the anxious and far too brief welcome he had received. Even Hamlet seemed far more interested in the food Ben had brought than in his master returning to look after him.

It was only after all the disruptions, that Tom could return to Rajini, still sitting, blankly uncertain, in his study. He looked at her for a moment or two, but found it quite impossible to realign his thoughts back to Britain in the thirties or to Rajini in the present.

'I think we had better postpone this lesson,' he said. 'My concentration seems to have gone.'

She grinned back at him. 'And that's a disaster of course for the all-powerful maestro.'

15

Alan was excited by the idea of Harriet joining the firm and needed to discuss the possibilities. He asked her over to lunch: 'Better if you could come here, rather than a restaurant, if you don't mind, because then we could work out some plans in the peace and quiet of my studio. Come on Sunday, we always have lots to eat on Sundays; Laura invariably cooks a monster meal to accommodate the various friends of the various children, and I want to show you something I'm working on anyway; something apart from boring old office stuff.'

'Heaven,' said Harriet. 'Not to have to worry about putting something in front of a sulky daughter.' She paused, 'You know Ben's gone back to Tom?'

'I didn't, no.' Alan paused. 'Temporarily?'

Harriet sounded irritated. 'How should I know? I presume he must have been bribed by some promise or other. Otherwise can you imagine why he would prefer to live in the squalor Tom's bound to have got himself into by now, than in the accommodation I've provided for them? So let him look after them for a change. He never has before.'

'You're totally unsuited, aren't you? Can't think why you married him in the first place.'

'He was so clever and so *logical*, that's what I liked. Quite different; I'd never met anyone logical before.'

Alan laughed. 'To marry someone because they're logical doesn't sound like a recipe for success.'

'I was escaping from boredom and family prejudices, but I have to admit that I find logic a bit tiresome now. It's easier to say "This is so because I say so." I did *try* with the children when they started questioning, but one only has time for so much.'

How pleasant, Alan thought, to be gossiping on the telephone. He couldn't remember the last time he had been relaxed enough to do so. It was something he had always nagged Laura for indulging in.

'I do so agree,' he said. 'I always resort to bombastic dogma, though Laura spends hours trying to make them see the logic of everything. Positive waste of time, as I always tell her, but she won't give up. I think it's the result of a massive anxiety complex.'

'But why should Laura have an anxiety complex?'

'Just in case she might upset somebody at some time. She has a pre-emptive conscience.'

'How absolutely appalling.'

'It's one of the things I fell in love with in the early days. My family had no conscience at all.'

'So escape to happiness?'

Alan screwed up his mouth. 'So escape,' he said.

He forgot to tell Laura that he had asked Harriet to lunch until the table had been laid for the Sunday feast.

'Did I tell you I'd asked Harriet?'

'No, you didn't. Did you remember your mother and father were coming?'

'Oh God – why didn't you remind me? You know I always forget.'

Laura said nothing; it wasn't worth it. 'Max, Louise,' she called out, 'more places needed at the table, please.'

There were groans. 'Why? Who else is there? There isn't any more room; this table only takes eight.'

'Harriet's coming.'

'Oh no,' from Louise. 'She won't fit in.'

'In any sense of the word,' said Hamish. 'She'll probably say our glasses aren't washed properly. She said that once you know.'

'Well they probably weren't.'

'But you shouldn't *say*,' this from Daisy. 'It's rude.'

'Harriet *is* rude,' said Hamish. 'Will Ben be coming?'

'No.' Alan's voice was terse. 'He's with his father, so he'll miss out on a good square meal.'

The four children simultaneously stopped what they were doing and looked at Alan.

'Gone back to Daddy?'

'Has he really?'

'Good for him.'

'But Emma says their new flat's terribly smart.'

'Will you get a smart flat for us all to live in, Mum, when you leave Dad?' Max asked.

Laura frowned: 'You'll have to get Dad to leave me if you want a smart flat. If I left him I'd probably have to apply for a council flat.'

'You could go to a home for battered wives,' Hamish suggested.

'Or we could be put up in one room of a seedy hotel,' said Louise. 'That would be fun.'

'Some of them are at the seaside aren't they? If you arranged to run out on him in the summer we could get a free holiday.'

'Lay the table with two extra places in case Emma comes,' shouted Laura above the din. 'You can put up the card table at one end and then there'll be enough room, and it will have to be family hold-off until we see if the food will go round.'

'That's not fair,' said Daisy. 'We're much more important than Harriet and Emma.'

'But not nearly so rich,' said Hamish.

Emma did come. She enjoyed Laura's family cooking, and now that Harriet had lost interest in providing smart, magazine-type meals for just the two of them, cooked meals had become a matter of much greater importance and some urgency.

Harriet drove slowly past the house, looking for a place to park and crawled down a side road before turning and repassing the house in the opposite direction. 'We shan't get there till tea time at this rate,' she said irritably. 'Ah – there's one.' And she drew ahead to allow the car behind to pass before she backed into the space. The following car, however, also saw its chance and pulled, awkwardly, into the space, nose first.

'Moronic bastard!' Harriet shouted in exasperated fury. 'What the hell do you think you're doing? Bloody skunk.' She drove on furiously and finally parked half over a double yellow line, still shaking with anger.

As they walked back towards the house, Alan's father, Bernard Sunshine, was just helping his wife, Esther, out of their very large Datsun. It had taken a considerable amount of manoeuvring to park it, especially when he had had to drive in nose first to claim the space. He saw Harriet and Emma and beamed at them, raising his hat as they passed.

Harriet's fury increased a hundredfold. Alan had just said come over and have Sunday lunch with us; it had sounded relaxing and casual. She had only met the Summerson seniors twice before, and the experience had been neither relaxed nor casual. His unpardonable behaviour in pinching her parking space confirmed her low opinion of them. She glared at Bernard Sunshine with distaste.

110

'Who's that?' Esther peered short-sightedly at her as she passed. 'Alan didn't say anyone else would be there. Is it a party or what?'

'It's the Turtle woman.'

'What?'

'Turtle – you know, those friends of Laura's.'

'Friends of Laura's? Why should I know friends of Laura's? So it's a party? Why didn't he say it was a party? I would have dressed different if he'd said it was a party. So thoughtless these young people. Laura should have told me.'

They all approached the house together, and Esther extended a gloved hand in Harriet's direction. 'How do you do; my son never said it was a party. I don't know if we've met . . .'

Harriet shook her outstretched hand: 'Yes, we have met once or twice, I'm Harriet Turtle and this is my daughter, Emma. Alan didn't tell us either, but perhaps it's just a family lunch.' She stared at Bernard coldly. Bad-mannered creep.

'Family lunch?' Esther bridled. What did the woman mean? She wasn't family.

Alan came out of the front door and took his mother by the arm, looking and feeling embarrassed. 'Hi, darling, you remember Harriet don't you?' He winked at Harriet and put his arm round his father's shoulders. 'Good to see you, Dad; let's go in shall we?'

The children arrived on the doorstep and there were kisses, hugs and general family remarks exchanged, while Harriet and Emma stood awkwardly, unable to join in or to make their way into the house through the jam in the porch. Harriet seethed inwardly.

'You didn't tell me it was a family do,' she hissed later to Alan under cover of taking her drink.

'I didn't know. Laura arranged it. I only learned about it this morning.'

111

That figured, Harriet thought sullenly. Laura would make sure that his family were asked to lunch at regular intervals and this was probably one of the regular intervals. There was a tremendous din of talk and a clatter of plates, in the middle of which Harriet felt more and more isolated and frozen into a furious block of resentment.

Bernard Sunshine approached her. And if he thinks he's going to chat me up he's got another think coming, Harriet intimated in her glare in his direction.

'Such a racket,' said Bernard. 'You forget what family life was like when you get old.' He obviously had no idea that she was the one he had deprived of a parking space with his boorish behaviour.

Harriet wanted to say that all family life didn't have to be like this but desisted because it really wouldn't be worth sounding critical and, anyway, she had no desire to start a fatuous conversation about children, nor on getting old, so she nodded, drew her eyebrows together in a gesture of pained agreement and hoped he would go away.

'I can't believe that beautiful daughter of yours ever made such horrible noises; she looks too calm and too self-contained,' he said.

'She screamed, off and on, for the first three years of her life,' said Harriet, shuddering at the memory of it. 'I wanted to have her adopted.'

Bernard laughed uproariously at the joke. 'That's funny,' he said, 'I like that, it's funny. Have her adopted! I like that.'

'What's so funny?' said Esther from the other side of the room. 'Can we share the joke?'

But Daisy pulled her grandmother towards the sofa and made her sit down. 'What have you got in your bag, Grandma?'

Esther was at once distracted from any further

112

attack, her face becoming creased with smiles. 'Wouldn't you just like to know, Miss Nosey, wouldn't you just?' She rummaged in the large tapestry bag she held and brought out an elaborately wrapped parcel. 'Something for a clever little girl, I shouldn't wonder.'

She presented the prize and rummaged further. 'And for Louise so that she shouldn't think I love one granddaughter more than the other.' More fumbling produced three more packages. 'And just to show I love grandsons as much as granddaughters.'

'Really, Mother Es, you spoil them,' Laura laughed as she said it. 'Anybody would think it was Christmas.'

Laura was the only one who was quite unaware of the minute Jewish hiatus in the midst of general sounds of unwrapping parcels and expressions of genuine approval of their contents. In spite of her conversion to Judaism, there were times when her early indoctrination popped to the top.

'So when's the bar mitzvah, boy?' Bernard pulled Max towards him. 'Your parents, they never tell me anything. It's a big day for you, next year, it's got to be next year, remember.' He looked round Max towards Alan, and Laura immediately became anxious and alert. 'You've started to make the arrangements I suppose? So why don't you tell me for God's sake? His grandfather, and he doesn't know when the bar mitzvah is; what a shame.'

Alan moved to Max's side fairly swiftly. 'We're dealing with it, Dad, don't worry; plenty of time. We'll discuss it with you, of course, don't worry.'

Bernard hunched his shoulders. 'Don't worry, he tells me. And what should I do but worry if the boy's education is being neglected?'

Max looked anxious that his father should be criticized for shortcomings on account of something to do with him. Harriet, on the other hand, was fascinated by a side of Alan she had not met before. He made a small gesture towards her that exposed his vexation, and she was amused by the transformation of a hard-headed, efficient business executive into a sullen son being told off by his father. But for the rest of the visit she was bored and irritated. No chance to discuss any problems of her own, or any subject that might have concerned her.

'You have sons too, I believe?' Esther was genuinely interested it would seem. Anybody's children interested her; families interested her and she assumed they must be interesting to everybody else.

Harriet stiffened: 'Yes, yes. Ben is twelve, like Max. He is out with his father today.'

'Benjamin, Benjamin – what a good name that is. My brother's name is Benjamin, called after his great-grandfather. Such a good name.'

The Summerson children all enjoyed the party along with their grandparents once Bernard had put his displeasure to the back of his mind. Alan and Harriet found neither the time nor the opportunity to discuss the job, and Laura sensed their irritation, so for her, Alan, Harriet and Emma, the afternoon was a tedious, monotonous disaster.

16

Tom rolled over to stop the alarm, and was at once very wide awake. He had always had the ability to wake immediately from sleep, and equally to fall deeply into sleep, wherever he might be and whatever time of day it was.

He lay, staring at the ceiling for a few moments, sorting out the day ahead, and then, inevitably, drifting into a contemplation of his present situation. Depression descended quickly, before he was able to summon up positive thinking or the alternative of attempting to discard all thought by switching on Radio Three and concentrating on the music. It was a fact that things had been getting on top of him recently. Much as he relished the pleasure of being able to live his life exactly as the spirit moved him, without having Harriet to shout at him, he recognized a certain blight that seemed to have closed in on him, which occasional whirlwinds of cleaning, washing and tidying in particular areas did nothing to dispel. There were moments when hope was temporarily abandoned, and it was distressing.

Now that Ben had moved back in, a degree of irritation had replaced the feeling of emptiness and led, naturally, to a sense of guilt. Was he actually considering Ben as an inconvenience? And if so, to what? It was only early in the morning that these questions brought on the depression. During the day, so many other thoughts and happenings occupied his mind that there was little time to consider the small trifles that would work themselves out in the general turmoil of everyday living.

Ben came into the bedroom with a cup of tea, and the guilt mounted.

'Tea! Ah, good chap. That's great. I was just about to get up and do your breakfast.'

'You don't need to; I had to get up at half-past-six to finish my Latin, so I had breakfast then. Does *cum* take the subjunctive, by the way?'

Tom probed his memory, '*Cum*? Er – yes, I think so – *cum cantibus in choro* – yes, of course it does.'

'Have you got anything to wash?' Ben asked,

'because I have to do my PE kit and I thought I might start the washing machine if you had something to do as well.'

'Yes – well, I'm sure to have something. Leave your stuff out and I'll do it later.'

'But you might forget; better if I put it on now.'

'I *won't* forget.' He shouted the words and then resumed, in control again, 'I won't forget, really. Put your things somewhere where I'm bound to fall over them and then you'll be certain.'

They looked at each other, sadly, without saying anything more, and Ben got himself dressed, took some food from the fridge for his lunch and packed his books into his case. Tom came downstairs as Ben was doing up his shoes.

'So what would you like for lunch?' Tom opened the fridge.

'I took some of that cheese,' Ben said, 'and the rest of the water biscuits and the last apple, and we need bread and butter and milk and I wouldn't mind some coke. I could get it on the way home if you're going to be busy and if you can give me some money.'

'No – I have to do the shopping today, anyway. I can get everything.' There was no excuse for being annoyed with Ben because he was super-efficient; absolutely no excuse at all; even if super-efficiency often became an end in itself and therefore self-defeating. But this was not the time to point that out. He gave Ben a hug and a five pound note. 'Don't seem to have given you any pocket money lately,' he said. 'And thanks for being such a help round the house. Makes all the difference.'

Ben returned the hug and smirked up at him. 'Thanks Pa.' No sense in saying that Ma paid pocket money into his building society account monthly. That would have sounded as though he was putting Pa down. 'And we need Chum and Whiskas when you do go to the shops.'

He went round to the back and cuddled Hamlet for several minutes before racing out of the front gate and down the road to catch the bus. It was good to feel in charge of both himself and Pa; neither Hamlet nor Pa could really manage without him.

Lexi arrived when Tom was in the shower and let herself in with the key that was kept hidden outside, under a stone. The hiss of the spray drowned her entrance and he stayed under the gentle needles that became gradually like tiny icicles making goose pimples of his skin as he turned the water from hot to cold. Exhilaration seeped through his body, and the lethargy, depression and irritation of the early morning sluiced itself away down the drain. New day, new thoughts, new stimuli.

Lexi, standing in the doorway watching him, on the other hand, spelt immediate deflation, and he exploded with fury at being deprived so suddenly and without warning.

'For God's sake, woman, can't a man have any privacy in his own house?'

He strode out of the shower and reached for his towel. It seemed he was making a habit of meeting young women while wrapped in a bath towel or less. Might be considered amusing if he had not been angry that Lexi caught him unawares and shattered the ebullience of the previous moments.

Lexi wilted, visibly. 'I'm sorry – I – rang the bell but you didn't hear I suppose.'

'So let's have some coffee.'

She slid past him in an obviously unobtrusive way, which he found intensely irritating. She should have shouted at him, told him to go and make his own coffee, pushed past him, argued with him – done anything that might have proved that she was man and not mouse. The sexism of the words amused him and he sat down on the lavatory seat and laughed at himself and Lexi and the whole stupid situation. Was he really missing being the long-suffering underdog?

When he had settled at his desk and Lexi returned with coffee, toast and a boiled egg, he became even more furious that she should have anticipated what he wanted for breakfast. He could as well have decided on Bran Flakes.

He pushed aside a heap of papers, books, pens and two dirty cups to clear a space for the tray. 'Not enough room here to eat, let alone swing cats.'

Lexi looked serious. 'Knowing your views on the time wasted in putting things away and tidying up generally, I never do it. But if you want me to . . .'

'Of course I don't want you to mess around with my belongings. It would be a disaster. I should never be able to find anything again.'

There was a pause as each considered the time taken to find anything anyway. Tom brushed away the thought. 'Having things visible and to hand is far less frustrating than filing everything away in forgettable files which have to be located, fetched, opened and rummaged through.'

'Yes, of course it is.'

It was an effort to restrain himself from shouting at her. If only she would disagree with him, he would be able to banish the slight feeling of uncertainty his own last statement had raised in him. She had only to express a doubt for him to muster up and expound his reasoning. Theories were easier to prove in dialogue.

The egg yolk was set hard, and he left it in disgust without saying a word. Lexi was hovering, waiting to see if he needed anything further: another cup of coffee, something typed, a letter written, a discussion, sex. He continued to seethe while keeping a stony silence. Let her work out for herself that he needed nothing, nothing at all, least of all her, on this morning that had seemed to be starting well in the sharpness of the cold shower, but which had been spoilt by her vapid self-effacing negativeness.

She stood, in complete stillness, at the other side of the room. It was obvious that she was not going to work things out for herself.

'Lexi, there is absolutely nothing I want done today, it's really not worth your while hanging around, you must have plenty of your own work to do.'

'Oh yes – yes, I have plenty of studying. Perhaps tomorrow?'

'Er – well, no. I'm going away for a few weeks – at least, I'm staying with someone, so I won't be here.'

The silence, this time, was full of disbelief.

'And Ben? He is going too?'

'Yes, he's going too.'

'Shall I come in to feed Hamlet and Gertrude then?'

How these small lies led on and on into others and a confusion of tangled falsehoods. A sequence like a geometrical progression or a game of chess: unless you planned ahead, it was easy to make a slip that would lose you the game.

'They're going with Ben; they're all going to stay with a friend of Ben's.'

It was so blatantly and obviously untrue that it made him want to laugh – except that it was sad and humiliating for Lexi, or would be if she realized the truth – or the lies. He almost exploded into laughter at the absurdity of it all. Lexi's arms drooped limply by her side, and Tom was struck by how much less efficient she looked when not carrying a sheaf of papers or a pile of books or a typewriter. He always thought of Lexi carrying something and was shocked to read such dejection into the sad stance at the other side of the room.

'I'll phone you as soon as I get back,' he said with forced cheerfulness.

Lexi continued to stand absolutely still for what seemed like a long time. So long that Tom began to find the silence and her stillness embarrassing. He tried to think of a light remark to make, but Lexi's explosion had merely been gathering momentum.

'You fucking bastard!' she screamed suddenly, 'I suppose you think I don't know about you and the schoolgirl you've taken up with. Well, you can bloody well get on with it and leave me out of things from now on. I've waited on you hand and foot for months, as well you know, so let her do it for a change. Take her on as your slave and see how she likes it, because I'm through. I've had enough – understand? And I think you're a shit.'

She turned into the door, slamming it open to pass through, crashing it shut behind her and careered down the stairs. Relief mixed with guilt flooded through him. But there was really no way he could blame himself for Lexi's devotion. He just hadn't rebuffed her, that's all.

He got up from his desk and paced round the room a little to minimize the nastiness of the confrontation. It was a day when he had no lectures and no supervisions, so no tiresome drag into town. Rajini came for her lesson later on, by which time Lexi already seemed to Tom someone from a previous life. The day had picked up from the moment the front door had slammed on her. He had worked on some new ideas for a play that was always at the back of his mind: a fresh approach, a real possibility of actually getting down to it. He had forgotten Rajini was coming, and had not eaten since the confrontation with the egg, boiled to excess.

Rajini climbed the stairs ahead of him and dropped her armful of books and her school bag on the table where his notes were spread out among the remains of the breakfast tray which Lexi had not removed. 'You may be able to live like this,' she said, stacking the coffee mugs back on to the tray and brushing toast crumbs to the floor, 'but I can't work in this sort of atmosphere. Let's tidy up.'

Tom was stunned at the cheek of the girl. 'I would remind you,' he said, 'that this is my study and my house and my way of living and . . .'

'There's no way you can organize yourself if you live in a pigsty.' Rajini collected together the notes he had been making and stacked books into a pile.

'Tidying up,' said Tom, in the pained, long-suffering voice he always put on when pointing out to someone how silly their ideas were, 'is a time-wasting habit, indulged in by those who use it as a means of proving that they have no time to do anything worthwhile.'

'That's the sort of stupid remark,' Rajini said, 'made by people too lazy or too disorganized to run their lives properly.'

She put her books in a pile on the desk opposite Tom's chair and arranged her file, pencils and rubber neatly beside them. 'Now, let's wash up these things and get ourselves some coffee.' She picked up the tray and started down the stairs.

'You are being impertinent,' said Tom.

'No I'm not. I just can't concentrate among crumbs and chaos, which means that you wouldn't be able to teach me, which means we would both work better if I cleared up first.' She walked past him through the door. 'And it would be a lot quicker if you came and helped me,' she added over her shoulder.

Tom stood rooted for a moment, wondering why he had not resorted to the bantering, disdainful comments he always employed when Harriet or Emma criticized his disorderly inactivity. Contemptuous logic was usually successful in gaining the upper hand in family arguments, driving them into fits of rage, but he thought cynicism would probably leave Rajini unmoved. He felt nonplussed and faintly amused by his own perplexity.

'You're extremely cheeky,' he said as he followed her downstairs.

It took the best part of an hour to clear the kitchen and, by the end of that time, they were both exhausted and in a state of giggling helplessness, with Rajini laughing at all Tom's jokes, and Tom indulging in childish slapstick to amuse her . . .

'It does seem slightly unfair,' Tom said, 'that I should charge your family a fee for giving you the privilege of cleaning my kitchen.'

'You could give me a free lesson to pay for my services,' said Rajini. 'Oh no, perhaps not, because then they'd want to know what services I rendered. Anyway, now I've made the place habitable, we could perhaps get on with the lesson.'

'But the time – you've been here over an hour already; won't they be sending out the CID in search of you soon?'

Rajini smiled at him expansively. 'No, no, they won't actually.' She filled the kettle and sat down at the kitchen table. 'They've gone to visit my aunt for the weekend because I said your wife had asked me to stay the weekend here, with Emma.'

There was a stunned silence for a moment or two. 'Of course, I *could* go back and sleep in the empty house,' she said, 'but they didn't like that idea which was why they wanted to take me with them. That was when I thought of this.'

Tom sat down opposite her and stared at her hard

122

and long. He saw, in his mind's eye, the lean brown body, imagined the excitingly young breasts and followed the line down through the navel. What, he wondered, did she look like between those sleek, smooth thighs?

He got to his feet quickly, clasped the back of his chair and held it against himself in order to regain his equilibrium and bring his heartbeat back to normal.

'What an outrageously amoral little person you are.'

'Not at all; you showed me last time I came that you had absolutely no physical interest in me; that you considered me a child whom you could patronize and take under your intellectual wing, so I knew I would be perfectly safe with you, that I could rely on you to look after me and that I would be in absolutely no danger in your house.'

'No danger whatsoever,' said Tom, regaining control. 'And Ben can be your chaperone.'

'Ben?' Her expression changed. 'Is he coming this weekend?'

'He lives here now, with me, and sometimes Emma comes for the weekends as well, so we'll be a nice family unit. I'm sure Emma won't mind sharing her room with you.' A silent prayer that Emma would decide to turn up.

Rajini gave a small shriek of laughter. 'Oh God! Is Emma really coming. She'll probably plunge a knife in my guts, she hates me so. But I really can't go home now; I'm far too frightened to stay in an empty house alone; death by stabbing would be infinitely preferable and much less horrific.'

The telephone warbled: 'Hi Pa, this is Ben. I shan't be back tonight, Ma's taking Emma and me down to Shoreham with the Summersons. We're going sailing.

You won't forget the animals, will you? There's not enough food for them unless you got it with the shopping, did you?'

'Yes, yes, of course I got it.'

Blast the lot of them. A weekend's sailing would have been ideal; just the thing to get rid of depression and lethargy. Was this another pleasure from which he was going to be excluded from now on? And what the hell was he going to do about the impudent child in his kitchen? He felt trapped and enraged but at the same time stimulated by the frustration into an aggressive impetuosity.

He strode back into the kitchen and was electrified to see the change that he and Rajini had wrought there. And the strange thing was, that the new, bright look did not in the least remind him of how the kitchen had been in Harriet's time. Harriet's whiteness and tidiness had been cold and forbidding, with nothing out of place and all the myriad wired-up machines seeming menacing and at the ready to chop, slice and mince at the inadvertent touch of a button. Everything now looked positively welcoming.

'I like it,' he said to Rajini, looking round the room. 'I really like it. Don't think I've ever seen it looking so nice. I might even try to keep it like this.' He put the coffee pot on a tray and wished he had thought to buy some of those delicious German chocolate biscuits. 'But now the intellect has to be called into being. English economy between the wars we were considering I believe.' And, picking up the tray, he led the way upstairs, back to his study.

Whether it was that Tom's self-pity brought about a desire to be comforted, or whether it was plain unbridled lust that induced the intensity of the sex drive that took him over from that time, he was not really interested in deciding. He did remember thoughts

124

flickering through his mind like: Fuck the lot of them – if they want to push me out, I've got a right to some pleasure . . . and: Why bloody should I control myself? . . . and: She wants it and I want it, so where's the harm for God's sake?

And immediately, back came the image of the naked Rajini he had conjured up before, bringing with it the compulsive tingling, the erection and all the accompanying disturbances. He saw, by the expression of delighted triumph on her face, that she knew exactly the effect she was having on him.

'You are very distracting,' he said, watching her pour the coffee, amused at the enticement she managed to put into her every action. It might be obvious, he thought, but it certainly worked.

Rajini glowed, quite visibly, and brought the cup over to him. 'So are you,' she said, and leaned forward to place the cup beside him. He realized that the move was calculated to emphasize the close proximity and the most tantalizing view of her breasts, and that the way she lingered in the same position longer than was necessary demanded a far greater sense of restraint than he was capable of at that moment.

There seemed to be no way out of the dilemma – not that he was actively searching for a way out – and once he had succumbed to capitulation, there then appeared to be no time at all for any preparation; no time for anything as they wound themselves round each other on the way to the bedroom through piled-up and discarded clothing and other clutter, to fall on to the unmade bed with its tangled bedclothes. They were part of the jumble of discarded clothing and tumbling erotic confusion themselves.

'How could you wear tights?' said Tom, struggling with the awkwardness of getting them off. 'Stockings and suspenders are so much more exciting.'

'I'll remember next time.' She scarcely smiled as she said it, as though this was far too serious a moment to admit to any sort of humour.

Her skin was the colour of dark heather honey and felt like cool silk, Tom decided, as he watched his own hand explore it, but there was nothing silky or controlled about her love-making, inexperienced though it might be. She reminded him of a wildly excited cat that writhed and arched its way all over him with startling speed. She exploded with such a frenzied delirium that for Tom it was like a first time, a mind-blowing experience; something quite new after twenty years or so of jog-along, everyday, rule-of-thumb coupling, enjoyable enough in its own way, but nothing, nothing at all like this.

He rolled away from her in a state of panting exhaustion. 'My God,' he gasped. 'What did you do to me?'

She leaned over him, so that he was at once aroused again but too fatigued to do more than pull her down on top of him.

'It wasn't me,' she said. 'I'm the pupil, remember, coming to teacher to be taught. This was certainly some lesson; I'll recommend you to all my friends.'

He laughed weakly; 'No teaching involved, you knew it all.'

'I didn't; that was the first time.'

He pushed her up, away from him, straightening his arms so that he held her at arms' length, and was immediately overwhelmed by the sight of his hands on her breasts. 'What do you mean? First time? You told me you weren't a virgin.'

'No I didn't. I said, who says I'm a virgin.'

'Jesus!' He let her fall on the bed beside him and raised himself up. 'But I . . . I must have half-killed you. Why didn't you tell me for God's sake?'

Rajini rolled on to her front and laughed at him. 'You mean why didn't I whisper, "Be gentle with me", and stare up at you with doe eyes half-blinded by tears? You must be mad, it's much more exciting to be raped. I like my sex to be violent. I've always imagined it that way and it's just great.'

She turned over, wound her legs round his neck and drew him towards her again. 'Fucking is really fun,' she said. 'I just love it.'

17

After a trial period in the office, the Alan/Harriet experiment was proving a great success, just as Laura had predicted. She was delighted, both for him and for Harriet. 'You are so exactly the sort of partner he wants,' she told her, 'I've never seen him so unfrustrated where work is concerned. It's a small miracle.'

'Hold on a minute,' Harriet was pleased at the praise, 'I'm not quite a partner, a mere employee, remember.'

'At the moment, I know, but he's always had great plans for setting up on his own, you know.' It was all part of the frustration; Alan really never worked well under people; he had too many ideas of his own and it was difficult for him to understand why others did not always enthuse to the extent that he did. Laura found it hard to understand also; he not only designed better than anyone she knew, but could also promote his ideas so brilliantly. It hurt her to have him depressed when the firm did not give him adequate recognition. 'It's jealousy,' she told him. 'You're so much better than the others.' But it was not her support that mattered; what he needed was a strong kindred spirit in the company. Harriet could become just that – was becoming so already, judging by Alan's much more relaxed behaviour at home these days. It was important to induce Harriet to stay with him, and not go dashing off on some new scheme of her own.

'I can see it now – Summerson and Turtle – what about that?'

Harriet laughed. 'It sounds ridiculous. Nobody can take a name like Turtle seriously. I've decided to revert to my own name. Now Summerson and Cheevers *would* sound impressive, but I think you're jumping the gun a bit.'

'Maybe, but he's in such a good mood at the moment, anything could happen. I'm deep in your debt, my dear, home life is positively idyllic, and that means he's happy at work. I've even sent off for Open University particulars,' she added in a conspiratorial undertone.

'Great,' said Harriet. 'Did he tell you about Rome?'

'Rome? No, what?'

'He has to go to Rome for some conference plus business and thinks I ought to go too.'

Laura brightened visibly. 'Oh wonderful,' she said. 'I thought for an awful minute you were going to say he wanted me to go, but I can't stand these business trips, even if they're in Rome. So there's another way you are helping me to avoid boredom.'

'I told the kids, and Emma wants to stay with you,' Harriet said. 'Would you mind very much? I really don't want her to go to Tom, and she doesn't either of course, and she absolutely refuses to go back to her grandmother, the silly girl, though I suppose it is a bit starchy for someone her age.'

'Of course she can come, what's one more among friends?'

'I've told her she must make herself useful and really help with everything.'

It could well be a help to have her. Laura was already committed to her new ideas and involved in form filling, interviews and preliminary study in the libraries. Home life was beginning to drift behind her, like a static shadow, and without Alan to cook for, to listen to and to pacify, freedom indeed began to seem more than a little enticing.

But Emma was not the sort to be a help around the house. She resented the fact that there was no congenial place for her to stay, and was not averse to showing it. She found that Hamish, at sixteen, was boringly too young to be of any real interest, and although they had grown up together in their various family encounters and get-togethers, they now had become slightly estranged and embarrassed with each other. The rest of the family tended to treat her as the hired baby-sitter. She felt herself to be in every way superior to them all and angry with Laura who went out and left her to cope.

Hamish was uncertain as to how much he was expected to organize while Emma was there. Was she guest or helper? She had suddenly become difficult to talk to. He called on Max and Louise. 'Mum's not going to be back till late,' he said. 'So I'll fill the dishwasher, and Louise and Daisy could tidy things up a bit.'

They all looked at Emma. She was annoyed that she hadn't said it first, but at the same time, it wasn't her place to boss them around. She started to stack plates herself, rather ungraciously.

'What's for supper?' Max said, looking back at Emma.

'No good looking at me,' Emma said sharply. 'Didn't your Mum say?'

'She just said there was enough in the fridge to make something. Salad, she said.'

'Ugh,' said Daisy. 'Can't we send out for a pizza?'

'Money?' said Max.

'We could pool what we've got, Mum'll pay us back.'

At that moment, Ben arrived with Hamlet. 'Pa thought I might pitch in here as everyone else has and he's lecturing late and might have to stay out the night. He gave me some money to buy pizzas.'

This reduced the tension, and the six of them became a party, much as they used to be a few years ago. Emma felt herself dropping several years in as many minutes. The pizzas were sent for and they prepared for a picnic-type supper on the floor with the record player going full blast. When Laura returned they were in the middle of a riotous game of racing demon with six packs of cards and the pandemonium was at its height. Hamlet stood beside Ben, barking to accompany the shouts, with his tail wagging amiably.

It was about the most depressing sight she could ever have imagined, and the noise jarred horribly on her ears. Only a short half-hour ago she had been bathed in silence in the library, deep in Thomas Aquinas and totally at peace with the world. Odd how she had never felt put upon before, because she did now.

'This place has to be cleared before any of you go to bed,' she yelled above the noise. The voices dropped measurably, but the game was too intense for her to be able to interrupt it.

'Pig,' squeaked Daisy, 'I've been waiting for that three of spades for ages.'

'You're not allowed to use two hands, it's not fair.'

'Where's the six of clubs for God's sake?'

'Four, five, OUT!' shouted Ben delightedly, and the noise immediately rose to deafening levels again.

'Oh NO – I've got millions left.'

'I bet you're cheating Ben, you always win.'

'I'm *not* cheating, I'm just much quicker than you.'

Laura felt unable to deal with any part of the situation. It must be tiredness; it had been a long time since she had used her brain to the extent she had done that evening; obviously wasn't used to it; she'd have to go more slowly. She had the sudden feeling that she disliked the lot of them – all these noisy and unruly children who had been dumped on her by their various parents. At the same time she couldn't believe she was being so irascible and peevish. Almost felt she wanted to cry. How stupid.

She went upstairs to the bedroom without saying anything further to them and dialled Tom's number; he could bloody well take them off her hands tomorrow because she wanted to go to a lecture.

His phone rang for some time. Must be out. She was about to put it down when Tom came on, sounding breathless. 'Hallo, Tom Turtle here . . .'

'Hallo, have I disturbed you? Were you at the bottom of the garden or in the loo or something?'

'No, no, I was just clearing up something, nothing important.' He didn't sound amused or relaxed. What had he been doing that he didn't want to tell her?

'I'm ringing to ask a favour.'

'Ask away.'

However justified, she didn't feel she could ask without some reason. 'I think I'm coming down with flu or a migraine or something, could you possibly take your two and my four over for tomorrow and Sunday? I'd be deeply grateful. There's something I've just got to do this weekend, and I can't face a house full of young.'

There was a fractional pause. 'Of course I'll have them; I didn't realize you had Emma so when Ben asked if he could spend the night with your lot, I thought you must have asked him – so sorry. Pack them all off in the morning, I'll be here the whole weekend.'

'You're a true friend. I'll do the same for you.' Why did she sense a distinct unease in his voice? Probably imagination. Perhaps he had a girl friend there and didn't want her to know. She felt a pang of guilt but stifled it; compassion for Tom must not be allowed to get out of proportion. He had to run his own life, after all, no matter how distressing the circumstances. He was possibly as glad to get Harriet out of his system as she was to be rid of him.

The tribe raised themselves from bed the next morning at varying times, according to age. Emma was the last down in accordance with the status symbol of being the eldest. Laura had already left for the library, marvelling at her ability to desert with scarcely a flicker of self-reproach. With Alan and Harriet living it up in Rome and Tom enjoying his freedom, the small core of resentment within her had not melted away overnight.

'We're going over to Pa's for today and tomorrow,' Ben told Emma as soon as she emerged, and waited with interest to see her reaction.

The reaction was visible: 'What? Who said?' Straight out of sleep, her expression was thunderous.

'Mum did, actually,' said Hamish, apologetically. 'She's not feeling well and she's got some studying to do.'

'*Studying?* What's she studying?'

'Open University,' said Louise.

'Something like that,' said Hamish. 'She's just started on it.'

Emma made an attempt to rearrange her expression, while feeling mortified with the embarrassment of imagining how her father would be able to deal with all of them, and wondering if she could possibly get there before the others in order to make the place look less like a down and outs' squat.

'Heaven help us,' she said. 'You'd all better be prepared to camp in the garden and eat out of tins; my father has no idea how to cater for himself, let alone six of us.'

'He does,' Ben said. 'We've got plenty of food in the freezer and our place isn't any more untidy than this is.'

They all looked round at the mess from the night before, which Laura had forced herself to ignore before she left.

'We'd better clear up a bit before we go,' Louise said, 'or Mum will have a fit; specially if she's not feeling well.'

There was a rather stilted air of sulkiness and bad feeling as they set to, as though each wanted to blame the others, even though there was no real thought that anyone was in the wrong. They were tidying up weren't they? Laura's unwellness was obviously not their fault, so no real reason to feel guilty about anything.

'I warn you,' Emma said, stacking plates in the dishwasher, 'it'll be dead boring over there; just nothing doing in back of beyond old Whetstone – talk about suburbia.'

'Just because you've moved into Regent's Park,' scoffed Max.

'Couldn't we have a party?' said Hamish. 'That would clear things up. A mix up of the King Alfred's lot with North London Collegiate girls could be great.'

They discussed the idea on the way back to Tom's and had become a well integrated animated group by the time they arrived. Tom found himself blasted out of any pretence of peace and quiet as soon as he heard them coming up the road. They seemed to fill the place with noise and aggressively rumbustious action, and soon spread all over the house in a lax, unconfined mass.

'My God, Pa, whatever's come over you? The place looks positively cared for. Have you got a woman in?' Emma slumped down on one of the chairs and took off her shoes. 'We're having a party tonight, is that all right?'

Backpacks and bags were dumped wherever anyone happened to be, and Hamish fiddled with the stereo and a tape. Ben turned on the television for *Grandstand* motor racing and Hamlet started to bark for his food.

'Can I have a drink?' Daisy asked, and she and Louise went into the kitchen to find it.

Tom realized he had not said anything at all since the invasion and that, so far, nobody had seemed to notice. It was rather like a nightmare. If Harriet had been there, they would all have been on their best behaviour and quite silent while she issued sensible, down-to-earth orders that nobody would seem to resent: not openly at least. He would anyway have been closeted in his study as soon as he had sensed their arrival. This was just a new experience, that was all; one that he was in and yet not a part of.

Rajini arrived on the doorstep some time later, when the whole company had settled in comfortably and were making continuous telephone calls to invite friends to the party. Others were considering what sort of refreshments they should get with the ten pounds they had elicited from Tom. Rajini and Emma confronted each other with guarded hostility.

'We're having a party,' Hamish joined them cheerily, 'Got any more of your North London lot that might come?'

'I suppose you've come for your history lesson,' Emma said in a venomously supercilious tone. 'Still got a crush on Pa?' She turned to the others: 'Can you imagine anyone having a thing about my pa? Isn't it a creepy idea?'

There was a lot of laughter, and Rajini felt herself grow suddenly taller and several years older than all these children laughing at her.

'Oh, it's far more than a crush,' she said, tilting her chin in the air. 'I am deeply and seriously in love.'

It had the effect she meant it to have: shrieks of laughter at an idea so preposterous, and a general relaxing of Emma's attitude to her. After all, the whole idea was absurd.

Tom froze with horror as soon as he saw Rajini, sitting on the sofa and talking into the telephone. For a moment he felt that all had been discovered and that a crisis was about to erupt, but as he watched from the door, before she saw him, he realized that she was part of them rather than a part of him. She looked up and blew him a kiss. 'Got some friends coming over,' she was saying into the phone, 'bring some beer . . .' and she described the way to get there. She put down the phone and approached him. 'Are you coming to the party?'

'I haven't been asked, have you?'

'Not until I arrived.' Her voice dropped to a whisper. 'I wanted to see you, so I told my parents that Emma and I needed to work together on some revision; they were quite impressed that I was so keen.'

There were too many people too near for him to make any sort of worthwhile comment; his feelings alternated between anger and anxiety. The situation was impossibly embarrassing and somehow humiliating, and he turned away and climbed the stairs to his study. What right had these children to make him feel so inadequate? He sat down, abruptly, on the edge of his desk, one hand thrust deep into his pocket while he chewed at the fingernails of the other.

Rajini slipped into the room and twined herself round him and against him. 'Shall we go to bed? They'd never miss us for a few minutes.'

He untwined her arms and tried to back away. 'You're mad, girl. Go back downstairs at once; of course they'll miss us. Don't even think of it.'

Rajini laughed. 'Doesn't matter if they do. You're a free agent, after all. Nobody has any right to interfere with what you do.'

'I have a right as to when I do what I do, and this is not one of those times. Go back downstairs.' He put his hand at the back of her neck and propelled her towards the door. 'Out of here this minute. OUT!'

'Damned spot.' She giggled as she made her exit. 'But you must come down to the party when it starts. You would add distinction and glamour to the proceedings.'

He sat down at the typewriter and attempted to get back to the work that had engrossed him up to four-thirty that morning, but the noise that gradually built up downstairs – the front door bell and the shrieks and screams of welcome yelled above the ear-splitting music – finally wiped out all serious thought. After two or three hours of mounting frustration, his tetchy irritation at the idea of his being trapped in his study by a crowd of noisy hooligans downstairs grew into an immense fury. Who did they think they were? Walking into someone's house and creating mayhem without a thought for anyone but themselves. It was outrageous. He realized that he was both famished and half-dead from a desire to sleep, having stayed up until four-thirty that morning and not having eaten all day. It was surely time for at least Ben and Louise and Daisy to go to bed. His confidence boosted by this realization, he made his way downstairs and entered the fray.

The ground floor of the house was a seething tangle of youth: some dancing languidly, others locked in erotic embraces, some eating, some drinking, some asleep and one throwing up on the floor. Daisy was standing by the door, near a worried-looking Ben with a can of beer in his hand.

Tom sidled into the kitchen in an attempt to get himself a drink without being noticed, and was daunted by the sight of the devastation. Was this really the same place Rajini and he had made so bright and inviting? The sink was piled high, and the hot water tap ran aimlessly. The fridge and freezer doors were open, and tables, chairs and the floor were littered with sliced bread, used packets of butter, cheese, open jars of mayonnaise, remains of chopped hard-boiled eggs, lettuce leaves and squashed tomatoes. The rubbish bin was crammed full and had pizza boxes, plastic bags and giant empty coke bottles balanced on top.

Tom took a furious step to turn off the running tap and slid from table to sink on a tomato. He looked for his stock of beer which he had replenished at the beginning of the week, but found nothing there. The little sods; but he should never have left it where they could find it. Oh well – open a bottle of wine.

The door of the larder, where he kept his small, but specialized wine cellar, was open and he saw, with mounting horror, that there were many spaces in the racks. How much had they pinched, for God's sake?

As his fury mounted, he turned to find Rajini standing directly behind him, smiling broadly, in a slightly drunken manner. She said nothing, but locked her arms round his neck and clamped her mouth to his in an impassioned kiss. In spite, or because of his frustrated annoyance, he felt himself rising immediately to the occasion and allowed his hands to wander down the back of her.

Within seconds, a roaring, flailing Emma set upon Rajini, pulled her off Tom, pushed her on to the floor and poured a full glass of beer over her head before falling on top of her and pounding her with fists and feet.

The party surged out of the sitting-room and gathered round the spectacle with the enthusiasm of a playground audience cheering on a fight between rival gang leaders, and Tom had no help in his efforts to drag the two of them apart. Hamish finally came to his rescue and pinioned Rajini's arms to her side, while Tom dragged Emma out of reach.

'ENOUGH!' roared Tom. 'That's it. It's finished. Everybody out – NOW. And for the ones who are staying, clearing to be done, sick to be cleaned up, carpet to be washed and disinfected, and noise to be abated.'

There was a slight, embarrassed movement away from the scene of battle, and Tom and Hamish released the wilting protagonists on to the floor, where they collapsed in tearful heaps.

Tom surveyed the scene with disgust, but at the same time enjoying the sense of authority that he'd regained in the past few minutes.

'Ben, Louise and Daisy, you can go straight upstairs to bed and, Ben, you will be in my room tonight, so that the others won't disturb you when they come to bed after clearing up. Put a pot beside the bed in case you're sick in the night, so that you don't wake me up.'

Rajini, whose nose was bleeding, sat up without raising her head. 'I shall have to stay,' she said in a whisper 'because my parents thought I was going to; where can I sleep?'

'That's something you and Emma can work out together,' Tom said. 'There's plenty of floor space.' And taking Ben by the arm, he marched him upstairs to the bedroom.

Hamlet, sensing that everyone had misbehaved themselves, followed guiltily behind them, his ears drooping sadly over his eyes.

18

'I really feel quite decadent,' Harriet told Alan over a Rome hotel breakfast. 'To visit Rome for the first time in my life, and spend the whole time in offices and restaurants discussing business. To whizz past the Colosseum two or three times a day on my way to meetings and not stop for a look, seems – well – rather disrespectful somehow.'

Alan smiled at her, full of the complacency of achievement. 'From tomorrow on we'll sight-see to your heart's content. We've clinched a fantastic deal, so we deserve a little holiday. We're a great team, you and I; make all the right impressions. I can't tell you what a difference it's made, having you along as the smart, sexy, intellectual type who oozes charm.'

'I'm not altogether sure I like that description.' In reality, Harriet was actually certain that she did like it. 'But I like the fact that you think I was part of what finalized the deal.'

'A big part,' said Alan. 'So what about a little holiday? Let's go to Venice tomorrow and wallow in culture for a few days?'

'Even more decadent; Venice is an outrageously

plush city with its Doges and its palaces – oh Alan, I should just love that. But shouldn't we get back?'

'Maybe we should, but business deals take time to clinch; can't hurry them, can you? I'll phone home and say we've been delayed. Easy. We won't be missed.'

'I certainly shan't, don't know about you though. You're still a family man remember.'

'More a provider I would say. Laura's in charge of the family.'

'What an appallingly chauvinist statement. You shouldn't even think it, let alone say it.'

Alan hunched his shoulders: 'Laura likes it that way. She thinks of home, meals and children as her job and she really enjoys it.'

'Very suspect; that's probably your interpretation of what she thinks. No woman actually enjoys domesticity unless she's a moron.'

'Now there's an absurd feminist assumption.' Alan poured himself another cup of coffee, and leaned back in his chair, to enjoy the argument in a more relaxed manner. 'Domesticity and child-rearing is not necessarily a vocation for the feeble minded.'

'Oh, I know there are some people who adopt it as a profession, and others who manage motherhood and a profession with a dedication that is tremendously praiseworthy.'

'As you did.'

'No, I didn't. I never managed motherhood at all. And Tom's no better as a father. He's for ever promising them things he could never possibly come up with.'

'A sad man,' said Alan.

Harriet glanced at him sharply. 'Don't you go feeling sorry for Tom. He's had every opportunity; got a great brain and no financial worries; he should have made it to the top. You know I sometimes think he didn't really want to. I can never forgive someone for that. Having all the opportunities and not making the best of them. I think that's a sin.'

'There speaks top management, lady.'

They spent the following day at the various more obvious monuments.

'Beautiful,' said Alan. 'Staggering, incredible . . .'

'But much too unbelievably ancient to be even remotely plausible. I find I just can't make myself realize it all happened. I mean to say – all those old gentlemen draped in sheets and Christians being chomped up by lions. It's all too unlikely, isn't it?'

Alan laughed and took her hand. 'So we'll leave Rome for the Romans and travel on in time. Venetian decadence is more us I think.' He tucked her arm under his, still holding her hand. 'I feel so exhilarated today. Haven't felt like this for ages. Successful business trip, the weather, a sense of freedom and the idea of a few idle, romantic days in Venice with one of my favourite women: what could be better?'

'What indeed?' Pleasure shot up her spine in the sure knowledge that she and Alan were at the beginning of a liaison. She had forgotten that extraordinary, sizzling excitement that attacks the nervous system when sexual attraction is suddenly and simultaneously acknowledged by two people. She'd never felt it with Alan before, probably because of being hemmed in by the repressive effect of easy and friendly relations over the years, and the fact that he had been just the husband of a friend for as long as she cared to remember. She had looked on him as attractive, flirted a little at parties, but never this, and the suddenness took her by surprise.

They both stood still among the Colosseum crowds and traffic roar of Rome, and said nothing at all for several seconds.

'A decadent double bed in a decadent bedroom in a positively depraved, but very expensive hotel,' Alan said finally.

'With brocade hangings round the bed and a mirror on the ceiling.'

'With putti everywhere and Titians on the walls.'

'Only small ones then, big ones would be too overpowering; might take our minds off making love.'

'Nothing could distract me from that.'

So there it was, out in the open, with no going back. In the middle of all the milling crowds of tourists and guided tours, two business associates who were also old friends, suddenly possessed with an unquenchable desire for each other. The kiss they shared only served to increase the urgency. Harriet felt herself taking off in a perfectly extraordinary exultation. Where *had* decorum fled?

'Taxi,' said Alan, turning suddenly from her and grabbing her arm. 'Quick.' And he started to run, pulling her along behind him, towards the surging traffic whirlpool that was eddying round the Colosseum. But no taxis were free and, in any case, a tremendous jam of cars seemed to be building up around them as they ran.

'It would be quicker to walk,' said Harriet, so they did, weaving frantically through crowds and traffic, running away from people to the privacy of themselves and their new, overwhelming discovery of each other. How, thought Harriet, can this be me, running through the streets of Rome like a mad woman, fired with a manic desire to get into a bed with Alan?

The lift was probably the most frustrating part of the sprint. On reaching the hotel, they were breathless and by this time weak with laughter as well. The idea of two flights of stairs daunted them and they stopped by the lift, a caged, antique affair, imprisoned in wrought iron, which moved ponderously and with tremendous hauteur. An impossibly old couple fumbled their way in behind them, and the cage-load slowly, slowly started the journey upwards. Alan clutched Harriet round the waist, and let out a great explosion of laughter, as the oldies rolled an offended and irritated gaze in their direction before crawling out at the first floor.

The great metal grille had scarcely clanged behind them before Alan and Harriet were back in their original clinch, with Alan groping behind his back in order to press the button for the second floor. It was all rather like a drunken revel Harriet thought, with the rush along the passage, the giggling struggle with the room key, and finally, finally, the bliss of anonymity, privacy and security, where the weight of imprisoned emotion and lust could be let free.

Thank God the dress slipped downwards and avoided the ungainly tug over the head. Thank God she'd kept her figure; nothing to be embarrassed about there. Then sudden shock to find that he had short, curly hair all over his body, something she had always professed to abominate. She remembered expressing disgust rather too loudly and obviously at the sight of all those great hairy apes disporting themselves on the beaches on their South of France holidays. So why did she seethe with excitement on feeling his warm, furry body pressed voluptuously against her now? Tom had a few meagre hairs to the chest and soft down on his shoulders. But this? This was like making love with a bear and it was fantastically erotic.

He was miraculously naked without ever seeming to undress, and easing her gently down on to the bed without her assistance or co-operation. They were joined, and moved as one person. No looking round to see where the bed was, no awkward, ungainly

143

positions with one sitting and one standing, unsure how to arrange themselves. And how the hell had he divested himself of clothes so elegantly and unnoticeably? What finesse!

They came together in a delirium of pleasure and stayed, without further movement, while their pulses simmered down and their breathing slowed and the deep content of total satisfaction took them over.

Harriet was afraid to let the moment go, never having experienced anything like it before; was it possible to have lived forty-two years without realizing such physical enjoyment existed? She lay motionless, marvelling at the realization that she was not, after all, the sort of woman who thought sex was overrated.

'What a revelation,' she said after several long and silent minutes. 'What a bloody miracle.'

Alan woke from immediate sleep with a slight start, rolled on to his side and drew her towards him. 'Absolutely right, you're a bloody miracle, my darling; not only a high tech business woman, but a six million dollar lover as well, something I thought didn't exist. Why did it take so long for us to meet? How, in God's name, did we manage to remain so unaware for all those years?'

'Circumstances I suppose. Home surroundings, everyday life. We were both drowning in our own little worlds and far too busy to look beyond.' She was seized with panic that all might revert when they returned. 'Perhaps we should stay here for ever and never go back to reality.'

He started to kiss her again, bringing back all the passionate frenzy within seconds. How was it possible? *Twice* in the space of less than an hour? Another eye-opener: she found it perfectly possible.

'This is not at all wise of course,' Harriet said, a long, long time later, as they sat together in the deep armchair in his room sipping Barolo and tucking in to delicious carpaccio with gusto. It would have been tidier, she thought, if they could have finished off the business side here, in Rome, and then started from scratch with the affair once they got to Venice.

'What is not wise?' He got up and stood behind her, sliding his hands down under the front of the bath robe she had wrapped round herself.

'Us. We are not being very sensible.'

His hands stroked upwards until they reached her throat, when he leaned down and enclosed her neck and her head with his arms, kissing from the top of her head, down past her ear and back to the point between shoulder and neck that sent her pulses racing yet again and shock waves exploding from vulva to crown. Wisdom and sense flew out of the window, along with tidy presuppositions of Rome being the place for business. There seemed to be absolutely no room at all for any thinking or talking that had nothing to do with the present situation. It was a wicked waste of time to attempt conversation.

'I don't see what sense has to do with it,' said Alan, with his mind on the business in hand, and neither did she, really.

Venice was the cream in the coffee. While Harriet basked in the new and momentous change in her life and outlook, Alan remained in the euphoria of having well and truly hit the jackpot. The coupling with Harriet had worked like a charm. With an asset like Harriet behind him, there could be no doubt about success. Asset? He smiled to himself at the idea of Harriet being one of his assets – part of his estate! Was he looking on her as a *possession* already?

They sat in St Mark's Square, drinking bellinis, as the light was fading and the sky became dark with wheeling pigeons. It was impossible not to think of oneself as part of a medieval painting.

'So where do we go from here?' said Harriet, elegant legs crossed, skin golden, to match all the gold of the Venetian frescoes, the heavy earrings he had just bought her, glinting in the lights as she moved her head; she fitted perfectly into this magnificent city, impeccably dressed in expensive clothes; bright, alert and painfully desirable. He was living with what seemed like a permanent erection.

She was so completely his sort of woman. He wondered how she had ever allowed herself to be attached to absent-minded old professor-type Tom? How had he, Alan, only thought of her as Tom's wife up till this moment? Attractive – yes, he'd always thought her attractive but, before this extraordinary magical week in Italy, she had appeared also to be a bossy, discontented loudmouth, who had got herself tied up in a disastrous marriage. In just seven days, she had changed into a different woman right before his eyes. He was staring at her without answering her question while the thoughts went through his mind.

'Are we going to call this a wonderful dream and slip back into our own little lives as soon as we get back?'

She knew quite well that it was impossible, there was no way back for either of them, but she was not yet completely sure that this sort of thing was not a fairly regular occurrence for him. For him, business trips might be two-a-penny. She simmered with jealousy at the thought. 'Do you do this sort of thing often?' Her voice sounded cold and angry: she heard it herself.

Alan clasped his hands and leaned forward. 'I have had other women when I was on trips away from home, quite often. No excuse, just needed them. And you?'

It seemed humiliating to admit that she had not slept with anyone other than Tom during their marriage. She was the woman who had had no time for sex because it was so overrated, wasn't she? She blushed, for probably the first time in her life, and felt like inventing a few adventures in order to appear more normal. But that was absurd.

'Never had the time,' she said, and they both laughed.

'Too busy working,' said Alan, 'and being a pillar of society. What a waste.'

'So what are we going to do?'

There was a silence between them, and then Alan said: 'It's all about Laura, isn't it?' and there was another silence.

'To start with,' Harriet felt the need to be certain. 'Are we more than a one-off?'

'I can't vouch for you, but as far as I'm concerned, you are one-hundred per cent all or nothing for me. No way could I treat this as a holiday lollipop.'

'And you are a mild expert on holiday lollipops?'

'Dabbler rather than expert. None of them have ever become more than the occasional treat.'

'And Laura? Does she go along with these holiday treats?'

'Laura doesn't know, at least I don't think she does. Laura is an angel; upsetting her would be harrowing.'

'Like me upsetting Tom.'

'Scarcely the same thing. Tom had it coming.'

Harriet felt suddenly annoyed, finding herself wanting to speak up for Tom in the face of criticism. She let it pass.

'So what are you going to do?' With an emphasis on the you. Disappointment was growing inside her. Had he not felt the same certainty about it that she had? It was surely mutual and unavoidable? Much too strong to be pushed aside and lost. Must hang on to it somehow until he was as certain as she was.

'Is there any way,' she said cautiously, 'that we could carry on in a triangular fashion?'

He glanced at her sharply. 'But Laura would never agree to that.'

'I didn't visualize her knowing about it.'

'Oh, I see.' And he shut up again.

'Otherwise, even though you might not consider me a lollipop, I might find myself becoming the business trip side-kick – i.e., fall into bed only when convenient to the boss, which I wouldn't enjoy.'

'If we weren't sitting out here under the stern gaze of St Mark and his church and all those horses and lions all over the place, I would insist, as boss to boss, that we consummated our partnership yet again, here and now, for the hundredth time in the past few days. This might serve to remind you that we both need each other continuously, day and night, no matter what. I think we have to face up to that and decide, when we get home, how we're going to bring it about.'

Harriet retained a waver of doubt that for her, like Cinderella at midnight, everything might change back to ashes and rags when they touched down at Heathrow.

19

'And everybody was sick on the floor,' Daisy told Laura after the Summerson family had returned home and left Emma and Ben with Tom. 'They were all drunk and kissing and everything; even Ben was drunk.'

Hamish threw a book at his sister from across the room. 'Lies,' he said. 'All lies. Anybody would think it was an orgy from the way you tell it. *One* person was sick, that's all.'

'As if that wasn't more than enough,' Laura said heatedly, horrified at the idea that she had foisted such scenes on Tom. 'How could you have been so bad mannered as to inflict such a thing on someone who was kind enough to put you up for the night when I wasn't well?' She cringed at the thought of having off-loaded her own irritations on to someone who had enough on his plate already. 'How absolutely disgusting of you.' She glowered at Hamish as she spoke because the others could just be considered too young to be responsible.

He responded with fury: 'It's not my fault. Emma suggested it—'

'No she didn't, you did,' said Daisy.

'Shut up you shitty little grass,' yelled Max. 'It was Emma's snooty North London lot that brought in the yobbos.'

'I can't imagine that your lot behaved any better,' Laura said, still full of anger and shame.

'Well, we did clear up,' Louise said. 'It was revolting. I hate parties, but it was quite funny at one point because Emma and Rajini had a fight.'

Laura had noticed the dewy-eyed Indian child entwined with Emma on several occasions when she had been at the Turtle house; she had not looked capable of anything but gazelle-like dignity and grace. 'A fight? What do you mean?'

Hamish smirked: 'Emma seemed to be accusing Rajini of having it off with Tom.'

'WHAT?' Laura swung round on Hamish again. 'Emma couldn't have been so stupid as to imagine such an absurd idea. It couldn't have been that.'

Daisy giggled. 'They were really funny, Mummy; kicking and scratching and pulling each other's hair and everything . . .'

'The whole thing must have been horrific, and not in the least funny. I shall never be able to face Tom again. I am desperately ashamed of the lot of you.'

She phoned Tom the next morning, early: 'Tom, what can I say? I had no idea they could be so uncivilized.'

Tom laughed. 'For God's sake, it was nothing to do with you. It was a new practical experience for me – all part of adult education today.'

'I always hoped that sort of thing only happened to other people's children.'

'What? Getting drunk and learning when to stop? One small step for them while we learn to sit back and watch them make the same mistakes that we did. I would suggest that we both take the day off, drive into the country and lunch at a pub overlooking rolling downs or a wild tempestuous sea, only you'll have to drive me because my absent wife won't let me use her car.'

The idea of escape filled Laura with quite overpowering desire. 'Lovely thought, but I couldn't possibly; Alan's coming back tomorrow and I have to organize myself about food and get the house into some sort of shape, and the family will expect me here when they come back from school.'

'It should take about half an hour for you to write notes for the kids, get the car started and be outside my house. It's now ten o'clock: see you at half-past.' And he put the phone down. He needed some fresh air and he felt that Laura possibly needed her resistance built up against what he was pretty sure Harriet and Alan were about to confront her with.

They strode along the front at Brighton battered by a mini-gale.

'So much for rolling downs,' Laura gasped.

'But the sea is definitely wild and tempestuous. As Harriet's nanny most certainly would have said, "This will blow the cobwebs away."'

'Cobwebs, maybe, but guilty conscience for leaving the children to cope, no.'

'Give it time, give it time. I'll take you to Beachy Head next, and that is bound to blow the guilt away or you over the cliff.'

'I do feel bad, though, just walking out on the children like this. I didn't even do any tea for them.'

'A hungry child will not go hungry long if there is bread, milk and cheese in the house.'

'But I'm afraid they'll eat the special things I got in for Alan's return tomorrow – asparagus and strawberries, and I was doing roast duck.'

Tom turned to look at her. 'What do you think of this team up between Harriet and Alan?'

'Best thing that ever happened to him; he's been a changed character since Harriet joined the firm. I suggested it you know, a long time ago. I always thought they'd make an ideal duo where that business is concerned.'

Poor innocent, Tom thought. 'Only where business is concerned?'

She put her hand up under his arm as they battled along the front. 'Oh Tom, poor Tom. You're naturally suspicious after the way Harriet treated you. I do understand, but Alan isn't like Harriet, you know. He's really a marvellous husband and father. He'd never do anything to upset the children, or me for that matter. He's such a family man. It's the way he was brought up. Family first, and let nothing come in the way of that. Harriet isn't his type at all; she wouldn't spoil him like I do. He knows that perfectly well. You're not jealous of Alan are you?'

'Only in that he has a wife who spoils him.'

'Poor Tom. It must be hard for you on your own. You were always pretty useless at housework weren't you?'

'I manage. Ben keeps me in order.'

'Ben is a dream of a boy. Was he really drunk that evening? I can't imagine it. And what's this extraordinary story they were telling me about Emma having a fight with her friend Rajini? That she thinks you're having an affair with Rajini or something? Wherever did she get that incredible idea?'

Tom found himself suddenly cold with a shocked anxiety. 'It's all in the mind. You know what they're like at that age. This Rajini has a crush on me it seems, and Emma took it to its illogical conclusion.'

Laura laughed. 'Well just you be careful. Young girls are not what they were. You might find yourself swept off your feet if you don't watch out. She's quite one of the most beautiful girls I've ever seen. Don't let your disillusion with Harriet get the better of you.'

'No fear of that; I was disillusioned with Harriet from the word go, but quite willing to put up with things for the sake of the children and a fairly quiet life. I just hate to see the way Ben is being torn to pieces by it. She could easily have waited a year or two until he was more able to cope.'

'I do rather agree,' Laura said. 'But everyone says now that the children are worse off if the parents fight all the time.'

'That's balls,' said Tom. 'And anyway we didn't fight. I just gave in.'

'You didn't you know, you fought like mad, only you did the fighting in such a gentlemanly well-reasoned way, that nobody noticed it.'

'Just pointed out to her how wrong she was, that's all,' Tom said with a chuckle. 'Which, of course, she was.'

They found their pub, overlooking a peaceful sweep of the downs, and returned to their housekeeping duties late that night, much refreshed and suitably calmed.

Harriet and Alan drove back from Heathrow in Harriet's car which she had long-term parked for the period they had been away.

'So, back to reality is it?' she asked, wanting to have the situation faced and cleared up at a time when it was impossible for sex to take over and suffocate clear thinking.

'Depends what you consider reality.'

'For me, reality is living with you, sleeping with you, working with you. I've changed my mind about a *ménage à trois*; I want you to myself, all the time. This is reality. So what do you propose to do about it?'

Alan slid his hand up her thigh under her skirt and found that the contact banished all uncertainty of what action had to be undertaken.

'I shall have to break it to Laura somehow. The thought of it appals me and I haven't an idea how I shall bring myself to do it, but it's got to be done.'

'When?'

'Well, not *now*, not just at the moment of return . . .'

'Why not? The best thing would be for you to come home with me, now, and tackle her in the morning. So that she could realize something was different from the word go, then she'd be far more ready to accept the inevitable.'

'I can't do that; she would never understand why I shouldn't go home. The kids will be expecting me. I can't just walk out without any explanation.'

'Much the best way because then you're dealing with things from a position of strength, away from all the hassle.' She squirmed sideways and her foot pressed down hard on the accelerator. 'For God's sake, darling – not on the motorway.'

'When's he coming?' asked Daisy, with her nose pressed to the window pane. 'What time is he coming?'

'Stop fussing,' Louise told her. 'A watched pot never boils.' Which was an expression she had recently learned from her grandmother.

Daisy stared at her with incomprehension. 'I'm not watching a pot,' she said. 'I'm waiting for Daddy to come home. And you're not to tell him about me coming first in poetry because I want to.'

'You can tell him I came last in maths if you like,' Max said. 'He'll like that.'

'When's he coming?' Daisy asked Laura.

'I don't know exactly,' Laura said, 'but there's a flight that should have got in two hours ago and he might have been on that, in which case he'll be here anytime now.'

She felt elated and depressed at the same time, or rather in intermittent bouts – up and then down. Full of interest to hear how the trip went, and whether he and Harriet were able to get on for the whole ten days, or whether they had fought together over the ways things should be approached; and then half-dreading the loss of freedom his return would inevitably mean. The day at Brighton with Tom had been so unbelievably free of anxiety; no watching one's step in case one blurted out something tactless, which she was for ever doing. Alan was often touchy when immersed in work; she frequently felt clumsy, not being able to sense what sort of a mood he was in. She had a bottle of red wine open and the duck was smelling delicious.

But by the time Alan and Harriet arrived back at the empty Regent's Park flat, they were both far too aroused to do anything other than fall into bed. Alan's taxi finally dropped him at his home at quarter to one in the morning, when everyone but Laura was asleep. She was lying in bed, sleepless and anxious, listening to the radio for news of a crash, and unwilling to ring the airline to find out if there had been a delay. Why else would he be late?

20

The recriminations at breakfast from Daisy were noisy. 'Why didn't you come back last night Daddy?'

'Well, I did . . .'

'Yes, but not in time. Mummy let me stay up till nine o'clock waiting and then I had to go to bed, and I wanted to give you . . .'

'But I didn't say what time I'd be home. I didn't know exactly . . .'

'But Mummy had looked it up and she knew and . . .'

'Flights get delayed, pet, you never can tell what aeroplanes will do next.'

Laura busied herself with pouring coffee: had there been delays in the flights from Italy last night? She had not really wanted to find out. He had given no explanations and she had not asked for any in case they should be painful for him to give. This stupid inverted protectiveness of not wanting to upset *him*.

'I have something very good to give you,' said Daisy, 'but it doesn't seem as exciting this morning as it was last night.'

'But it's exciting for me,' Alan said, 'because I didn't know about it at all last night which means I couldn't be excited about it until now when you're going to tell me about it.'

Daisy considered this for a moment. 'Well,' she said sulkily, 'I made something.'

'So can I see it? How very exciting. Will you show it to me? Please?'

'All right.' Daisy was still grudging, but allowed him a little more information: 'Miss Steel held it up in front of everybody and they all clapped.' She produced a small clay thumb pot from behind her back.

Alan hugged his daughter, and felt his throat constrict into a ball of pain. An immediate reflection formed in his mind: and I have something very bad to tell you and it seems far more traumatic this morning than it did yesterday morning.

Alone with Laura after the exodus to school, he stood silent and waiting for the obvious questioning to start. You can't just blurt out something like that, without a good, solid row and some sort of goading from the other side. Can't just say, Darling, I have decided that I am about to leave you and go and live with Harriet. Harriet said that she just went upstairs and started to pack and told Tom on her way out, but this situation was too fraught and unresolved for Alan to be able to take such a decisive step. He couldn't even set off to the office in the usual way, with a smile and a wave, and just never come back. The questions stayed unasked but they were there, just the same, almost animate objects hanging between the two of them.

'I'm sorry,' he said finally.

'What for?'

There was the question: so answer it. But the flesh was extremely weak. 'For messing everything up last night and not letting you know.'

'Letting me know what?'

His innards continued to writhe and churn with

distress. 'Er . . . well, Harriet – Harriet and I . . . we . . .'

Laura could not let her mind admit to what she was hearing. She remained totally, unhelpfully silent.

Alan blundered on: 'We – er – I'm afraid we had a little sort of affair.'

As the words tumbled out of his mouth there followed another long, embarrassing silence, and as he watched Laura in a kind of awful horror, he saw her crumble in front of him. Her face appeared to crease and disintegrate into minute jigsaw lines and cracks. The colour drained from her cheeks and her skin suddenly looked like parchment. He was frozen into a painful numbness with the shock of the effect he seemed to have had on her. Was it possible that his small statement could have done so much damage in such a short time? He wondered if she was going to be sick – or perhaps just drop dead there and then. He had the sudden certainty that nothing in his life was ever going to be the same again.

Laura heard her voice, sounding fairly normal, say: 'So thank God you told me about it. It does make it slightly better to know that we can be honest with each other.' How was this voice able to carry on while her whole being remained numb and without thought? She felt as though someone must have switched her on so that speech was automatic. 'But I do see,' the voice went on, quite amiably and in full control, 'that the fact of being in Rome with someone as attractive as Harriet might have had its problems.'

But then the clockwork suddenly ran down and she burst into tears. 'No, I don't see, I don't see at all. After all these years, how could you? How could either of you? What sort of a position have you put us all in now. Did you think? Did either of you think of the consequences? What have you done to us all? What awful damage have you done?'

The storm of weeping in which she indulged, after running upstairs and hurling herself on the bed, gave great relief, at the same time as tearing physically at her throat and her chest and her tear ducts.

Alan sat, slumped, in the kitchen, arms hanging limply, drained and not at all relieved. Life had gradually returned to his physical body, but his mind remained dead. This was only the first step, there was still a long journey ahead. He felt hopelessly divided and unsure, but there seemed to be one thing certain, sudden death was not a feasible answer. Harriet must be made to see this; ruthless amputation was not the answer in this case. Put off the inevitable just a little bit longer, when it was sure to be easier to adjust to. Things must surely work themselves out in time.

He went upstairs and sat on the bed and forced himself to talk to Laura. 'I know it won't make things any better,' he said, 'and I don't mean it to sound like an excuse, but we did pull off the most fantastic deal which will probably put us on the map as an independent company in the very near future, and we were both so elated that we sort of went overboard in our celebrations.' The excuses spilled out in an automatic fashion; he didn't have to think about them.

Laura had stopped crying, and was lying face down, stiff and intractible.

'A one-off you mean.'

Scarcely that. 'Not exactly; a kind of culmination of effort and exultation and relief.'

The silence was frigid.

'It was a very physical thing,' he added, after a moment's hesitation, wondering whether that might not make it sound worse. Could it sound as though he was denigrating their own, rather cosy, married sex? He had an immediate twinge of anxiety that he would not now be able to respond to cosy married sex ever again. There was no way, at that particular moment, that he would be able to perform should Laura make an approach as a possible gesture towards an amnesty. Would he ever be able to? Apprehension made him retreat into himself and curse that he had brought the idea up in the first place. Nothing was ever going to be the same again.

'Meaning you love me while making love to her?'

That was a possible explanation, but put like that made it sound far more reprehensible than it actually was. There was no suitable answer, and they lapsed into tense silence again.

'So what do you intend to do?' Laura said at last. The question he had been waiting for, but which now, he decided, must be evaded for the time being.

'That depends on you, darling. It depends whether or not you can forgive.' But if she forgave him, then surely she would expect him to take up where they had left off? What a stupid thing to suggest.

Laura sat up and stared into his face. Trying to read truth into it? He looked back at her, unflinchingly he hoped.

'If you mean,' she said, 'do I intend to walk out on our life and our children because of what you've done, then of course I don't; but it will take time to adjust, and I can't vouch for what I might do if I come across Harriet. I shall have to depend on you to keep her out of my way. And I shall also have to depend on you not to carry on from where you left off. I shall consider it a one-off, whatever you think it was – and I do really mean was, not is.'

He squeezed her hand. 'You're very generous,' he said, and wondered what the hell he was going to say to Harriet. He had achieved precisely nothing apart from tearing himself to pieces by seeing Laura collapse in front of his eyes. All the good bits of their life together screamed at him from behind her set expression. Was anything worth this terrible anguish he was causing someone he was fond of? Who said splitting up was easier than making do with compromises?

There was no way he could tell her more at this moment.

'Well?' Harriet looked up as he came into the office. 'What happened? Did you tell her? What did she say?'

She watched him put his brief case on the desk and snap it open.

'You didn't tell her, did you?'

'I told her we'd been to bed.'

'And?'

'She's looking on it as a one-off and forgiving me.'

'Oh God – you're such a wimp you know. A step at a time policy is just not the one to use here; just spreads out the misery. It's not being kind, if that's what you think.'

A secretary poked her head through the door. 'The boss is in and wants to see you as soon as possible.'

Alan ran his hand through his hair, and began to sort papers. One bloody thing after another. Got to start the hassle of beginning to edge himself out of the firm and into their own organization. Harriet was dead set on it. She wanted them together in partnership as soon as possible, and she was probably perfectly right. They could make it together in all senses of the word, but taking that first step brought on spasms of abject terror. He felt assailed on all sides. Why didn't they leave him alone to enjoy the pure pleasure of just creating a beautiful piece of furniture without the bother of trying to cut corners in order to make it cheaper, or easier to make, or less outrageous, or more like the popular one they did last year. Why did life have to conform always to what other people wanted or, at least, thought was acceptable. Harriet was right; they had to break free and be on their own to produce the sort of stuff they had just proved they could easily sell in Italy and all over the world for that matter. He must overcome this initial fear of taking direct action.

Emma had been staying on at Tom's for the night of the return from Venice but went back to Harriet's flat from school that afternoon with feelings of relief liberally tinged with guilt, though why guilt she found difficult to understand. She travelled back on the train with a friend as far as Baker Street. 'I can't see why I should feel guilty because I'm going back to stay with my mother instead of my father,' she complained. 'I mean it's not my fault that they choose to live apart.'

'You probably like living with your mother because it's much more comfortable,' said the friend, voicing the obvious which Emma had been at pains to suppress.

'I don't see that there's anything wrong with that,' said Emma.

'Well, if you don't want to side with either of them, then you usually feel sorry for one of them more than the other and so you think you ought to be a bit nicer to make up.' Her parents had split five years previously.

'It's his own silly fault,' Emma said, stonily.

'Sort of you are awful but I like you situation?'

This made Emma laugh, and that helped her to push guilt into the background and thank God she was going back to a state of order and organization. The irritation at the lack of system in the last few days had edged her into furious despondency.

Alan and Harriet were both there when she got in, and her assumptions of a period of uncluttered living evaporated in the atmosphere of interrupted anger and shock at the unexpectedness of her arrival.

'Hallo,' she said, feeling that she should perhaps apologize for being there. 'I didn't come back last night because I didn't know when you were arriving.'

'Quite right,' Harriet recovered herself from the tension of her argument with Alan and repeated herself: 'Quite right; we didn't get back till late.'

Emma looked from one to the other, wondering what was wrong. 'Have a good time?' she said, for want of something better.

'Fine, fine. It was a business trip you know.'

'Yes, I know.'

'So I mean we didn't get much time for sight-seeing.'

They all laughed, and Harriet pulled herself together sufficiently to prise them out of the awkward void in which they were floundering. 'So we had better look in the freezer to find out if we have to go out for supper. I haven't had time to consider shopping yet.'

'Ben's all right,' Emma said, in case Harriet remembered later that she hadn't asked about him. 'Do you want me to go out and get anything?' she added as Harriet searched the freezer.

'No, no – plenty in here.'

So Emma went to her room and shut the door, stunned by the unfamiliar situation. If you had been away, did you not come back with news and colourful descriptions of where you had been? Did you not want to know how everyone had got on without you? Weren't you pleased to see people? She felt a shudder of apprehension crawl up her spine. Was somebody dead or something? She wondered why this morbid thought always cropped up when she was confronted with something she could not quite fathom. She turned the CD player up loud, and listened to M. C. Hammer, tipping out her books, magazines and make up on to the table. Best get dug in to some work straight away so

162

as not to allow her thoughts to dwell on possible un-
pleasantnesses.

It was a good hour later that she started to feel
hungry, so she switched off the music and prepared
herself to emerge for supper. The voices in the flat
were raised, angry and strident: Emma stood in front of
her closed door and listened.

Harriet: 'The only way you can come back here, my
dear, is if and when you have told her the truth. I've
said that so many times. I will not and cannot be the
mistress on the side.'

Alan: 'You could never be the mistress on the side, we
both know that bloody well. All I'm asking for is a bit
more time – even a week would be something. It's no
use thinking we can bludgeon our way through
everything, and it's no good setting the divorce in
motion before organizing the business side. We have
to do the two things together so that it can be seen to be
one and the same thing. It would be less shocking to
everybody if they are seen to be connected.'

Harriet: 'Seen by whom? You can't make it respectable, you know. No-one will think any better of you for
attempting to prove that it's really only a business
deal.'

Alan: 'So are we going to call the whole thing off just
because you can't wait a week?'

Harriet: 'There's no *sense* in waiting a week.'

Alan: 'No sense? No sense? God dammit, woman, what
does sense matter when we're dealing with people's
suffering?'

Hunger probably had a lot to do with it, but at that
moment, Emma felt suddenly that she might quite
possibly die if she stood behind her door a moment
longer. Her heart was racing painfully, which made
her head throb in a simultaneous action. Her throat
was constricted and dry; she felt an overpowering

certainty that she was about to vomit and, as she flung open the door, her stomach quite literally rose up in an agony of retching. Immediately the flat rose up with it and reeled round her head, so that she fell on the floor in the glorious anaesthesia of a dead faint. It could scarcely have been a more dramatic protest.

21

Tom's coaching sessions with Rajini continued with increased frequency. 'It's perfectly all right,' Rajini told him when he suggested that two and three times a week might be considered excessive. 'The parents are so dead keen on my getting in to Oxford that they wouldn't question anything I say might help. They're quite impressed that I'd even want to spend my holidays working.'

'Even so,' Tom said, 'I can't help feeling perfidious when they pay me for making love to you.'

Rajini laughed without any sense of perfidy. 'Don't be so silly; I couldn't learn nearly so well if I didn't get all the lovely excitement as well. I am succeeding because I love you and so remember everything you say. You can charge them for the hour and then give me another hour of your valuable time absolutely free. They would appreciate that and think you were most generous.'

'That's what makes it so dishonest.'

'What my parents think is good for me and what actually is good for me are two totally different things. You are good for me in every possible way, and if you are doing me good, then there is no reason for you to feel guilty, whatever my parents might think.'

'Convenient and comfortable reasoning,' said Tom. It would surely be most unreasonable to stop the affair when both he and she were benefiting so obviously. He found that the relationship still surged like a fire when they were together. It made him feel quite capable of achieving objectives he'd had no energy to strive for previously. Talk about new leases of life – it was as if he had stepped off the edge of a cliff and found he could fly.

All the uncertainties about his writing, which had prevented him getting down to it in earnest, now seemed to melt miraculously away. So much inspiration filled him that he had difficulty in dragging himself from his typewriter. The play that he had had in his head for years, but which he had never been able to finish to his satisfaction, he was now able to adapt and rewrite because of the new ideas and enthusiasms Rajini had inspired. Childish and immature, possibly, but he was suddenly confident that the play was good enough to produce.

He had always been heavily involved with student theatre groups and had, over the years, produced plays for a particular group that had had moderate success in fringe productions. His readiness to involve himself meant that his time was increasingly overfilled. Without Harriet there to answer to, there seemed less and less reason to refuse any request for assistance. He found it difficult to admit that anything was impossible to achieve, and he enjoyed the knowledge that every moment of every day was packed with action so that no time was wasted.

'Time, Rajini my dear one, is a precious asset,' he told her. 'One we must on no account waste because we'll never get it again.'

'You talk in clichés,' Rajini said, leaning her head against his shoulder, 'which is pretty disgraceful for a writer of ace plays. But I have to admit that I agree with the essence of what you say, so I will forgive the cliché. Has the company agreed to put this play on, by the way? And am I going to play the lead?'

'They want the play,' said Tom, 'but it's not easy to introduce a rank outsider with no experience for a lead part; you'll have to win it on merit, plus a glowing recommendation from me. If we decide to give you the part, the rest of the group will hate your guts and probably be very nasty to you.'

'I'm perfectly willing to put up with that. I shall be brilliant.'

Having written the part with her in mind, Tom realized that there was no possible doubt about that. 'You'll choose me because I'll be the best.'

'Maybe *I* will think you would be the best, knowing you as I do, but if you start criticizing my clichés, I'll vote for someone else.'

She kissed him and slipped her hand under his shirt, sliding it down his back to the bottom of his spine, which induced spasms of sheer delight. It was just when it was apparent that there was no turning back that the front door slammed and Emma's voice called up: 'Pa? Pa? Are you in?'

Rajini was the first to recover: 'Jesus,' she said, springing away from him and buttoning up her shirt, 'she'll kill me.' And moving like a scalded cat, she sprang out of the window, dropped on the flat roof of the bathroom below and swung herself down the apple tree into the next door garden. Tom was left breathless, unzipped and sick.

'Yes,' he shouted weakly. 'I'm in.' And he descended the stairs shaking quite visibly.

Emma was sprawled, untidily, over the sofa in the sitting-room, her head enclosed within her arms, shoes off, coat, books, bag and money from her purse scattered on the floor round her. Her long, straight hair was spread like a mantle over her shoulders, her arms and the sofa.

Tom sat down beside her, the previous few minutes dissolving at once into the new crisis. 'So what's all this? Whatever's the matter, love?'

'Oh Pa, oh Pa, what's happened to everybody? And nobody telling me anything. Why didn't you tell me? Surely I'm old enough to be told?'

Tom pulled her towards him and held her in his arms. 'Told you what, darling? What haven't I told you?'

'About Ma and Alan – why didn't anyone tell me? Why did I have to find out like that? It was such a shock. I actually fainted with the shock of it – at least I suppose that was what it was. You know they sent for the doctor. Can you imagine anything so silly? He gave me something that made me sleep half through today, and when I woke up there was no-one in the flat so I just ran here. Why didn't you tell me? I suppose everyone else knows except me; is that it? Do all Alan's kids know?' She sat up, with a startled look on her face. 'Oh, but I suppose they don't, because she was saying that he'd got to tell Laura and that she wasn't going to be the part-time mistress . . .' She looked at him suddenly. 'Did you know?' she whispered.

Tom smiled, and took her hand, feeling that a blow to his midriff had winded him. 'No, I didn't actually.'

Emma flung her arms round his neck. 'Oh Pa, I'm so sorry. But I suppose you don't mind that much, because you're not involved any more, are you?'

'I don't think one stops being involved for a very long time – perhaps one never stops really. Loving and being loved is a funny thing; you can never quite fight your way free, however hard you try.' He kept seeing the vision of Rajini leaping out of the window and felt the desire to laugh and cry at the same time.

They had coffee and biscuits together and, for the first time for many years, they both had a feeling of a sort of affection which was warm and comfortable.

'It's a bit of a mess, isn't it?' Emma said, 'I mean, Alan as a stepfather – ugh; and then all that crowd as step-brothers and sisters, and what does that make Laura who's the nicest of the lot? Even if she is a bit soppy.'

'Poor Laura,' Tom said sadly. She had been so sure, even though he had envisaged what was coming. Must be Harriet behind it rather than Alan; it was bound to have been her insisting on having her own way. They could surely have been discreet if they had to have an affair. There was no need to disrupt so many lives. Poor Laura.

'Think I'll stay here for a bit,' Emma said. 'Until I get used to the idea. Shall we tell Ben?'

'It might be better to wait until we know for certain.'

'If you think so, but I hate going round feeling I'm deceiving someone. I feel as though I'm lying all the time.'

'I know what you mean; but sometimes telling somebody something that's going to upset them is better avoided until it becomes absolutely inevitable. And this might blow over.'

'You don't really think it will, do you?'

'I don't know that it won't. Let's wait and find out a bit more first.'

'Ma can't marry him at the moment anyhow; she's still married to you, after all.'

Tom smiled. 'So she is, I almost forgot that. Not that I think that is going to stop your mother when she has her mind set on something.'

'You're so biased.' A bit of the old irritation showed.

'I don't deny that.' Tom looked at his watch. 'I have

to go or I'll get the sack. Will you be all right on your own? Ben will be back at tea time. There's enough in the fridge for supper. I shan't be in till late, I've got a meeting to attend . . .'

'A meeting? What are you up to now?'

'A student theatre group production I said I'd help with.'

'Oh Pa, you're hopeless; why do you take on so much when you never have time for everything anyway? Do you mean you leave Ben on his own all the time?'

'Ben is a very able boy; he looks after me more than I look after him.'

'But he shouldn't have to; if you're not careful, I shall report you to the NSPCC or Esther Rantzen or something.'

'But you'll baby-sit for him tonight will you?'

'Only if you promise you're not just pandering to all those boring girl students who dote on you, by making them believe they are all possible Judi Denches. I know how you enjoy having a trail of worshipping disciples hanging on your every word. You care more for them than you do for us.'

'Not true, my dear Emma, but I have to admit they do often seem to need me more than my own family does.'

Emma looked angry. 'Now you're criticizing us, in your usual annoying way.' It was scarcely fair to blame Ma for being so much more efficient than he was. He was so unreasonable.

Alan sat down with Laura to a meal she had hurriedly and delightedly prepared. The fact that Alan had rung her, from the office he said, to say that he was coming home at lunch time because he wanted to talk to her, had filled her with a new hope; it was obvious that he

169

wanted to talk things over and probably try to make everything better between them. It was good that he wasn't going to box things up this time and she welcomed the chance to discuss ways of making their life together more satisfactory than it had been. It sometimes needed a crisis to get the situation straight.

She made a good soup with the stock she had prepared the day before; he always enjoyed her soup, and this one was a special favourite of his. She cooked sole bonne femme and new potatoes and still had time to put on discreet make up and be actually sitting down knitting when she heard his key in the lock.

They had a drink together, sitting in their own special chairs, as they used to do when Hamish, as the only other member of the family then, was packed away in bed.

'Long time since we did this,' Laura said, her heart beating uncomfortably heavily.

Alan looked at her with overwhelming dread and unhappiness: why the hell couldn't she make a scene and shout at him? It would be so much easier. He tried not to think of the way she had seemed to disintegrate when he had first told her about the affair. But there didn't seem any way round it this time and, in any case, the actual ending of all things past had happened then; there was no hope of ever getting back into life as it had once been, he could only move forward from now on.

He gulped down half his scotch: 'Laura darling, Harriet and I have decided that we are going to have to move in together to make a go of this whole partnership business.'

The silence was very dead, and lasted through the loud ticking away of several long drawn out seconds on the clock. Sufficient waiting time to allow his mind to consider whether he or Laura would get the clock in the division of the spoils. He kept his eyes on his feet, and noticed, with distress, that he had stepped in some mud or dog shit. By now the silence had become agonizing. 'I really am desperately sorry.' And he put his hand over hers.

For Laura, it was that gesture which gave her instant momentum to let fly all those feelings that had lain dormant for so long. 'I can't believe what I'm hearing,' she said. 'Do you actually mean that you intend to move out on me and the children and set up house with Harriet?'

Alan opened his mouth to say something, but closed it again, realizing the futility of inconsequential apologetics.

Laura approached him with the velocity of a tornado and caught hold of his ears: 'You dirty, rotten, stinking bastard,' she screamed, shaking his head backwards and forwards with furious vigour. 'How could you? How could you *dare* to treat us like that? Get out of my sight, or I'll kill you.' She turned to the table and picked up a knife. 'Go on – go! Go back to that two-faced whore, you just about deserve each other!' She raised the knife above her head and plunged it downwards, but Alan had mercifully got the message some few seconds earlier and stampeded, in panic, out of the door, down the steps and into the car.

The knife sliced through a cushion and stayed, poised in the back of the chair, with Laura's hands still grasping it. All she could think of at that moment was: 'What a bloody disaster. I missed him.'

22

Tom and Laura sat alone in their various houses, staring at their telephones.

'I won't do anything unless she actually asks,' thought Tom. 'To offer assistance would seem too much like poking my nose in, or saying I told you so, or even the conventional attempt to take advantage of a lonely, unhappy woman.' A smile rose inside him but did not reach his face. He felt ridiculously unhappy for Laura.

Laura was staring at the telephone without seeing it; it could have been the wall or the door or the window. She sat on her bed and was unable to make any attempt to stop the swirl of devastating thoughts that were passing, unheeded, through her head. She could only take in what was her immediate thought, because as soon as it had passed, there was no recollection of it. A kind of black void kept steady pace with what was going on in her head: now she saw a telephone but, one instant later, she forgot what her reaction to seeing it actually was. But she was able to realize that this state of affairs was wrong and that her mind had obviously ceased to function; that she was in great danger; that she was probably mad.

She kept seeing the telephone as her eyes gazed round the room, and she began to connect it in some way with help. She picked it up and stared at it. Tom would help. Her finger pressed certain buttons unerringly at precisely the same moment as Tom dialled her number. Both numbers were engaged which made Tom think better of making any further move and Laura realized that help was not forthcoming after all.

She lay back on the bed, where she had lain since the episode of the previous day, ignoring queries from the children when they came back to tea. 'I'm ill,' she had said in answer to their demands. 'Go away. You'll have to look after yourselves.' They had retreated in distress, recognizing something more than a migraine in her tone of voice.

'I don't know what's wrong,' Hamish said to his brother and sisters the following evening, 'and I don't know what to do about it.'

'Where's Dad?' Max asked. 'He wasn't here last night or the night before.'

'We have to tell him about Mum being ill.'

'Shouldn't we ring the doctor?'

'I said that to her but she just shouted at me to leave her alone.'

'We could see if Dad is at his office.'

'I tried that, three times, only he wasn't there any of the times I did. They said they'd tell him I called.'

There was worried silence from all of them, and Hamish felt his eldest son position to be suddenly onerous rather than privileged.

'We could ring Harriet,' suggested Louise. 'She would know where Dad is because she works with him now, doesn't she?'

'She probably won't be in.'

'But Emma might be, and we could ask her to tell him to ring us because Mum's ill.'

So Hamish dialled the number and Alan answered the phone.

'Dad? Dad? We've been trying to find you. Why didn't you come home? Mum's ill. She can't get out of bed. She's shut herself in her room and won't let us in.

173

What shall we do?' He felt an explosion of grief and anxiety making its way up through his chest and throat and filling his eyes with unexpected tears. Embarrassment stifled him, and he stopped speaking.

'I'll come right over,' said Alan. He put the phone down. 'I have to go home,' he told Harriet. 'Laura has evidently . . . seems to be . . . er . . . ill. The kids don't know what to do.'

'Ill? What exactly? More like a spirit of revenge I would say. An "I'll teach him to leave me" sort of thing. You shouldn't go. I know you only too well, you'll just give way to her.'

'I can't leave the kids on their own. It's their holidays soon, someone has to be there if Laura's ill.'

'So what are you going to do with them? There's no room for them here. Darling, I *know* it's difficult for you, but doing things by halves is just madness in a situation like this. I mean, I could be having hysterics about Emma and her little scene last night, but I think it's best to let her get over it with Tom. The doctor said she would feel better after a long sleep, and the note she left us sounded perfectly rational and self-contained: "Going to Pa's for a while." What could be more mature and sensible than that? It's far kinder in the end to let them work out their own solutions to the facts of life; we can't go on living their lives for them and guarding them from anything nasty.'

'You may be right, but I find it impossible not to do what I can to help them over the nastiest parts of life, no matter how grown up or sensible they seem to be. Perhaps they'll do the same for me when I'm old and feeble.'

'There speaks a truly selfish parent. Just thinking of his own dotage.' Harriet swung him round to face her, wrapping her arms tight round him and kissing him. 'If you have to go, then I suppose I must let you but, remember, I don't approve; I think you are just making things more difficult for everybody.'

Alan allowed sex to blot out anxiety for a few moments, but then broke away. 'I'll just go and see that everything is all right. Then I'll come back. I'm sure I can arrange things somehow; get a doctor to Laura, do something about food for them all. Maybe contact my parents if necessary.' But the thought of breaking the news to his parents sent fresh surges of anxiety through him. He'd have to think of something else. He kissed Harriet lingeringly with his hand on her breast. 'I won't be very long, darling.'

'You'd better not be.'

But before Alan set out, Tom overcame his reluctance to interfere, and rang Laura's number. Laura shrank back in shock at the sound and Daisy answered from downstairs and immediately started to cry. 'Oh Tom, Tom, please will you come and save us because there's no-one here and Mummy is very ill and won't come out of her bedroom and Daddy isn't here yet and we don't know what to do.'

Tom ordered a mini-cab and explained to Emma, who was not impressed. 'I can't see,' she said, 'that they need you any more than we do; their mother's ill, our mother's left us for their father: so what?'

'I think their immediate need may be greater than yours – ours – at the moment.'

'So what do I tell Ben? He doesn't know of their need yet.'

'Perhaps you could explain to him?'

'No, I couldn't; you've got to do that.'

The taxi driver rang the front door bell. 'All right, I'll tell him about it as soon as I get back.'

Emma wheeled round and stamped upstairs to her room, slamming the door.

Ben appeared on the landing as Tom opened the

front door. 'Hallo – what's the row about? Where are you going, Dad?'

'I have to go over to the Summersons for a while?'

'The Summersons? *In a taxi?* Whatever for? Can I come?'

'Well – no, not really. I'll explain when I come back. Shan't be long.'

'What's for supper?'

'Oh – not sure – I'll bring back a pizza.'

'And we need some more Chum.'

Blast the bloody dog. Tom collapsed into the taxi, confused, unsure that he should be following his immediate reaction and angry that his children should be so unsympathetic – well, Emma anyway.

The journey was fairly quick but very expensive; he had left himself short of money, as usual, and realized he would not have enough cash for a pizza. He felt in his pockets for his cheque book to find that he had forgotten that too.

Louise opened the door to him, and looked a little shocked: 'Oh. Oh. Daisy said she'd asked you to come. She really shouldn't have. We don't want to bother people and Daddy says he's coming as quick as he can.'

Tom's spirits sank lower. 'Ah – well – perhaps I'd better leave it to him.'

Louise looked distressed, and the other children appeared behind her. 'Thank you very much for coming,' Hamish said. 'We are a bit worried you see, and we weren't sure where Pa was . . .'

Tom stood in the hall with the anxious circle clustered round him. He had a great urge to put his arms round the lot of them and expound comforting words of wisdom and good cheer. 'As I'm here, shall I go up and see if your mum might like to talk to me?'

The relief that made itself felt was very obvious, and

Tom knocked on Laura's door. 'Laura? This is Tom. Can I talk to you for a moment?'

There was a long silence during which time questions came and went in Tom's brain: how long shall I wait before knocking again? Did she hear my knock? Was it loud enough? Is she actually in there? Has she taken an overdose? Could she be dead? Does she resent my poking my nose in?

He didn't hear any movement until, quite suddenly, the key turned in the lock. As he had not tried to open the door, he had no idea as to whether the sound indicated locking or unlocking, but he turned the handle and found the door opened for him.

Laura was standing with her back to him, staring out of the window, fully clothed in what she must have been wearing since the original débâcle. He went up to her and put his arms round her without saying anything, his mouth against her ear, rocking her very gently from side to side.

The confusion in Laura's head seemed to swirl and settle and come to a deadening, silent stillness. 'I don't know what's the matter with me,' she whispered eventually. 'I seem to have become someone else. Do you know what I did?' She turned to look at him. 'I tried to kill him; did you know that? I took a knife and tried to stab him. I wanted to kill him and it was only because he escaped that I failed. Am I really the sort of person who would kill someone? I daren't allow myself out of the room in case I might do it again. Oh Tom,' she clung round his neck and wept into his shoulder. 'I'm going to have to finish myself off; I'm too dangerous to be with anybody – but I don't know how to do it; pills will make me sick and won't work, so I think I must hang myself, only I'm so silly, I don't know how to tie that sort of knot. Will you show me? You have to help me because of the children; they wouldn't be safe with me around, not knowing what I might do next.'

Tom picked her up, and sat down on the bed with her on his lap. 'Of course I'll help you,' he said, unbuttoning her shirt and talking gently as he began to undress her and get her into bed. He was shocked to find that she smelled strongly of sweat and dirt and urine. 'First of all, you must have a little rest in bed or you won't be strong enough to do anything at all.'

'You'll show me the sort of knot I have to tie?'

'Of course, if that's what you really want.'

'There doesn't seem any other way.'

'We'll talk about it when you've had some sleep. I can think of some other ways which I think would be just as good in the long run.' He took off her shoes and her jeans and was just pulling the covers over her when Alan burst into the room with a deal of commotion.

'Laura! Are you all right?' And to Tom: 'What the hell are you doing here?'

Laura screamed and crouched at the end of the bed behind Tom. 'He's come back to punish me! He's come to kill me because I tried to kill him. Don't let him kill me, Tom.'

'Alan wouldn't dream of killing you, Laura. You're not well and he wants to get the doctor to see you, that's all.' He looked at Alan. 'You're just going to ring the doctor now, aren't you, Alan?'

Laura still clung and watched Alan with wide black eyes. 'He'll kill me if you go, I know he will. And of course I deserve it, but I'm frightened, that's all. I'd rather do it myself if you show me how to tie the knot, Tom. Please don't leave me with Alan because he might hurt me.'

Alan's emotions formed themselves into some sort of intangible knot: all he could feel at that moment was fury that Tom should seem to be doing what was clearly not his business; he found he was quite unable to speak or even move. If he moved, he thought he might well fling himself at Tom and attempt to strangle him. What the hell was Tom Turtle doing with his wife?

Tom felt the aggression of the long silence and was afraid both for himself and Laura. Was Alan going to attack him? Was Laura justified in her fear? He called out, sharply, to break the black silence.

'Alan?'

At the sound of the sharp bark of Tom's shout, Alan finally turned, in a state of stunned confusion, and went out of the room to do as he was told and telephone the doctor.

Tom laid Laura down. 'There, he's gone now, and I'm still here,' he said. 'I'm going to find some medicine to give you so that you can sleep before we decide what to do.'

Laura made no attempt to get up again, but lay, with wide staring eyes, while Tom searched the bathroom for sleeping pills, which he eventually found and gave her a dose. He held her hand and stroked her head until she slept, and then went downstairs to face the next phase of the battle.

23

Alan, resentment and feelings now under some sort of control, met the doctor as he came out of Laura's room and ushered him, rather possessively, into the studio. He was the one to deal with the situation from now on;

it was his responsibility, not the doctor's and certainly not Tom's.

'She seems to have a loss of consecutive thought,' the doctor told him, 'added to which, she believes that she might lose control and harm someone. Something must have triggered off a small spasm that could have caused a sudden restriction of blood or oxygen to the brain; might be a form of epilepsy; we shall have to do tests.'

'Epilepsy?' Alan said aggressively. 'Laura doesn't have epilepsy.'

The doctor looked at him over his glasses. 'The disease can manifest itself in one form or another at any time of life. Did your wife suffer some sort of shock before this attack started?'

There was a moment's hesitation, then Alan said, 'We have been having some marital difficulties. She was upset.'

'Might have been connected.' The doctor wrote a prescription. 'She mustn't be left,' he said. 'Are you able to take time off in order to be with her? The condition may pass off in a day or two though one never can tell.'

'I – I'm not actually living here at the moment.' It was easier to face the doctor than Harriet's displeasure. 'Is there a possibility of a private nursing home? I would prefer her to have the best possible care.'

She was admitted to an aggressively expensive nursing home that evening, and Tom stayed with the children while Alan took her in the car. He cooked them spaghetti bolognese, and wondered what his two were eating while he parried questions from Daisy and Louise.

'How long will she be there?'

'Will Pa be here to look after us?'

'Even if he is here, Pa can't cook. And will he have

time to do the shopping? He's always so busy, he never gets back early enough to do it.'

'One of us can do it when we get back from school,' said Hamish. 'We might even get let off homework if we plead dire distress. Anyway it's the Christmas holidays in a minute.'

There was a deathly silence for the few moments that it took for everyone to imagine Chanukah and Christmas without Laura, something that was too painful to be discussed or even considered just now. They had always celebrated both with gusto.

'Won't we get any presents?' Daisy asked in horror.

'You don't have to worry,' Tom said. 'There are lots of people who will see that you and your father are looked after properly, and of course there'll be presents.'

'They might give us a home help and meals on wheels, I expect they can do Christmas pudding,' said Daisy, and the others laughed far too loudly, because the relief of having responsibility lifted from them by Tom and others turned the anxiety into mild hysteria.

'That's only for crinklies,' said Max. 'Pa's not that far gone.'

Alan and Harriet talked the next day: 'I shall have to go back and live there while Laura's in the nursing home, there's no other way.'

Harriet was incensed. 'She's doing it on purpose; it's blackmail.'

'Oh come now, darling. Laura's not that sort of woman.'

'How would you know? You could never admit someone you've lived with for some twenty years could be anything but a paragon – otherwise why would you have chosen her?'

'As I'm the obvious one at fault in this case, I think I

have to do something about the kids. They'll be on holiday next week; I'll have to be there.'

'At fault? At fault? That's no longer relevant in a case like this. You want to live with me and not with Laura – whose fault is that? We should thank God we've moved out of the dark ages of being forced by law to spend the rest of our lives with someone we can't abide.'

'It hasn't happened because I can't abide Laura, it's . . .'

'Oh don't quibble, you know exactly what I mean; and the kids will be far better off in the end. Everyone says so. Get a housekeeper for them if Laura can't manage, or an au pair or something.'

'Maybe later I will, when Laura comes home and needs support. I shall have to go back until then.'

'Well, if you do,' Harriet said, 'I shall come with you. We may as well start as we mean to carry on. It will give the kids a chance to get to look on me as a step-mother.'

Alan was speechless for a moment or two. 'But they don't even know yet. At least give me time on my own with them to explain. Then I could perhaps say that you had offered to help out, if Laura has to stay in for any length of time. After all, she may only be in for a few days.'

But Laura's depression hung on for more than a few days and Chanukah and Christmas passed in a dreadful trough of depression which even Daisy was unable to break out of. Laura was not well enough to be able to face their visits nor to appreciate their presents.

It was the year that Bernard and Esther Sunshine traditionally spent the holiday in Glasgow with another part of Esther's large and far-flung family, so the Summerson children felt further deprived of a share in seasonal activities. Chanukah with Bernard and Esther was always a warm and cosy affair and, though presents had been distributed before they went, it wasn't quite the same since Grandma Sunshine always wanted them opened while she was there and that wasn't nearly so exciting as keeping them for a great splurge of present-opening on a special day.

Alan, on the other hand, was greatly relieved that he was able to put off explaining the whole débâcle to his parents – for the moment at least.

'I never realized,' Louise said, 'that it's really more exciting to give presents than to get them.'

There was a silence while each mulled over what an untrue statement that was.

'Odd how you can't really have a good time when something's bothering you,' Max added.

'It's like being in disgrace,' said Daisy, full of tears.

'It'll be better when we're back at school,' Hamish told them. 'Only two more days.'

Alan stayed on with them, and Harriet took to going back from the office with him, staying to supper, and then deciding it was too late to go back to her own empty flat.

Daisy was the only one young enough to express disapproval out loud.

'Did you sleep with Daddy in Mummy's bed?' she asked as Harriet came down after breakfast in Alan's bath robe, her hair drying in a towelling turban.

'Your father and I are both too old to sleep on the floor or in the bath,' Harriet said, smiling at the joke. 'The bed was a natural alternative.'

There was an embarrassed silence as Daisy worked out what a natural alternative was. Nobody said anything further, even when Alan attempted some over-hearty conversation, and they all left for school hurriedly, without looking anyone in the face.

'It's horrible,' Louise said through tears as they

walked to the underground. 'Harriet's trying to push Mum out; trying to steal Dad while Mum's ill. She's a bitch.'

'I think we've got to realize,' Hamish said, 'that we're probably going through what a lot of our friends have had to go through – including Emma and Ben: Mum and Dad are splitting up. That's probably what has made Mum ill.' There was a shocked pause, and they all stopped walking. Louise, Daisy and Max started to cry.

'But that's awful,' Max said, trying to force his voice to sound normal. 'I mean, think how miserable it will be to dance backwards and forwards between the two of them all the time.'

'Other people do it and they don't seem to mind much,' Hamish insisted, thinking how much he disagreed with what he was saying. He had always counted himself lucky that at least his parents were kind and together and that their home was happy and a good place to go back to each day. He was not at all sure that he would be able to cope with the unknown strains of divided households.

'I hate Dad,' Louise said, blowing her nose and resuming, with the others, the trek to the underground and normal, everyday living. 'When you think how beastly he's been to poor Mum. I shall never forgive him.'

'It's more Harriet's fault than Dad's. Just because she's walked out on Tom and so hasn't got anybody of her own, she goes and steals someone else's husband,' Max said. 'I think we ought to show her what we think and how we don't want her around us.'

Hamish didn't argue, though he felt uneasy, and decided to ask others how they had coped with the experience. They each continued their journey silently, with a dark sense of dread and misery clinging to them and stultifying all their activities throughout the day.

*   *   *

'Your bloody children are about the rudest, most bad-tempered lot I've come across,' Harriet told Alan as they sat in her flat one lunch time, after a week of the Show Harriet Where She Gets Off campaign. 'Giving up my time and falling over backwards trying to please them is just a no-no situation. Can't you at least try to show me some support?'

'Give them a chance, Hattie, they're having a pretty rough time. They see you as a threat to Laura.'

'Oh, thank you very much; I come to help out in a time of stress and you call me a threat to Laura.'

For the first time since the show-down, Alan laughed out loud. There was something so outrageous in Harriet's way of thinking that made his own credibility seem quite impressive. It reduced the weight of his guilt slightly.

'I can see nothing whatever to laugh at,' Harriet said. 'Moving in with you was obviously a mistake and, when Laura is let out, will be an impossibility, of course. I think we'd better sit down and decide on our next move. Our business is suffering; we've made no progress at all with the way we opened up in Rome, and if we don't start moving in that direction immediately, we're going to miss all the opportunities we set up for ourselves over there.'

Back came the insecurity; Alan immediately saw the rationality of her argument: she might not be able to consider the other person's point of view, but her single mindedness at least led her straight to the underlying problem.

'You don't need to get a divorce from Laura,' she said. 'She's not going to plunge back into matrimony in the immediate future, so you don't have to go through the ding-dong battle that Tom and I are going to indulge in any minute now. That should make things a great deal easier.' She paced round the sitting-room of the flat, finding herself irritated by the position of certain pieces of furniture: she never should have bought that low table, it didn't fit at all; must get rid of it. All this waiting about before getting down to the details of the divorce put her on edge. Trying to get solicitors to move was like trying to run in a dream.

'I don't see that not getting divorced is going to make that much difference to Laura,' Alan said.

'But of course it will.' God, Alan was almost as bad; needed a bomb behind him. 'I mean you won't have to employ solicitors to dig about and discover nasty bits of her nature which would absolve you from paying her irrational sums of money for the rest of your life. I shall have plenty of cash for both of us until we get the new business under way, because I'm not going to let Tom get away with all our assets. I shall insist on selling the house so that we can divide everything down the middle. He gets a good salary and is perfectly well able to do his bit in paying for the children too. It's only fair.'

'But you don't need the money, Hattie. Wouldn't it be less fraught to keep things as they are, legally, until the kids are a bit older? Your Ben is going to be torn apart if his home is swept from under him at this moment in his life?'

'And at what point in his life do you suggest he will stop being torn apart?' She was stung by Ben's decision to move in with Tom, but convinced herself it was obstinacy about the dog that had brought it about. 'Kids are adaptable, as I've said before; they may make a fuss at first, but they soon adjust. And anyway, I'm only insisting on what is fair. Just because I happen to have more money behind me than Tom does, doesn't mean that he should get away with being able to deprive me of my fair share of everything.'

Perfectly rational thinking: she would have made a

good lawyer, but Alan could not bring himself to enjoy the idea of being dependent on Harriet, even if only for a short time, until the new business became stable. A bit of his upbringing hovered in his mind: You must be the boss, boy, and that means you earn the money, never forget that. Silly, old-fashioned stuff, perhaps, but it wouldn't go away.

'We'll see,' he said, pushing it back a little until he had time to think. 'But perhaps I'd better see about getting in some sort of help while Laura's ill.'

Harriet shrugged. 'If that means you'll stop being so absurdly conscientious and old womanish about your offspring, then it's a good idea, though I can't imagine anyone will stay very long if they continue to behave in the way they do at present. You must insist on her living in, because otherwise you'll be popping off every evening to be with them instead of me.'

She undid the bath towel that she had wrapped round herself while she dried her hair, and approached him, smooth, brown and lean, her silky, loose hair down to her shoulders and covering part of her face. 'And now I want you,' she said. 'So enough of the bickering and excuses and half-measures. Come here immediately and perform your lover's duties, or I may divorce you without even marrying you.'

She caught hold of him and pulled him roughly towards her, tugging at his shirt, so that buttons flew and material ripped. 'All that lovely fur,' she said, rubbing her face against his chest. 'It drives me mad.'

Alan responded voluptuously, and allowed Harriet's dominance to take over. The eroticism of resigning the mind and the body and of relinquishing all responsibilities to one who was sufficiently tyrannical was irresistible. He lay, supine, in submissive joy and they indulged themselves, with what appeared to be never-ending energy, well on into the afternoon until Harriet

187

rolled on to her back in a state of helpless exhaustion and started to laugh weakly. 'Oh God, Alan, we must be a bit mad I suppose, to carry on like this when we should be concentrating on work. We're never going to succeed in business at this rate.'

'Don't talk such crap,' Alan said, climbing back on top of her. 'A good fuck works wonders: clears the air, clears the head and fills you full of energy and the spice of life.' Life with Harriet was the only life that was possible for him; it was obvious.

24

Overcoming his diffidence and a certain embarrassment, Tom had managed to get the student theatre group to accept his suggestion of Rajini as a lead player in his play. What if there were muffled grumbles about the director's couch methods – the part, and indeed the play had been written round and about her. They were already beginning to admit she was right for the part, which was hardly surprising, and there was no doubt that she was an obvious natural on stage. Rehearsals were now building up, and Tom, as director, became steadily more immersed.

A visiting lecturer from Canada, attached to Tom's university for the year, had joined the group. His approach Tom found unsettling at first.

'Hi there,' holding out a large pink hand. 'I'm Claude Columbo from Montreal and I'm told you're in charge of the theatre group. I run an arts festival back home, and I'd be interested to get involved with your little set-up if you'd have me.'

Tom mistrusted the condescension – little set-up indeed; who did he think he was? But in spite of the brashness, the Canadian Columbo, as he was known, became a dedicated and enthusiastic member of the group, fell deeply in love with Rajini and ended up as Tom's right-hand man.

'You should treat your pink Canadian slave far more kindly than you do,' Tom told her. 'He's extraordinarily useful and might well get us an invitation to perform at his college in Montreal.'

Rajini perked up. 'Really? That would be fantastic. But he's a bit crass, isn't he? I don't see why I should have to work for the benefit of the community. You're the director – *you* go to bed with him for the honour of the side.'

'Would you be jealous?'

'Might be, might not.'

'Jealous or not,' his mind switched back to the present interest, 'that last rehearsal we did was great. With a bit more polish, this production could be really good.'

'It could be, or I could be? You never seem to like what I do. You like what everybody else does; it's dire. You give me an inferiority complex.'

'Rubbish.' Tom took her hand in his. 'Nothing could give you an inferiority complex; that's partly what makes you dramatically good.'

'Dramatically as in drama student of the year or as in over-the-top ham?'

'Bit of both.'

'Supposing I decide to throw up the idea of university and try for drama school?'

'You'd be mad. The competition is dire and the training pins you down to spending your time sitting by the phone waiting to be hired. Acting is an impossible life.'

'There you are you see, you don't have any faith in me. You think I'm hopeless. Can't see that a degree in English or history or maths or whatever is going to do me any more good, job-wise. I mean I don't want to end up like you, a boring old lecturer who daren't move out of his narrow little world for fear of being destitute.'

'So I'm just a boring old lecturer?'

They were on their way to a rehearsal together, and Rajini stared out of the window from the top of the bus. They chose buses rather than tubes these days because the opportunities to talk were so much greater and the journeys more leisurely. Tops of buses were anonymous, especially the front seats; in the underground, those who had not brought books or papers to read spent their time summing up the people opposite them, and listening to their yelled conversations.

'You're not boring to me,' she said, 'because you make love to me and I know what you're really like underneath.'

'So what am I really like underneath?'

'You're full of damped-down excitement and fire and just dying to break out of the sort of life you find yourself in at the moment, but you haven't the guts to break free. You're a miserable old bum.'

'You think so?'

'I *know* so. Just look at the way you are when you're poncing around directing us all; absolutely full of ideas and fervour. You positively inspire everyone to perform, and you love it, you know you do.'

'So you think I should throw up my university work and plunge into the ever-welcoming world of theatre?'

'In a word, yes. Your plays are brilliant so you could at least spend a bit of time concentrating on getting them accepted and put on.'

Tom smiled down at her, rather benignly, for

knowing what had been in his visionary mind for so long. 'Crazy child,' he said kindly.

'Condescending old hypocrite,' said Rajini. 'This play ought to be seen by thousands; should be in the West End. It's a *great* play I tell you. Why don't you *do* something about it?'

Why indeed? Fear of rejection? Fear that his reputation as a doyen of politics and economics should be damaged by the knowledge that he wrote plays that might not be as good as he hoped? Lack of sufficient time to give his writing the concentration it needed. Or mere laziness?

'It's easier to stay in the rut,' he said.

'*Exactly*,' said Rajini.

The rehearsal, that day, and Rajini's observations roused in him all the old enthusiasm he used to feel before Harriet's lack of interest and insistence that he shouldn't waste his time writing plays had made it seem easier to persevere with the daily grind and the common task. So perhaps the lethargy *was* just laziness. He had been writing this play, intermittently, over the last few years, and it was only when Rajini came into his life that it seemed to take off. He had rewritten the whole thing in a great drive of energy and had finished it in three weeks.

'I have to admit,' he told her on the bus going home, 'that you were quite magnificent today. Makes me feel as though I might be a good playwright after all.'

'I told you,' said Rajini. 'And thank you, that's the first real compliment you've ever paid me. Am I good? Really? I do think I want to act for the rest of my life. It's so *great*, it really is. Makes me feel brill – really goodly.'

Tom put his arm round her and felt a deep contentment – a childish contentment that was spliced with an equally childish excitement. 'I feel pretty brilliantly goodly myself,' he said.

'We make such a marvellous team, you and I,' Rajini said. 'As soon as I decide whether to go to university or drama school or whatever, we must get a place together so that we can be shot of all this family business, and then you can write plays and I'll act in them and we can spend all our time just *living* and doing what is best for both of us. If you lived just with me, then you wouldn't have to bother about your silly old lecturing job and keeping up appearances the way you have to now. I wouldn't mind not having much money at first, and we'd be bound to earn a lot as soon as your plays got known.'

The child was crazy, but the idea was pleasantly flattering and she would grow out of it in a few months; grow out of him, in all probability, in the same few months. He immediately felt deflated, but the chance that she might *not* tire of him was so remote as to be honestly inconceivable. No sense in arguing about it now. Wait and see what happens and, in the meantime, make the most of what you've got, Tom Turtle.

'Lovely pipe dream. But I do have the children to support.'

'You'll die a death if you go on as you are now, and then you'd be no use to anybody.'

'I'm not much good now.'

'Exactly; and that's because you just drift along, miserably, without ever letting your real self show.'

'Such wisdom from the mouths . . .'

'. . . of babes and sucklings. There you go, spouting clichés all over the place. Per-leeze Mr Turtle, sir, stop being your age and come down to earth for once. And you might also stop all this pomposity and condescension, or I shall give you up as a bad job.'

'I would hate you to do that.' Good sense and fair play began to melt away in the face of the delectable physical attraction that took over whenever she was around. He wanted her there and then and wished they were sitting at the back of the bus, where mild or even heavy petting could proceed unnoticed, instead of the front where the eyes of all the other passengers would be on them.

'What time did you say you'd be home tonight?' he asked.

'I warned them I'd be very late because of the show being so near. They half-hate me doing this play and are half-pleased that I've got the lead. They are very confused, poor things, because they can't help being impressed by you and all your qualifications, but at the same time thinking play-acting, as they call it, is time wasted which I should use for studying.'

'Emma said she would be staying with Harriet and Alan tonight and Ben will be in bed.' He felt uncommonly like an eager teenager setting up a session behind the bike sheds, and was slightly sickened. Hole-and-corner sex was ignominious.

He let himself into the house, piqued that he felt compelled to make the effort to be as quiet as possible. So much better to be able to shout out: Hallo everyone – just come back to enjoy a session of love-making. Shan't be long, but we don't want to be disturbed. Instead, he ushered Rajini in and closed the door noiselessly.

He had reckoned without Hamlet. Ever ready to defend, the heavy bulk of liver-and-white springer spaniel hurled itself from a basket in the basement, up the stairs with a skittering of nails on the floorboards, and into their legs in a frenzy of angry barking. The barking changed to howls and moans of delight with the embarrassing realization that the intruder was actually beloved Lord and Master and his guest. The commotion had upset Rajini's balance, and she fell against the umbrella stand which strewed its contents on the floor beside her. Hamlet was overjoyed to be approached at his own level, and greeted her with licks to face and neck and any other exposed parts of her, groaning with pleasure.

Ben appeared, peering over the banisters: 'Hallo, who is it? Oh Pa – hallo. What time is it? Shut up Ham, you ought to know it would be Pa; you ought to be able to smell him a mile off. Who have you got with you?'

Rajini picked herself up, together with sticks, umbrellas and a butterfly net.

'Rajini came back to collect her books,' said Tom, angry with the compromised explanation, and further put out by the fact that Emma had also suddenly appeared on the stairs.

'I don't believe it,' she said. 'Go back to bed, Ben. Pa and Rajini will probably need at least an hour or two to collect all her books.' And she slammed back into her room.

Tom was incensed. Why *should* he feel guilty all the time? He felt very much inclined to take Rajini straight upstairs to his bed and indulge in lengthy, noisy and uproarious sex for the rest of the night. But the spontaneity had gone and the awkwardness refused to go away. He didn't have the gall.

'I'll walk you home,' he said grimly to Rajini. 'Pipe dreams tend to have disastrous side effects.'

Emma sat on her bed, biting her nails and trying to sort out her feelings. This sense of outrage, was it actually justified? Yes, it damn well was: everyone had let her down; there was no-one she could trust or even talk to. She had thought for a moment that Pa was an ally. There had unexpectedly been that comforting bond of sympathy between them when she had come back home, but now—? The distressing image of Rajini and her father locked in a naked embrace made her cheeks flame and a gagging stricture clutch at her throat. *How* disgusting! It was obvious that he was not really interested in *her* unhappiness, nor particularly bothered by Harriet and Alan's behaviour. Much more concerned with getting into bed with Rajini, a dirty old man chasing after young girls. No wonder Ma had left him.

The thought of Ma and Alan cropped up then, and fury and humiliation rose up like a wave; all this sex that seemed to overpower these old people when they ought at least to be gaining some control over themselves. What Alan and Harriet had done to Laura and the family was unforgivable: shameful. Almost as bad as what Rajini was doing to Pa. How couldn't he see what she was playing at? She might even be doing it for a bet, or to look big or something. And suppose, suppose he really fell for it and she'd take off when she got tired of him and just leave him high and dry. *Surely* he had more sense than to fall for it and get really hurt?

The thoughts seethed through her head, along with a bitter hate for Rajini and Alan as the instigators, and furious disappointment that her parents should have fallen so far short of her belief and pride in them. She remembered in what contempt she often held the parents of many of her friends, and it did not please her that her own parents could now be looked down upon in exactly the same way. It was mortifying. Sleep came a long time later and brought nightmares with it.

Ben took Hamlet up to bed with him that night; strictly not allowed, but he felt depressed – not for any real reason that he could think of, or at least that he wanted to think of, but something hovered at the back of his mind; something connected with Emma's slammed door and general air of anger, just when he thought she and Pa were beginning to get along again. The last few weeks had been fine with Emma there most evenings soon after he got home. Sort of eased off the loneliness and the empty kind of feeling when Pa didn't get back till late. Not that he minded being on his own all that much, but just lately Pa had hardly been there at all. He saw him at breakfast though, that was something. And he was always very kind about organizing some sort of day out at the weekends – though he often had some-one else there whose car they were borrowing, and they usually had to drop off somebody Pa had prom-ised to drop off, or they had to go to the rehearsal of the play Pa was doing. Often quite boring, except that they allowed him to work on the computers while he was waiting. That was the trouble with Pa, he was so kind, and so everyone took advantage of him and got him to do things for them.

He had heard, from Emma, the news that Alan had moved in with Ma. Emma was furious about it all, but it didn't trouble Ben that much. He quite liked Alan and, if Ma liked him too, there didn't seem much wrong in their being together. Could be tough on Alan's family, he supposed, having their father walk out on them, but then Laura was the only one that counted with them because she was just always there and doing things for them all; life without Alan wouldn't have been all that different for them. He was for ever working, even when he was at home, and that wasn't often. Emma did tell him that Laura was ill, though he had thought it rather odd that Pa should have gone off in a taxi to see them. He supposed that Laura had got over her illness when Pa had returned home; they must have all settled down again the same as he had.

He found he didn't miss Ma so much really. He had always had the idea that he was wasting her time – she was always rushing off to do something. He quite enjoyed being on his own actually, especially now he had his own computer and Hamlet as well. Life wasn't so bad, apart from little depressions and anxieties now and then.

25

Grandma Sunshine arrived at the Summerson house one afternoon unannounced, when only Daisy and Louise were home.

'Hallo, my darlings,' she said, hugging them to her. 'Thought I'd surprise you all. Just on my way back from a lovely shopping spree in Harrods. Brought you some of their lovely chockies too, and some special beigels for Daddy and Mummy. Daisy I do believe you've grown since the last time I saw you. You must tell me all about school and how you're getting on. Where's Mummy?' She bumbled cheerily past them into the sitting-room, which was in a terrible state. 'Oh my,' she said, covering her mouth with her hand. 'Whatever's happened here?' She looked round at the girls. 'Where's Mummy then? What have you been up to, to get the place like this?'

'Mummy's in hospital,' said Daisy.

Esther Sunshine gave a small shriek: 'Hospital? What do you mean, hospital? Why didn't anyone tell me? What's the matter with her? Is Daddy there with her? Is she in danger? What hospital? A public ward do you mean? Oh my goodness, what a shock.' She collapsed heavily into an armchair and fanned herself with her handbag.

'She got ill one day and Daddy was away . . .'

'Tom came over,' said Louise.

'Tom? Who's Tom?' Grandma Sunshine asked.

'You know Tom; Tom Turtle. He's the father of our friends who live in Whetstone, and he came over and then we found Daddy at Harriet's and he came too . . .'

'Who's Harriet?'

'You *know*, Grandma, you've met her hundreds of times. She's Tom's wife – at least she was, but she isn't now, because she and Daddy work together . . .'

'And so Daddy stays with her most of the time.'

Esther Sunshine moaned and rocked herself back and forth in the chair.

'My God, what am I hearing?' she said. 'And who is looking after you?'

'Well, Daddy does when he's here – and Harriet came as well for a bit,' Louise was cautious in what she said, afraid of letting slip something she thought her father might not want Grandma to know.

'But we didn't like that,' said Daisy, remembering the horror, 'because we thought she shouldn't sleep with Daddy in Mummy's bed, so we wouldn't do what she said.'

Louise kicked Daisy, who cried out in pain. 'Daddy's trying to get a housekeeper to look after us until Mummy is better,' Louise said hurriedly.

'A housekeeper?' Esther was crying now, and searching for a handkerchief in her bag. 'What does the boy think he's doing? Not to tell his own mother? And think of a housekeeper without consulting his father or me? What am I hearing?'

Further explanations and revelations were postponed by the return of the two boys.

'Grandma's here,' shouted Louise, to warn them, as Grandma struggled to her feet to enclose them in emotional hugs and kisses. 'My poor little loves,' she wept, 'what's to become of you all? But never mind, I will care for you, Grandpa and I will come straight away. I will phone him and tell him to come. Get me the phone, Hamish; God knows where it is in all this mayhem. What a disaster. What does Alan think he's doing? That my only son could treat us all like this? I always said it would be no good from the start. She's not right for you Alan, I said, but would he listen?'

Max found the phone under the sofa and handed it to her. Hamish raised his eyes to the ceiling and jerked his head in the direction of the kitchen. 'We'll go and make some tea,' he said, and they escaped with a feeling of relief.

'Daisy told her *everything*,' hissed Louise as Max filled the kettle. 'You're such an idiot, Daisy; you needn't have said that about them sharing the bed.'

Daisy turned red. 'Well she shouldn't have and I don't see why Grandma shouldn't know, otherwise she might blame Daddy.'

'Nobody should have told her anything,' Hamish said crossly. 'She ought to have heard everything from Dad when he thought it right to tell her. Now he'll get it doubly in the neck, poor sod.'

'You shouldn't call Daddy a sod,' said Daisy.

Alan returned home at eight o'clock to find both his parents waiting for him. Esther had told Bernie to come over as quickly as possible, and he had obeyed at once. 'Left the children to starve,' she said as soon as Bernie arrived. 'What is it with your son? Is he a monster or what? That he couldn't tell his own mother – so what do I have to feed my grandchildren on? Chocolates and beigels from Harrods.'

'But Grandma,' said Hamish, 'we aren't starving – really.'

'I am,' grinned Max. 'Can I have some money for fish and chips?'

'No you can't,' Louise said. 'It's Hamish's turn to do supper, and he said he was going to do a cottage pie and I like that better than fish and chips. Hamish is good at cottage pie, Grandma, and we had some mash left over from the sausages and mash yesterday so it won't take long.'

'You and Grandpa can have dinner with us,' said Daisy. 'That would be really nice.'

Esther shook her head: 'That my grandchildren should have come to this,' she said, sitting back again in the armchair and dabbing her nose and eyes with a handkerchief. 'Having to cook for their grandparents.'

Bernie smiled round at the group. 'Cottage pie is one of my favourites,' he said. 'Can you really cook it?'

'Just you wait and see,' said Daisy. 'We're really good at doing supper. I lay the table and we take it in turns to fill the dishwasher.'

'Poor destitute little darlings,' moaned Esther.

The cottage pie looked impressive and the table was laid faultlessly.

'Not that I could eat a crumb,' Esther kept saying, but Bernie was impressed. 'What a chef we have in the family,' he said to Hamish, 'and I never knew it before. Eat up, I tell you Essie, the boy's a genius.'

Alan froze in shock as he saw both cars belonging to his parents in front of the house. His immediate thought was that something drastic had happened to the children. A burglary? A fire? An accident?

He ran into the house: 'Hallo? What's the matter? What's wrong?'

They were all sitting round the table, the children smiling, glad to see him; glad not to have to make further conversation with their grandparents; happy to shift responsibility on to him.

'What's wrong he asks,' Esther raised her hands to her head. 'The very question we would like to ask you, son. I come here to see my grandchildren, and what do I find? I find them living in a pigsty with no-one to care for them. All alone they were, with nobody to look after them.'

Max laughed out loud, but the others stifled their giggles.

'Grandpa thinks I'm a first class chef,' Hamish said.

'So we shall have to move in at once Bernie,' said Esther. 'It seems this boy of yours can't organize his life.'

'Please Mumma,' Alan said through gritted teeth. 'We'll talk about everything later . . .'

'But why couldn't you talk to your mother before . . . ?'

'I'm sorry, I'm sorry but – well – anyway, I have today managed to engage a housekeeper to help out for a while.'

'But you can't trust these people,' Esther complained. 'Most of them are just in it for the money – and what money, my God – so how can you trust them with your children? My own son, and he never tells us his troubles – employ a housekeeper, he says. How do you know she won't beat the children when your back's turned? How do you know this? Alone in that big house with all those expensive things; so easy just to take something and not be noticed. Why don't I come over every day and keep an eye on her?'

Bernard patted her hand. 'Stop worrying about it, Essie. With you there following her round the house, she wouldn't stay five minutes. Let Alan decide what's best.'

'And the next thing,' Esther clasped her hands over her stomach and leaned back in her chair. 'Who's this Harriet they tell me about?'

'She's my business partner, Mumma. You remember her, you've met her several times. We're setting up a business on our own. She's extremely able and she wants to put her money into a new venture. We pulled off a big deal in Rome with her help. It's a great opportunity, the sort I've been angling for for years.'

Esther squinted at him through narrowed eyes: 'You're walking out of a good job to set up on your own? You hear that Bernie? To walk out on a good job.'

'Alan's all right, Esther. You don't have to worry. He knows what he's doing, always did. If he thinks it's the right thing, it's the right thing, please God.'

Esther hunched her shoulders. 'The right thing? The right thing? God knows what is the right thing. So is it the right thing for Laura?' Nobody moved for a moment, but all eyes were on Alan. 'This –' Esther waved her hands in the air, 'this – Harriet person; does Laura think that she is the right thing?'

'Mumma, we'll talk about this later. Look what I've got, kids.' He held aloft the special ice cream they were particularly fond of. 'I think we all need a treat.'

'And the beigels,' Daisy said. 'Grandma brought some beigels and chocolates, let's eat them all now.'

The end of the meal was edgy because the ice cream wasn't kosher and no-one could eat it for fear of upsetting Grandpa. The adults and the older children were conscious of what was really uppermost in everybody's mind but nobody wanted to broach the subject for fear of emotional scenes. Esther sniffed and dabbed at her nose throughout, pushing away the food with distaste, but Bernie kept up a smiling and amiable conversation with each grandchild in turn.

Alan finally got to his feet: 'I have to talk with Grandpa and Grandma,' he said. 'We shall be in my studio, so you can turn the television on if you want to.'

Another hateful confrontation.

'Laura and I have decided to part,' he said quickly as soon as the door was closed. 'It's been building up for some time, and we really have so little in common these days.'

'So little in common?' Bernie raised his voice for the first time. 'You have the past twenty years and four children in common, is that so little?'

'You hear your father?' Esther's voice rose higher and louder than Bernie's. 'Though I said at the beginning it would never work, that doesn't mean you give it up after all this time; you make a commitment – you keep it.'

'Mumma, we're living now, not fifty years ago.'

'So fifty years makes a difference to commitments?'

'That's not what I meant, you know quite well. Things – people change in twenty years. We've moved in different directions.'

'So your father and I haven't changed? With the golden wedding coming up? You think we haven't changed? That we didn't sometimes disagree? But we made commitments, and these we don't break – twenty years after, thirty years, fifty years; we don't run away from commitments.'

Bernie took her hand. 'Things are different now, Essie. It's not the same.'

Esther turned her head away furiously: 'That's what I'm saying; things are not the same and what a disgrace that they are not. What does Laura have to say? Is she the real reason? Has she been playing around? If so, then perhaps you have an excuse. Who has she been playing around with? Is it this Tom person the children talked of.'

'No, she hasn't – Tom is just a friend, we've known him for years.' He nearly reminded them that he was Harriet's ex-husband which he thought they had probably forgotten, but thought better of it. The complications would surely prove even more difficult for them to sort out. Get this over as quickly as possible; quite enough to tell them the bare facts.

'But why did you have to do it when Laura was ill?'

his father asked. 'Surely you could have waited? Must have been a shock, or does she go along with the idea? You have got to shelve the idea until she is better. And why don't you tell us what's wrong with her? Can we go and see her? Do you spend your days with her?'

Alan held in his irritation and impatience. 'She refuses to see me.'

Esther sat up straight. 'Won't see you? So why not? That's no way to mend a marriage. If there's trouble between you, then the trouble should be worked out by talking. No sense in refusing to talk. Something can be worked out between you. I'm sure it can.'

'Mumma, Harriet Turtle and I are teaming up together. We find we are perfectly suited, not only in the business sense but also in our lives. We have decided to live together. That's all there is to it; we have made the decision and nothing is going to change our minds.'

He found he was suddenly able to stifle the tremors and the anxieties and come out fighting. All this idiotic talk of something being worked out between Laura and himself was a lot of interfering rubbish, and he felt a great rage against being preached at. 'Laura says that if I so much as put my nose round the nursing home door she will kill me.'

Not strictly true, of course, but it would do since she had made the attempt once. Not necessary to say that she had been insisting that the only person she wanted to see was Tom.

The nursing sister who informed him of this fact that same afternoon was one of the steely smiling types; reminded him of *One Flew Over the Cuckoo's Nest*. He could sense the hostility behind her smile: 'I'm so sorry Mr Summerson, but Mrs Summerson is still very disturbed; I think it would be best if you didn't see her today. She is insisting that she is afraid of – er – something.'

She wanted to say she's afraid of you, Alan thought, but is making some attempt at tact. He was furious that she should dare to consider herself to be in a position to have to be tactful to him.

Esther gave way to near hysterics when she heard of Laura's threat to his life.

'Oh my God, Bernie, you hear that? She says she'll kill him. Is she mad? So you see what you have done to her, Son? And this is what happens with young people today. You call this progress?'

It took time, some brandy and comforting phrases from both Alan and his father to pacify her sufficiently for Bernard to be able to shepherd her past the children, through the door and into his car to drive her home.

'We'll fetch her car tomorrow,' he told Alan. 'Goodbye kids; look after your father.'

Alan stood, drooping at the door, watching the car drive away down the road. The children were grouped in a sad pack, watching him from the sitting-room, emanating, he assumed, silent accusations and unspoken interrogation. His rage and seething resentment of the afternoon had dwindled into an exhausted despair. What was happening to his life?

26

Tom planned his day in detail. Life was so enjoyably full at the moment that he found it difficult to fit everything in. He made studied calculations as to how long it would take to get from A to B in order to work out how much time he could give to each commitment.

But, in order to fit everything in, he habitually under-estimated travelling time and so was never on time for any appointment.

'I couldn't do half the things I do do,' he said in answer to Rajini's complaints that he was always late for rehearsals, 'if I allowed time for what *might* happen on the way here. Think of the time I would waste if I got to places too early and had to hang about doing nothing.'

'But that means other people have to hang about waiting.'

'Just because they don't employ the same logic as I do,' Tom said. 'They make allowances for all those things that might never happen; and they don't really mind wasting time either. You, for instance, if you have to wait for me, you don't get worried about what you might be doing, you just get irritated because you think that I'm not conforming the way you think I should.'

The day following this conversation, Rajini was waiting after school at an appointed meeting place sufficiently remote for them to feel unrecognized and safe. She was cold and hungry and hoped he would bring something for them to eat before the rehearsal started. She kicked at loose stones under her feet and thought how stupid she was being, putting up with all this waiting. At moments like these, she saw her life with Tom as being impossible, no matter how much she loved him. The thought of the ghastly struggle that they would have to launch themselves into once the situation became public knowledge was a nightmare. Could someone like Tom ever face up to that sort of thing? He would never get involved in a discussion about where their relationship might be leading, only teased her gently about her intensity: 'Just let things happen,' he would say. 'No good anticipating before they do; waste of time.' She might be sure of herself, but how sure was she of him? She shivered a little, and tried to think of something else.

As she paced up and down, head lowered and arms clasped round her school bag, a motor cycle roared up beside her and stopped. Her heart lurched with anxiety: was she about to be raped? But the cyclist removed his helmet, and underneath there was Tom. She gave a yell and collapsed, laughing, with her arms round his neck.

'I decided you were right,' he said. 'Must do something about my unpunctuality, so I went and bought this. Even remembered to get a helmet for you. So armour on and climb aboard.'

'Oh Tom, you're ace, you really are.' She climbed on behind him and clasped her arms round his waist. 'I've always longed to be a ton-up groupie.'

'And I've never really grown out of the James Dean era,' Tom said as he roared away down the street.

The thrill he felt as they tore through the traffic, her arms tight round him and her legs clamped round his bottom was something he had only dreamed of. It was, as Rajini had pointed out – ace, or crucial or brill or safe or even, from his own era – fab.

And the excitement and sensation of riding on cloud nine carried on right through the rehearsal that evening. Tom felt inspired and elated and could almost believe in his own brilliance. This is what I am – kept surging through his mind – this is what I *really* am.

A telephone call to the rehearsal hall cut suddenly through the exuberance: 'Pa? It's me – Ben.' The ferment froze solid at the sound of Ben's queried 'Pa?', just as though Tom's heart ceased beating at that precise moment. What catastrophe had prompted a telephone call?

'What's the matter? What is it? Are you all right?'

'Yes, yes, of course I'm all right, but I thought I ought to ring you because they said it was urgent.'

'Urgent? What's urgent? Who said it was urgent? Is it Emma?'

'No, Emma's gone out. It's nothing to do with her, but they rang from the nursing home where Laura is; they said she was asking for you and they wanted you to go straight away, now, this evening. I said I'd find you and tell you.'

Tom's agitated senses simmered down inside him like boiling milk taken off the heat. The premonition of guilt melted away: anything to do with the kids would probably be his fault, he couldn't possibly be to blame for Laura's troubles. The creative energy, though, which had made itself felt during the evening had immediately evaporated with the introduction of an unrelated situation. Tom's mind switched at once to Laura's problems with sympathy.

'I have to go,' he told the cast. 'Terribly sorry, but someone is ill and I seem to be needed. Columbo, will you take over?'

'Ill?' said Rajini. 'Who's ill? Is it Ben?'

'No, no – nothing to do with my own family.'

He began to collect his things and put on his jacket, and Rajini broke from the scene and joined him by the door. 'Who is it then? What's so urgent? Has there been some sort of accident?'

'No, it's Laura Summerson.'

'But she's been ill for ages, hasn't she? Why do you have to go now because of that?'

'I'm not sure; they rang me from the nursing home, wanted me there at once.'

'But why? What's it got to do with you?'

'I don't know; it seems she's asking for me.'

'Asking for *you*? Why?' Rajini bristled with suspicion.

'Can't imagine.'

'So off you go. Some woman beckons, so you run. And how do I get home?'

Tom paused with his hand on the door. 'Oh – sorry. But there's sure to be somebody.' He raised his voice: 'Columbo! Will you see that Rajini gets a lift home. I'd be most grateful. Apologies everyone, but it's a bit of an emergency. See you next Tuesday; same place, same time. You're all doing marvellously. It's going to be a smash hit.' And he sped away, full of satisfaction that he would be able to fulfil this mission in a quarter of the time it would have taken before the advent of the bike.

At the nursing home, the receptionist glanced up at the helmeted, leather-jacketed visitor, and waited for an express package to be delivered.

'Yes? Can I help you?'

'Mrs Laura Summerson please.'

Even when the helmet and huge gauntlet gloves were removed, the receptionist visibly doubted that Tom could actually be visiting a patient, and there was some delay before he was shown Laura's room.

She was sitting in a large armchair in a pale blue filmy dressing gown which Tom thought strangely incongruous; flimsy négligés did not accord with his own impression of Laura. She looked white, thin and very frightened when he first went in but, as soon as she recognized who it was, relief appeared to spread right through her. Hands that had clutched the arms of the chair softened and relaxed, she melted back among the very white pillows letting her head sink into them, and the smile that spread slowly across her face released the cord-like tendons down her neck.

'That's better, Mrs Summerson,' the nurse adjusted the pillows slightly and twitched at the blanket over her knees. 'Such a nice smile; we don't see it often enough.'

She left them alone, and Laura held out her hands to Tom. 'Thank you for coming,' she said. 'There's nobody else I can talk to. Were you able to organize somebody to cope with Ben while you were out?'

Tom adjusted his mind to her question; he had never consciously organized somebody to cope with Ben because Ben was so obviously capable of organizing himself. Wasn't he?

'Ben's fine,' he said, holding both her hands, 'but what about you?'

She was far less disturbed than he imagined she would be, remembering the evening when she had been carted off, heavily drugged, to the nursing home. She looked, he thought with anxiety, rather as though she was dead. There was a blank pallor about her he had never seen nor ever connected with her before. Laura had always been the pink, dreamy, smiling creature who was the hub round which the whole Summerson family revolved, efficiently and amiably. She was not the sharp, splintered individual sitting here, draped in a mushy disguise of pale blue transparency that completely obliterated her normal rosy good health.

'It's just that I have nobody I can talk to,' she said. 'I have realized, you see, Tom, that I am quite unnecessary. Harriet can look after Alan far better than I can and the children are so competent and grown up, they don't really need me at all any more. But if I said that to them, they would all protest and pretend that I was still of some use and I have discovered that the one thing I can't stand in life is being lied to. I want to kill people who lie to me. So I think it would be so much better for everyone if I were to die now, don't you see? And you said you would be able to help me. I am a danger to everyone as I am, because if the children pretended to me, then I might want to kill them like I wanted to kill Alan – don't you see? And Alan knows this, so he could be forgiven for wanting to get me first and I can't help being frightened of that; frightened of being killed by Alan I mean. I'm such a coward, so I would far rather do it myself when I was ready for it, I mean I couldn't bear a gun or a knife – a gun would make so much noise and loud noises always frightened me, and a knife would be so painful I thought – that dreadful slicing, and the blood . . .' She started to cry, and Tom lifted her from her chair, sat her on his knee and rocked her backwards and forwards in his arms.

It was the beginning of daily visits to the nursing home, when Tom's senses were in constant turmoil. Laura's illness and its consequences became the sudden centre of his life, and the thing to which all other responsibilities and commitments were subsidiary.

'You're such a bum,' Rajini complained. 'Leaving us all in the lurch like this. After all, it is your play; you seem to have lost interest. It's a bit much, just because you feel you've got to visit some woman in hospital. Are you turning into a health visitor or something? A bit morbid I call it.'

'Rajini, dear . . .'

'Stop it! You're about to be condescending.'

Tom rearranged the smile on his face. 'She's a great friend. She's desperately ill and she won't talk to anyone else. You think I shouldn't respond?'

'You really do think you're so important, don't you?'

'Well I am important to her.'

Rajini rounded on him in fury: 'Important to her? And what about me?'

The smile crept back and he wondered how he could stop it looking condescending. 'Am I as important to you as I am to her?'

211

'It depends, doesn't it?' Rajini was tense with anger. 'On how often you sleep with her.'

He allowed the smile to change to a laugh. 'Idiot. One can be fond of people without necessarily going to bed with them.'

'You're being impossible. I hate you when you argue in that snide way.'

'Sorry.' The smile was still there and he knew perfectly well it could be termed condescending, but he decided that there was nothing much he could do about it.

The daily visits to Laura began to show beneficial effects. Alan was kept informed by a fairly embarrassed doctor. 'It does seem, Mr Summerson, that this Mr – er – Turtle is, at the moment, being quite helpful in encouraging your wife to co-operate with our medication. All being well, she should be able to return home in the next few days, provided that you could ensure Mr Turtle is willing to act as – er – some sort of – er – go-between.'

Alan was thrown into an angry confusion, torn between resentment that Tom and Laura had something going that he knew nothing of and relief, in spite of that, that Tom might be of some use in solving the difficulties connected with Laura going back home. It would be impossible to leave her with the efficient but detached housekeeper he had employed temporarily who, he envisaged, would be resented and probably immediately sent packing by Laura.

Tom broke the news to Laura of her release from the nursing home: 'They say you can go home.'

Laura looked panic stricken. 'Home? How can I go home? I'm not ready; I'm not cured. I still feel I want to kill Alan sometimes. And what would I do if ever I came in contact with Harriet? There's no knowing what I might not do to her. And the children will be frightened of me – quite possibly with good cause. I'm not in control, Tom.' She was shaking violently and appeared full of terror. 'Don't let them make me.'

'But it's no use staying here in these unreal surroundings, darling Laura, now is it?' He knew at once, within himself, the obvious solution. 'Suppose I came and stayed with you for a bit, just until you got settled in and found you could cope?'

'Oh Tom – would you?'

Of course he would; just for a bit. Ben could come too, and Emma if she wanted to. The house was plenty big enough. It was only Rajini who wouldn't fit in, but she could be made to understand that this was an emergency and wouldn't last very long; just until Laura found her feet. His confidence diminished a little as he thought of Rajini, but she could surely be reassured, and they could always go back to his house to make love; an even better arrangement than the present one, where Ben and Emma's presence was always an anxious possibility.

It took no time at all to convince himself, but a little longer to satisfy everyone else. Alan was affronted, but could think of no other way out. He was offended by Harriet's amusement.

'But darling, what a great let-out!' she said. 'I think it's a fantastic idea and funny into the bargain.'

'But did you know about it? I mean how long has it been going on? If she's been playing around with Tom, what right has she to make all this fuss about us?'

'Oh Alan! You mean to say you know so little about Laura after all these years? She would *never* in a hundred years look outwards from you and the family. She's much too innocent – guileless – dutiful – call it what you will, to behave in a normal, unrepressed way. Probably all that church upbringing she had. She would never have dreamed of having it off with Tom. I can't vouch for him of course, but I would have thought he was far too wrapped up in himself and his work to hanker after someone like Laura. He just loves helping lame dogs, that's all. Makes him feel powerful.'

Ben rather liked the idea of staying with the Summersons, since the cold solitariness of living so much on his own had begun to pall in the winter bleakness of February, and Hamlet liked the Summersons' mongrel bitch. The Summersons weren't a bad bunch on the whole, and their house was big with a good closed off garden at the back, safe for Hamlet to wander in and out of. It would be a real holiday for Hamlet, and Gertrude would adapt. 'Are you going to come too?' he asked Emma.

'I might; this place is pretty dire with just us coping and I can't stand the idea of Alan and Ma somehow. I never thought she'd come down to his level. So demeaning, somehow.' She remembered her first reaction and was embarrassed to think how disgusted and upset she had been then. It had been immature to react in that way.

Ben tried to imagine his mother and Alan as a couple but found it much too ludicrous to consider so blotted it from his mind. 'Might be quite fun for a bit,' he said.

The Summerson children welcomed the news with varying degrees of enthusiasm.

'Ben's all right,' said Max, 'but Emma – ugh.' Max found Emma made him feel much younger than he actually was.

'Good of Tom to do it,' Hamish said.

'I like Tom,' said Daisy.

'I hope old Bossy-lady-paid-help stays to do the cooking,' Max said, 'if Mum isn't well enough.'

Grandma Sunshine made her weekly telephone call to know of any fresh disaster that might have befallen her grandchildren and Daisy answered.

214

'We're quite all right thank you,' said Daisy. 'Mummy's coming home tomorrow, and she's bringing Tom with her because she doesn't like Daddy much at the minute so she's having Tom instead for a bit, but we hope that Mrs Bossy (her name isn't really Bossy you know, but we call her that), we hope she's staying too because she cooks very nice things and Tom says Mummy won't feel like cooking for a bit and he isn't much good at it either. And Ben and Emma and Hamlet and Gertrude (she's their cat) are all coming too so we think it will be rather fun; perhaps you would like to come to tea with Grandpa, would you?'

Esther looked across at Bernie in total incomprehension. 'What am I hearing?' she said, with the telephone poised in mid air away from her ear. But Daisy had gone, so that Esther was able to convince herself that what she had heard must have been in her imagination.

27

Alan continued to find it impossible to join in the general feeling of relief that seemed to pervade the whole group at the idea of Tom's good-hearted gesture. The anger he had felt at first had shrunk to a sense of melancholic despondency at the realization that he had so alienated Laura that she had let herself fall straight into the arms of someone as unreliable as Tom. Probably into his bed too; this idea incensed him whenever he thought about it, no matter how illogical it might seem.

Most of the anger that remained, however, he

managed to channel into petty irritation against his parents, whose nagging accusations buzzed in his ear continuously. His father, with: 'How could you upset your mother like this?' While Esther was so completely confused that she phoned him constantly at work and at Harriet's flat to demand, yet again, just who was living with whom, and why.

'So why doesn't this Tom live with his wife. Why does he leave his wife alone in order to stay with someone else's? What sort of a man would desert his wife to set up with someone who doesn't know her own mind? Is he after her money or something?' The outrage and anxiety she felt took charge of her thinking. She tried hard to recall who this Tom might be, remembering, in short spasms, that he had been mentioned recently – she even thought she might have met him at some time. In any case, his scandalous behaviour in alienating Laura's affections, making her reject Alan in this disgraceful way, was unforgivable.

'Mumma, Tom is – was – married to Harriet . . .'

'So what's this Harriet doing that she doesn't look after her husband properly?' The name Harriet brought immediate hostile reaction and a clear memory of Alan telling of his connections with her: 'Can't she stop him running after other people's wives? Is this what you're telling me? When poor little Laura is in no state to resist him. What a scandal. What a disgrace.'

'Harriet is living with me, Mumma, you remember, I told you about her.'

Something she would rather forget; the thought of her son involved in anything so unwise was better pushed into oblivion – couldn't really be true. 'You see? This is what I am saying; what sort of a woman would run off with my son and let her own man wreck the lives of so many others?'

At this point – or others like it – Esther would sob noisily into the telephone.

'Put it down,' Harriet directed Alan from across the room. 'Just put the bloody thing down. What's the good of holding on while she wails away at the other end.'

But Alan found it quite impossible to hang up on his mother. It was just one of those things you didn't do.

'We really have to get this whole thing sorted out,' Harriet said later. 'This situation will drive us all insane. Personally, I think it would be an excellent way out for everyone if Tom and Laura got together. I mean really got together; they'd make an ideal couple. Why you've got cold feet I can't imagine. I shall tell the solicitors to inform Tom that I'm selling the house and then he'll have to get on with deciding whether or not he's going to move in to your place permanently. You can settle the house on Laura until the kids are grown, and we can buy something together. I really cannot see the problem.'

Alan was perturbed; the idea of Tom and Laura together permanently had not occurred to him. But the sense of Harriet's hard words penetrated his confusion like a plunge into a cold pool: half shock, half clear-headed relief from the mayhem of his conflicting instincts. They cleared his mind sufficiently for him to be able to collect together concise and pithy arguments for or against. But discussions like these also seemed to generate, in both of them, a fervent sexual arousal.

'Do you do it on purpose?' Alan asked, holding her, forcibly, so close that it felt as though their bodies were blended through clothes and through skin.

'Do I do what?'

'Disrupt any serious talk by becoming a lascivious, lustful, heaven-sent *femme fatale*.'

'Don't be so silly, it's nothing to do with me. You're

the one that sets everything in motion at every possible opportunity – discussion or no discussion.'

'With your explicit encouragement.'

'Of course. If it wasn't for the sex . . .'

It was difficult to talk for the next forty minutes or so.

'You were saying,' Alan said, sprawled under her in voluptuous satisfaction, 'that if it wasn't for the sex . . .'

'Did I say that? What a crazy thing to say. As long as you and I are together, the question doesn't really arise. No part of you and me could operate if it wasn't for the sex.'

'A frightening statement that.'

'Not really, because, whenever we are together, sex is the driving force; that's why we are so totally compatible. United we stand, sort of thing.'

'But divided we fall.'

'Precisely; so we don't get divided.'

A sudden tremor of anxiety made itself felt way down inside her: scarcely noticeable, but there all the same. Alan was one of the certainties of her life; she had never been quite so sure about anything before. There had never before been any reason to consider certainty: you did or said something because it was obviously the right thing to do or say. But in the case of Alan and her, that certainty had been there, almost like an insistent voice in her head, since those first days in Rome. It really was a case of until death do us part, and death just now seemed a highly unlikely possibility.

'So we forge ahead, no matter what, because we simply have to stay together – *that's* the essential thing that we have to keep in mind.'

It was all so easy and straightforward.

Tom reviewed the enormity of the task he had taken on and wondered, as he had wondered many times since he had suggested it, why exactly he had done so. There did not seem to be an adequate answer except that Laura had needed help and he thought he could probably provide it. Sitting at home he attempted to explain the plan to Rajini, a few days before Laura was due to leave the nursing home. Rajini became distraught and unreasonable.

'It will mean all your time will be taken up seeing to that Laura woman and all those dreadful kids. You just haven't considered me at all, have you? I don't understand how you just could have said that you'd act as her live-in nurse without giving it a second thought. It seems I'm just not a part of your thinking.'

'You are as much a part of my life as you ever were, darling Rajini. But I do have several parts to my life – you know that. You, my job, my writing and my family – all parts of my life that have to be reconciled.'

'Pompous old fool, of course you have several parts to your life – doesn't everyone? The trouble with you is that you can't seem to work out what's important and what isn't. You're shit scared that you might be missing something; got to do everything; be kind to everyone; save the world; rescue mankind – the lot. Mr Marvellous, Superman, God – you want to be all of them put together.'

Rajini's large brown eyes somehow looked twice their normal size with tears acting as magnifiers. Tom's solar plexus literally lurched with emotion at the sight, and he pulled her towards him to hug her.

'My adorable, completely beautiful darling: you are the unbelievable, exciting, mind-blowing part of my life which surely is most important; it's the part that has thrown me badly off course, anyway.'

'But it's obviously not *the* most important part for you, and that's not fair, because for me, you are my whole life.' She continued to look woebegone and appealing.

'Only because you haven't had time to consider what else lies in wait for you just round the corner.'

Rajini leaped suddenly from the childish and appealing to the raging termagant: 'Treat me seriously, you pig. You have no more idea than I have what's waiting round the corner, even though you may have one foot in the grave. At this minute, I want you, and I'm no more likely to change my mind than you are. So stop treating me like an infant in arms.' She was shaking with rage.

'All right, all right. Keep calm. But you must admit, it's highly likely that someone better will turn up before too long, in which case you'll leave me high and dry, won't you?' In spite of clinging to the snatches of hope that this might not be so in their case, Tom felt the need to voice the obvious every now and then.

Rajini still seethed noticeably. 'And if I do fancy someone else, it'll be because you insist on treating me like a child.'

'I see every possibility of it happening, however I treat you.' Jealousy brought hostility with it; 'Unless you come to realize how much older and wiser I am than you are and decide to put up with me as I am.'

'Not without a struggle I won't.' Rajini's fury began to melt a little. 'I shall mould you into a decent shape so that you become bearable.'

Conversations like these helped, fractionally, to lessen the uncomfortable twinges of conflicting responsibilities from which Tom suffered. The few occasions on which he could convince himself that their relationship might be an exception to the rule that widely differing age groups were incompatible instilled in him an idiotically youthful feeling.

And then, the idea of combining two families into one, with him in charge, seemed to him a bit like directing his play: at the head of operations, helping the story to unfold. So now he had three big projects on hand – Rajini, the Summerson family and the production – a very satisfactory situation, on the whole, which would occupy his whole time.

'Emma can have the spare room,' Hamish said, when the idea of the two families combining had been accepted, 'and Ben can be in the old playroom upstairs.' He looked at Tom. 'You could go in what Mum used as her workroom-study sort of thing; it leads out of her and Dad's bedroom.' He felt heat crawl up his neck to the top of his head. But even if it wasn't their bedroom any more, he didn't want a Harriet-type situation starting up between Tom and Laura. Make it quite clear what should and should not be done. He waited a fraction to see how Tom would react.

'Splendid,' said Tom. 'I appreciate your help. What about beds and blankets and things? Do we need to bring some with us?'

There was a general air of excitement among the young except for Emma and Max.

'You're in the spare room,' Hamish told Emma when she arrived at the house with a very small bag of her belongings.

'Well, it won't be for long,' said Emma, guardedly. 'I might go back to my mother, or I might stay with a friend.'

Ben's arrival gave cause for more interest. He turned up on the back of Tom's motorbike, holding Gertrude's cat basket, with Hamlet strapped into a carrier behind him. The Summerson bitch started a cacophony of barking which caused Gertrude to hiss and growl from her basket. Hamlet joined in the barking with great good nature and tail wagging, eager to renew acquaintances. The animals and the motorbike came in for

221

equal interest and admiration. Tom thought how sensible he had been to decide to settle everyone in before he fetched Laura.

He brought her back the next day, to a house empty of everyone, with only the dogs as a welcoming committee.

'I feel like a bride,' she said, not looking at him.

He picked her up; 'So I'd better carry you over the threshold.'

There followed a moment of awkwardness as he bore her into the sitting-room and lowered her on to the sofa. Neither of them wanted to continue with that line of talk; it had somehow slipped out unexpectedly.

'So, coffee and chocolate biscuit time,' Tom said, escaping into the kitchen. 'I bought some of those special expensive German ones to celebrate.'

It was all rather forced and embarrassing and he felt a slight tremor of anxiety that Laura might expect too much. He checked himself: what, after all, was too much? It was quite straightforward at the moment, just something he had taken on in a spirit of friendship, and in his spare time.

But there persisted for several days an artificial, slightly hysterical atmosphere when all the children were at home. They prowled round each other like hostile dogs, keen to play but aggressively ready for any suspected affront.

To each of the Summerson children, in their various ways, Laura came back to them from the nursing home as a transformed personality. She had become someone who was *not* always able to cope; someone who might not, after all, have all the answers; someone who possibly needed *their* support on occasion; someone, in fact, who could be done without. It was an eye-opener to each one of them. She even looked different; it alarmed the younger ones to realize that the rock of ages could, after all, be undermined and vulnerable.

'What do you think of this arrangement?' Max asked, rather miserably, after two days of Tom's infiltration; the Summersons were closeted in one room while Emma and Ben sat, behind closed doors, in Emma's provisional sanctum.

'I don't see,' Max said, 'why it's necessary for Tom to be here any longer. I mean, we could look after Mum perfectly well on our own.'

'I don't know that we could,' Hamish said. 'She may be better, but she isn't right, not like she was, and if she thought she had to look after us it might send her round the bend again.'

'But she wouldn't have to look after us,' Louise said. 'We would look after her.'

'Not when we're at school all the time we can't. She'd be on her own all day.'

'So's Tom out all day, or most of it, and evenings too; I can't see that he's any use at all,' said Max.

'And Emma's such a pain,' Louise said. 'She makes me feel somehow as though I should always be making sure she's not upset about anything; as though I ought to say sorry about something or other the whole time.'

'She ought to be saying sorry to us really,' said Daisy. 'After all, her mother's taken Dad away from us, she ought to feel guilty about that.'

'You can't be blamed for what your parents do,' Hamish reminded her.

'No, but you can at least feel guilty. I would. I wouldn't go around being stuck up like she is.'

'She probably does feel guilty,' said Hamish. 'That's possibly what makes her so bad-tempered.'

'You only say that because you fancy her,' said Max.

'Oh, belt up do,' Hamish threw a book at his brother in a fairly unchallenging way.

'I like it here,' Ben was saying to Emma at this same moment. 'It would be quite good if Pa married Laura; I would quite like that.'

'Don't be so revolting,' Emma told him. 'How can you imagine such a bizarre situation? It's creepy. For God's sake, grow up.'

'I don't see why it's so bizarre; if Ma and Alan get married, then why shouldn't Pa and Laura? There's nothing *wrong* about it.'

'Just because people have affairs, they don't necessarily have to get married. Just because that wretched Alan has induced Ma to have an affair with him doesn't mean Ma won't see sense eventually. Things might get back to normal again.'

'Do you really think they will?'

Emma paused and studied her nails. 'No, not really.'

'Well then?'

'Well then what?'

'Well, why couldn't they just change partners? It would be better than having some completely unknown person moving in.'

Emma felt suddenly like crying, but didn't want to show her emotions in front of Ben, so she got up and emptied her books out on the table. 'The whole thing's just a bloody muddle. Why can't they organize themselves without getting everyone messed up like this? They're so selfish and childish and – and – so undignified.'

She opened a book and cupped her face in her hands so that Ben could not possibly notice a tear running down her cheek. It was all so stupid, why should it make her feel like crying? There seemed no real reason to be upset. Life at home had been pretty boring before all this started, and very restrictive too. She had been itching to get away to university – or anywhere else for that matter – and leave it all behind her. This upset would probably make that a whole lot easier, so why the pangs? It couldn't all be pre-menstrual. Something to do with disillusion – but what illusions had she had about Ma and Pa? Surely she had outgrown them by now. They weren't any more saint-like than anyone else's parents. Pa was a wimp and liked young girls and Ma was a hard-headed, sexy cow on occasions. They were just people, after all.

Ben wandered off and found Hamlet playing strange games in the garden with Flossie, the mongrel bitch. He felt quite disgusted that Hamlet should do such a thing, but was far too embarrassed to call him off. Instead, he crept quietly back upstairs to his room, hiding whenever he thought he heard any of the Summersons approaching. Once inside, with the door shut, he sat on his bed, his hands between his knees, and rocked gently backwards and forwards, feeling completely alone and strangely unhappy. It was quite a new experience.

28

As final rehearsals for the play became more frequent and more frantic, Tom, as head of operations, swung from one emotional extreme to the other; a feeling that he was, momentarily, a creative genius was immediately dispelled by the certainty that he was crassly stupid. It was not always possible to blame the problems of a particular rehearsal on the amateur group with which he was dealing; often it seemed probable that it was his own writing that was at fault. Ideas that had been brilliant when they first made themselves felt, drooped and died when taken over by the non-actors who spoke the lines. Whose fault? Player? Director? Playwright? The plot was so closely connected with his own present situation, that he occasionally felt like God, directing himself and his characters through reality?

'Make it LIVE Melanie – you hate the man, remember, you want to kill him; make him feel frightened of you, for God's sake.'

The tensions among the cast, by this time, were at their peak. The jealousy that Rajini engendered was scarcely hidden, even though most had to agree that her acting abilities were marked.

Under the breath remarks were rife: 'I would have thought she had enough talent to get on without going to bed with an old man.'

'*Two* old men, dear, what about Claude?'

'She's got them both completely under her thumb, hasn't she? They daren't criticize anything she does.'

'The mutant Turtle is certainly besotted. But then he's not likely to get anyone else of that age if he lets her go.'

'Oh I don't know, he's quite dishy really.'

'Well, I think it's positively immoral of him to take advantage of a babe in arms like that.' This from one of the men in the cast.

Rajini smarted under the occasional overheard barb. 'They're so two-faced,' she said. 'Nice to me on the surface, and then they say things behind my back.'

'You can't really blame them,' Tom said. 'The director brings in his girl friend who has had no experience, it's very unfair. I wouldn't have done it if I hadn't known you were going to be a smash hit. So I'm relying on you to prove my point. Things always get hairy in the last few weeks of any production. Just put up with it and smile at everyone.'

226

'It's all very well—' said Rajini.

'All part of the neurosis of being an actor. On the other hand, they are bound to see, sooner or later, that you're head and shoulders above them. You're so good, you make me believe what I've written.'

'Do I? Do I really? Oh Tom, we're such a team, aren't we? But we must be careful, the parents are getting fidgety, and I don't want them to wreck things before we're ready to face them.'

Tom smiled at her earnestness. 'Quite a few years before that eventuality, lovely.'

She glanced up at him quickly. 'Not all that long. Once I'm well into the next bit of my life – university or drama school – then we don't have to be so paranoid about being found out. I think my father will probably tackle you before very long about how I should be concentrating my mind on my exams and preparing for university life, rather than frittering away my time on dramatic productions.'

Tom's thoughts swung into the future: where would things stand two years from now? Scarcely credible that Rajini would not have moved out of his ken by then. He gave her an affectionate hug. 'I'm well schooled in persuasion; it's one of my outstanding attributes. I'm sure I shall be able to convince your parents that deep study of the plays of Thomas Turtle is a must for a successful life at university.'

Rajini didn't answer at once, then she said: 'Tom, I really don't want to go to university, you know. Oxford or Cambridge, maybe, but to trail off to some boring second or third choice, no, no, I really don't need that. I was talking to Canadian Columbo the other day and he was saying that even if we don't get over there with this play he could get me a really good start in Canada if I went over next year, and I should like that because I want to go all round the world before I finally settle.'

Tom's insides gave a half turn – so underneath there was a subconscious plan that did not really include him at all. The idea of Columbo being a rival was ludicrous though.

'Don't tell me you've finally fallen for the cajolings of Canadian Columbo,' he said, trying not to sound anxious.

Rajini giggled. 'He's not so bad. And anyway, you told me to encourage him.'

'For the sake of the company, not to further your own ends.'

'Can I help it if he's madly in love with me?' She hugged him. 'Don't be silly. He could really be quite useful though, because he travels around with his own company out there; been to New York and everything. I keep reminding him what a brilliant playwright you are, and he agrees. He loves you too.'

Tom was irritated with himself; this was exactly what he had told himself to expect; she *would* take off before long – so why feel hurt when a possibility of it happening showed up? Anyway, it might *not* happen – not for a bit, at least. And surely not with Columbo.

'So,' Rajini said, 'I'm going to go up for auditions everywhere, from now on, and I want you to start to prepare my father for this eventuality.'

'That might be very difficult, and not really my responsibility.' Let her see how far Columbo would get with Papa Bhairavi.

'But I'm right, aren't I? I'm good – you keep saying so – and it's what I want, I know it is.'

'Acting is an impossible profession. I told you before.'

'Not for those who make it.'

'Even for them; you can't rely on it.'

'So what can you rely on? Being a university lecturer? Think of the time you've wasted being just that, when you could have become one of the great writers of the age.'

'A great starving writer.'

'So then you could have married a rich wife, just like you did. She would have supported you in exactly the same way as she has done for the last twenty years, by the end of which time you would have been a very rich and famous playwright and film director with a life of your own, instead of a slightly rich and rather unfamous lecturer with nothing at all of your own.'

Tom cringed a little. All possibly true.

'You just won't concentrate on one thing, will you?' Rajini got into her stride: 'Just have to do everything, don't you? Jack of all trades and master of none. My mother keeps quoting that at me because she wants me to concentrate on being a good wife and mother and thinks it should take up all my time.'

'Did anyone ever tell you you are impossibly cheeky?'

'Yes, you did and do, constantly, and it's very boring.'

Tom arrived back at the Turtle/Summerson commune quite late that evening to find Hamish and Emma still up and standing awkwardly round a weeping Laura.

'You're so late,' Emma said. 'She's been crying for hours and we can't stop her. Where have you been all this time?'

'I had a rehearsal.' And the last forty minutes had been spent snogging with Rajini in the bushes near her house. How reprehensible and how utterly childish; leaving two children to cope with a weeping Laura. How unacceptable.

'We were worried,' Hamish said. 'Didn't quite know what to do because everything we said she shouted at us and told us we had to find you, but you'd left the rehearsal hall when we phoned.'

Laura got up from the table and hung round Tom's

neck. 'I'm so sorry,' she said. 'Really, I'm so sorry. Can't seem to stop crying. I know it's silly. Emma and Hamish have been so patient with me but I – they – I got – I mean, *I just couldn't stand them, Tom.* And you know how that frightens me; I don't know what – I mean – I might . . .' She clung tightly and sobbed noisily and uncontrollably.

Tom smiled over her head at the two strained faces. 'Don't worry about it. I'm here now so you two get to bed. I'll deal with things. You don't have to worry.'

It took half a bottle of brandy – of which Laura had one small glass and which Tom finished off – and a considerable amount of time before the hysterical anxiety was appeased, but after two hours of Tom's quiet listening and gentle cajoling, Laura lay silently in his arms, staring up at the ceiling.

'I'm so useless,' she said for the tenth time. 'Why didn't I die when it all started? Things would have been so much easier for everyone.'

'That's a lot of bullshit,' Tom said. 'Just think of all the problems of organizing a funeral, not to mention the expense, and all those flowers left to wither on your grave; what a waste. And, apart from anything else, I would miss you horribly if you weren't here any more; there would be a great gap in my life that I should never be able to fill satisfactorily.'

Laura came back to real life then, with a slow smile. 'Dear, dear Tom,' she said, pulling his face down to hers, 'I don't think I could live if you weren't around either. At the moment you are my only reason for living at all.' The kiss began by being affectionate, but changed fairly rapidly into a sensual, tongue-touching arousal.

Tom found it gentle and pleasant and full of relief after the ferment and the tension of the whole evening, first with Rajini and later with Laura's hysteria. All

Laura wanted now was affection, love and reassurance. She had to feel needed; her self-esteem needed boosting and what better way to do that than to make love to her? The brandy swam round in his head and he felt as though he was sinking back into a comfortable, if temporary, cloud of peace and quiet. He was helping someone out of a state of misery. That was something he was good at.

'Bed,' he said amiably, pulling her up and guiding her, in a stumbling, amicable sort of way, up the stairs. 'Bed cures a multitude of ills.' And he set about undressing her in much the same way he had done on the night when she had given vent to all her rage and frustration. Only now the whole situation had changed; a simultaneous and urgent desire in both of them was taking over, and it expressed itself in a soft, voluptuous session of love-making that carried them both through into six hours of deep and satisfied sleep, wrapped in each other's arms like two middle-aged and exhausted babes in the wood.

The morning brought a continued sense of well-being and a complete absence of regret. They sat up in bed, holding hands and smiling at each other.

'That was one of the most satisfactory experiences of my life,' Tom said, with a genuine sense of surprise. 'And you have no idea how much I need satisfactory experiences just now.'

'Flattery will get you absolutely anywhere you want with me at the moment,' said Laura, finding herself brimming over with warm, satisfactory feelings herself. 'You're actually saying that you needed me, and to be needed by anyone, specially by someone as adequate as you are, is balm to the soul.'

'Needed is perhaps the wrong word.' He did not have to pretend, in order to boost Laura's self-esteem this morning: it was already boosted. 'I would say that you are necessary to my well-being if it weren't such a mouthful – last night, today, tomorrow. You are extremely necessary to me.'

And it was true, he let his thoughts catch up with the words: Laura had overnight proved herself essential to the balance of his life; the soft, incestuously maternal love, which he had left behind all those years ago, had nostalgically flowed back in and he found it comfortable and restful.

'After last night, I feel as though I might be able to face the world again,' Laura went on, lying back among the pillows. 'Probably won't last of course, but I really believe I am beginning to come alive again for a moment or two at least.'

They drifted down to breakfast a little while later and found organized chaos reigning among the young, over which Laura suddenly took smiling charge, clearing and stacking dishes, checking on lunch boxes and locating anoraks. All were startled into silence until Hamish ventured a rather superfluous 'Feeling better Mum?' just before they left for school.

'What on earth did Tom do to change things?' Louise wanted to know as soon as the door closed behind them.

'I bet you it's a miracle,' Daisy said, suddenly starting to skip in order to keep up. 'They do still happen, you know, even if you don't go to Lourdes or anything. My friend knows someone whose brother was . . .'

'Perhaps they have fallen in love,' said Ben. 'That would make Laura feel better. Making love to someone is supposed to make you feel great, so I expect that's what Pa did.'

'Shut up, cretinous jerk,' shouted Emma. 'Stop trying to be funny.'

'I'm not being funny,' said Ben.

'I hardly think Mum would have – er – allowed . . . I

mean . . .' Hamish looked straight ahead as he walked, in evident distress.

'And Pa almost certainly wouldn't have . . . no way,' said Emma furiously.

'I don't see why not,' Daisy said, 'if he thought it would cheer Mummy up. She wants people to love her now that Daddy doesn't.'

'Exactly,' said Ben. 'They both need people just now, and I can't see why they shouldn't get together just to cheer each other up.'

'On the rebound,' said Max, chuckling a little, 'and then we'd all end up step-brothers and sisters.'

Everyone, except for Emma, started to smile a little, and Daisy increased the height of her skips and then ran a little way ahead of them all. 'They could marry each other,' she said. 'That would cheer everyone up and I could be bridesmaid.'

Emma turned abruptly and crossed the road, while the others broke up into their individual groups and hurried quite cheerfully towards their respective forms of transport. It suddenly appeared that there might be possible ways out of the mess.

29

'No way,' said Emma to Hamish, 'would I go to see that little Indian sacred cow poncing about in some rubbishy play my father's written for her.'

'Can't see why you're so jealous of her,' Hamish said. 'What's wrong with the girl having a yen for your Dad? Probably lots of his students do. No reason to think he returns the compliment.'

'I am NOT jealous of the cunning little slag . . .'

'So why do you hate her so much if you're not jealous? And suppose your Dad does have it off with her, what does it matter?'

'Of course it matters if your father shows himself up as a gullible fool just because he's been egged on by some no-good go-getter. How would you feel if your Pa did the s . . . ?' She cut the sentence short. He might consider that his father had done exactly the same.

They looked at each other, and Hamish began to laugh. Emma was further incensed: considered her mother a slag, did he? Actually dared to compare the two things in his mind, did he?

'So don't mind me,' she said. 'You go, along with everyone else; organize yourselves into one big happy family party and watch my father make a fool of himself. Thinks he can write plays does he? I bet it'll be crap.'

There were moments when the strain of trying to deal with the various and separate parts of his present existence did make for some confusion and fatigue for Tom. There was never enough time. He slept less and rose earlier and earlier in order to fit in all he had to do.

'Darling Tom,' Laura, drowned in sleep, complained, 'it's only half-past five; you'll make yourself ill if you don't sleep enough.'

He returned to the bed to kiss her. 'Napoleon got it down to five hours a night, no reason why I can't. There are some notes for the faculty lecture I have to check up on and the last act needs some technical adjustments. Early morning is the best time; no other distractions. Go back to sleep.'

He remembered his mother telling him he would make himself ill if he didn't sleep enough when he was trying to make sure he would get into Oxford. Laura was already asleep again, and he laid her back gently, before creeping across to the room Hamish had prescribed for him when he had first taken over the rescue of the Summerson family a month or so ago.

Papers, clothes and books were strewn over the floor, and he trod, cautiously, searching for what he needed. They were under the chair, surely; he'd put them there when he had run out of space on the table that stood in for a desk.

A good five minutes later, after rummaging round everything on the floor and on and under the bed, he found the notes, neatly stacked and in a folder, back on the table. Things on the table, in fact, he then realized, were all neatly stacked and arranged: a new desk tidy held all his pens and pencils in ordered groups, books stood between bookends in order of height and colour, and a new pad of rough paper lay waiting, with ball point, pencil and rubber on the right hand side, all ready for him to pick up and start.

Dear Laura! She had begun to get back into her stride. Tom realized that he should have been over-joyed that she was really on the mend but instead he was reminded, rather chillingly, of the way his mother had always tidied his room when he had left for school, so that he was never able to find any of his most precious possessions when he returned home.

He pushed the thoughts to the back of his mind and the lecture notes on to the floor, searched for and found a tattered exercise book in which he began to write down stage directions to resolve a weak moment in the play he had noticed yesterday. Rajini spoke the lines he had written for her with such conviction, that she brought home to him meanings he had not actually understood himself when he had written them. He had to find a way to adjust the movements of other members of the cast to fit in with her brilliant interpretation.

More irritation to the rest of them, of course, but it was sometimes possible to keep the changes to mere technicalities to resolve such moments.

When he had started to revise the play, soon after he had met Rajini, it had been her personality and background that had set him off on the rewrite. What had been boring political dogma in dramatic form had become a living realism, with Rajini as its added ingredient. New ideas now cropped up so continuously that it was difficult to keep pace. Little pieces of paper with writing all over them filled his pockets; notebooks, the back of his cheque book, old envelopes, anything at all that was to hand, were filled with ideas for dialogue, stage directions and odd thoughts. So many exciting ideas jostled in his mind.

The actual performance, when it was finally presented, was as good if not better than most amateur productions ever are, and Rajini shone as an obvious and out-of-place star. A natural, as the local student paper later described her. Quite remarkable, outstanding, amazing, were epithets heard at the end of the performance. Claude Columbo was wildly enthusiastic.

'Superb, superb,' he crooned, clasping Rajini towards him. 'You were truly fabulous. And what a play! My God I *cried*; after having seen it a hundred times, I actually *cried*.' His eyes filled with tears as he spoke. 'I'm going to get you all over to Canada if it's the last thing I do. Tom, we must talk about dates.'

'I'm negotiating for a venue at the Edinburgh fringe,' Tom said, making the decision, as he spoke, to take up the tentative arrangement he had made. 'But I dare say we could fit you in somewere within our hectic schedule. Provided, of course, you make it worth our while.'

Claude laughed uproariously and hugged Tom,

along with most of the members of the cast. 'Just you wait, darlings,' he said. 'I'll positively bombard the university VIPs with demands for your presence.'

To Rajini, Tom heard him say: 'You have a great future ahead of you, lady. Go to drama school rather than college – please.' And he watched him kiss her rather too lingeringly, at which he experienced a stab of anxiety because Rajini seemed to be enjoying it a little too obviously.

The Summerson contingent, with Laura in smiling control, though lacking Emma, included Tom's parents, proud but uncertain. Laura was surprised that she had never met them before. There had been plenty of talk about and even contact with Leonie Cheevers, but practically nothing had been spelt out about the Turtles as either parents or grandparents.

'A bit outspoken,' said Millie Turtle, smiling.

'And this idea that life is worse if you're coloured, might make for bad feeling, showing it up in the theatre,' said George, laughing and coughing at the same time. 'Too much argy-bargy going on in real life as it is. But then our Tom was always one for shocking people. That little dark girl was a star though, weren't she? What a beauty, too.'

Laura tried to adjust to the idea of Tom shocking people, and to the fact that Millie and George were Tom's parents, but found it almost impossible. 'She was quite outstanding, wasn't she?' she said, remembering that the star of beauty and Emma had actually fought physically on the night of the party. Whatever could that have been about?

Tom was surrounded by the cast, and friends and relations of the cast which included Monisha and Ashoka Bhairavi with their son, Ravi. They stood at the back of the small crowd, looking blank and saying nothing. Tom looked over heads to talk to them.

'What do you think of your brilliant actress daughter, Dr Bhairavi?'

Monisha Bhairavi's smile was not real, but Ashoka was manifestly bursting with pride. He wagged his head from side to side. 'Good, good. A splendid performance I have to say.' He put his arm round an excited Rajini, who was almost hidden by sheaves of plasticly wrapped gladioli and roses interspersed with asparagus fern. 'But what about her studies, Mr Turtle? Are you sure her studies are not suffering with all this play-acting?'

'And what about this play, Mr Turtle?' Monisha Bhairavi spoke loudly to make her point more firmly. 'I don't think Rajini should take part in something that criticises Indian customs and where she ends up by defying her parents.'

'Amma, *really*!' Rajini looked round to see who had heard among the eulogizing crush. 'Mr Turtle *wrote* the play. It's a super play, he's a brilliant writer.'

'That may well be,' said Mrs Bhairavi, 'but it is not suitable for a young Indian girl to act in.' She twitched her sari up over her shoulder with a flourish of anger.

Dr Bhairavi looked embarrassed. Ravi let out a burst of laughter, which was about the only sound he had made the whole evening, and Max and Hamish and several of the younger group of admirers joined in. Tom felt anxiety that he had inadvertently upset the Bhairavis and Rajini's expression of triumph changed noticeably but she induced her smile to remain.

'You were brill, Rajini,' Ben said, his eyes bright with admiration. 'So was Pa's play.' He hugged Tom. 'Much better than the ones you get on the telly. It was so real, just like things really are. And I bet Rajini will become a famous film star.'

Tom put Monisha Bhairavi's remarks out of his mind for the moment. 'I do think,' he said, looking

238

hard at Dr Bhairavi, 'that there would be a very good chance of her making a big success should she choose to continue her studies at a school of dramatic art. There's no doubt about that.'

Tom beamed across at Rajini, and there was a miracle flash of mutual pleasure between them. She knows exactly what I am feeling, Tom thought. We both know how exhilarating this fiery, triumphant ebullience can be when it surges through us at times like these; it makes all negative thoughts and feelings burn up in the blaze.

They went their separate ways, once the post-performance excitement had died down a little, parting with a chaste kiss and a hug, as with all members of the cast.

'Sleep well, bright star,' Tom whispered in her ear. 'You shone with distinction.' And then it was on with the helmet and gloves and a buckling up of leather jacket before the altogether satisfactory deafening exit of successful writer-producer-director-Tom following, on his motor bike, his adopted family to the Summerson home and the other role he was called on to play.

Rajini, in her father's car, crowded herself into the back seat with her brother, still surrounded with the effervescence of success and achievement, and the physical presence of the fruits of that success: flowers, cards, presents, theatrical make up and hot, uncomfortable sweat that dripped off her forehead and upper lip. She was thus shielded and quite impervious to the silent disapproval of her mother, emanating coldly, from the front seat of the car.

Tom was greeted with hugs, kisses and shouts of praise from the whole family and a special supper of smoked salmon and champagne for which everyone was allowed to stay up.

'That was a fantastic play,' Laura said, when everyone

had retired to bed. 'I never realized how good you were. Can't think why you haven't been recognized. How many more have you got tucked away?'

'None really; haven't had time to finish any. This one only got done because meeting Rajini gave me the idea for a racial slant on the harassment of women idea I'd been playing around with for so long, and then I discovered what a first-class actor she was.'

'She certainly is.' Laura watched him tugging himself out of his clothes and plunging under the shower. She felt, suddenly, a little shocked at the idea of Tom being so influenced by a schoolgirl.

'And the plot – very topical isn't it? The PLOT,' she repeated as he emerged, 'very topical.'

Tom laughed. 'I suppose you could call it that, with its wimpish males coming under attack from its dominant females fighting back against overall male supremacy.'

'Do I take it,' said Laura, 'by the way you ended it, that you think too much female supremacy is not altogether a good idea either?'

Tom sat down beside her, damp and smelling of soap, shampoo and shower gel. 'Writers have artistic licence along with active imaginations. The fun is trying to discover what's real and what isn't. Play endings are always the bits that disagree with reality. They're either happy endings or sad endings. The difference is that real things don't end pat, like that. They don't end at all unless one side or the other gives up the fight or unless one or other of the combatants die.'

'Till death us do part in fact?'

'Something like that,' said Tom, feeling perfidious, because it was nothing at all like that; it was not till death us do part but till death doth life take in order to solve an insoluble problem. But how to explain that now? Why, in fact, have to explain it at all? It was just a play he had written round certain aspects of life which he had found particularly interesting at that moment. Much easier to make gentle and affectionate love before the euphoria of the evening wore off.

So they did.

30

Harriet returned to the flat, fresh from a meeting with her solicitors, fired with new determination to get on with things and seething with irritation that her solicitors were so dilatory and inefficient.

'Makes me spit,' she said, removing draped silk jersey and a Hermès scarf and peeling off the gloves they had bought in Rome. She kicked off her shoes and let her toes spread out into the black mohair rug. 'Keep me talking for an age at a hundred and fifty pounds an hour and tell me nothing I don't know already, better than they do. The whole thing is a racket.'

'Were you able to sort anything out with them?' Alan asked, looking up from the rather cramped table top he was using for his drawing board and implements. His spirits were at rock bottom, and he pined for the space of his studio back home.

'Against them, rather than with them; I finished up by telling them what to do rather than them telling me. Such an absurd waste of money. I told them that I was selling the house and that they were to tell Tom he must move out straight away.'

'It seems he has already done that.'

'Himself, yes, but I want all his things out or I shall

sell them too. He doesn't even bother to let me know what he wants to do but, if he's going to quibble about keeping the house, I can't see that he'll have a leg to stand on because I shall obviously get the custody of the children *and* care and control, so I'll get the house because of that.'

'But – I thought you didn't want the house, and hasn't Ben chosen to live with Tom?' Harriet felt a qualm catch at her. Was Alan actually showing disapproval of what she was doing? A shiver of anxiety forced its way up through the secure belief that what she had decided to do was the right thing. Doubt was the last thing she needed at the moment. The exasperation and the irritation she had been experiencing over the past few weeks were only held in check because of her belief in her own decisions. Did Ben really prefer living with Tom? Surely it was just pig-headedness, or even a misplaced sympathy for Tom.

'I don't think Ben really knows what he wants,' she said, with the uncertainty showing in her voice. It was difficult to hide how much she wanted him to choose her rather than Tom. She cleared her throat to restore the firmness of her tone. 'It's fairly obvious,' she said, 'that I have far more to offer than Tom, where the children are concerned, and the courts usually act in the woman's favour in these cases. Anyway, I can't think that Tom will really *mind* not having them round his feet all the time. I should have thought he would have welcomed the idea. Of course I shan't object to their going to see him whenever they want to, as long as I get custody. It isn't that I'm being vindictive.' She wondered to herself why she wanted to convince Alan of this. It should be obvious. 'I just think that Tom isn't really capable of bringing them up properly. He doesn't consider their real needs . . .' Get the conversation back to generalities. 'The whole thing is so messy at the moment, I just have to get any loose ends tidied up. I mean I shan't mind sharing the proceeds of the house sale with Tom, but he can't be allowed to let the whole place go to rack and ruin, which he will do if he stays.' She thought of trying to sort out the jumble of Tom's belongings and shuddered.

Alan felt defeated and deflated: if Harriet was able to look on the whole thing as a case that now just had to be argued in court, then why could he not do the same thing? As far as he was concerned, no matter what the lawyers said, he had become convinced over the past few weeks, that nothing could really be sorted out satisfactorily; nothing was ever going to be bearable again. The whole mess had become a desperate shambles from which there seemed to be no escape for him. Harriet might be certain and confident, but he could see only disaster ahead. Even the idea of Tom searching for somewhere to store all his rubbish became an insoluble problem that was somehow sure to affect Alan. There were suddenly no answers to anything at all.

'I hope he finds somewhere to put all his rubbish then; I don't want it littering up *my* house.' But Tom had already invaded his house and his family, hadn't he? Tom had managed to deprive him of his whole life.

'If only he would organize himself properly,' said Harriet, 'he could rent somewhere and store the furniture while he looked round for somewhere else. I've decided that the only way to get him to stir himself is to sell the house over his head. It's in my name of course – a wedding present from Father.'

She looked across at Alan who sat slouched, his head in his hands, over the drawing board and her irritation spilled out on to this nearest tangible object in her path.

'You're so gloomy these days,' she said, after a few

minutes of arid silence. 'You really must try not to worry so much, darling, or all our little schemes may go up the spout. I can't be a fantastic sales person and back-up if you don't provide designs for me to sell or back up. Things really aren't as bad as you seem to think. Painful for a time, but nothing that we can't all recover from after a decent period of readjustment.'

Alan didn't look up or move from the drooping, boneless position into which he had sunk. There was no possible hope of recovery, for him at any rate, he decided. He was quite simply not able to do what everyone expected of him. He was not going to be able to live up to Harriet's strength. 'You don't have to remind me,' he shouted at her. 'You think I don't know it's all my fault?'

Harriet shivered suddenly and moved to turn up the central heating. What was the matter with spring this year? Even the beginning of April seemed as though it had become stuck in an endless winter. She did not, at that moment, want to face up to the idea of Alan shouting at her, so concentrated on the fact that the flat felt cold. She remembered that she'd had her doubts, when she was first viewing the flat, as to whether the white walls in the sitting-room might not look warm enough in the winter. In her mind's eye she saw the current ivory-tinted curtains transformed to a rich vermilion, with perhaps a large Hoyland painting on the main wall; pick up one or two of the colours of the painting in cushions here and there. She narrowed her eyes and saw the room between a fringe of eye-lashes.

She brought her mind back to the here and now, and glanced over at Alan again. He was sitting in exactly the same position, and she noticed, with a sense of dread, that he was on the verge of tears. A tremor crawled up her spine again. He was surely not the type to suffer from neurosis; he was much too good a businessman to be neurotic.

'Don't be so dramatic, darling,' she said, taking hold of a handful of his hair and pulling it gently. 'You've just got a bit of a block, that's all. It's not the end of the world. Nothing we can't overcome.'

Best to put chivvying to one side for the moment. With Easter coming up, there would be nothing much moving in the business world until after the holiday, by which time he should be well over any depression he might be in at the moment.

'Why don't we go away for Easter?' she said. 'A holiday in the sun would be good for both of us. What about the Bahamas? All those lovely shares Daddy left me all that time ago have just produced another little bonus. I feel very rich.' And soon to be richer still when their plans started to take shape.

'But I – but – what about the kids?'

'*The kids?* Well, what about them? It's better to take them on holiday in the summer, though we could take Hamish with us if you like, with Emma to keep him company, but I would say the others are too young to appreciate a Bahamian break. And anyway, Laura would love to revert to her Christian upbringing and organize Easter eggs for everyone to make up for the way she messed up Christmas for them.'

'Laura and Tom,' said Alan, quite unable to keep the venom out of his voice.

Harriet laughed. 'Laura and Tom – of course! What an ideal arrangement. Tom is a sucker for the traditional Easter morning egg hunt.'

'It's Passover,' Alan said shortly, touched momentarily with nostalgia and memories. 'We sort of did both: Passover with my family and Easter eggs with Laura.' She surely wouldn't allow the Jewish side to lapse; she couldn't; the kids were Jewish after all.

245

'How sweet; but they're all getting a bit big for that sort of thing now, aren't they?'

Alan winced, and resentment surged up again at the idea of Tom possibly wanting to change the status quo that had always been a part of his family life in *his* house.

'We could ask them which they want to do,' Harriet said. 'The older ones might plump for the Bahamas; much more exciting.' She pictured Alan and herself lying in warmth and luxury on a sun-drenched beach. That would surely bounce anyone out of a depression.

The idea was rejected out of hand by all, though Emma was tempted. 'It would be quite nice,' she said to Hamish, 'but I can't stand the idea of being there alone with them. I know it's silly, but I somehow can't get used to this mix-up. If they'd gone off with someone we didn't know, then I'd find that much easier to take. All this incestuous inbreeding seems totally immoral.'

Hamish was impressed by what he considered a rather sophisticated way of describing the situation. In spite of his denials to his brother, Hamish admitted to himself that he did actually fancy Emma, but he was very conscious of the wide gap between a male of seventeen and a female of eighteen. If Hamish was impressed, then Emma had achieved her aim to impress.

Daisy and Ben were conspicuous in their eagerness to plan the important first holiday get-together, having few inhibitions about what should or should not be done.

'We can all go to Grandma and Grandpa's Passover party,' said Daisy. 'They won't mind Tom and you and Emma being there because after all you are part of our family now.'

'But we're not Jewish so what do we have to do at

Passover parties?' Ben was suspicious. 'If we don't know what to do we shall look silly.'

'No, you won't; you'll get presents just like Christmas presents and you light candles and eat lots of nice things.'

Esther Sunshine was more worried than Ben: 'Our son goes abroad at this special time, and we are supposed to invite all these strangers to our home,' she complained to Bernie. 'And here's Daisy saying she wants this Harry and his children to come to us for Passover.'

'Tom,' Bernie prompted.

'Tom, Harry, George – what's a name, I ask you; just the same a *stranger* taking the place of our son, Bernie; it's not decent. You must tell Daisy we just invite *family* to Passover, not outsiders; it's not the custom, tell her. She must understand these things.'

'But it would make Daisy and the kids feel good, Essie. I think we could stretch the hospitality a bit, couldn't we? Tom and his kids must be feeling a bit low in the present circumstances at this time of the year. We could give them the chance to enjoy Passover with us, couldn't we?'

'Bernard Sunshine you are too good to people, but what about your son, I ask you; we leave him out of Passover then?'

Bernie hunched his shoulders. 'He chooses, Essie, he chooses his own way of life. Nothing we can do.'

'*He* chooses, you say? *He* chooses? More likely this Jezebel, Lena – Lorna – whatever her name is – more likely *she* chooses. That poor boy, always easily led, he was, never had the strength. Much too easily led.' Tears came into her eyes as she remembered the years when he had acquiesced so adorably to her every wish and suggestion.

Tom escaped the preparations for Easter Sunday lunch. He had received a letter from Harriet's solicitors and was furiously angry at the injustice of the whole system. He went back to the empty house that was so full, not only of memories, but also twenty odd years of his life, in tangible form. He stared round at the plethora of posters and photographs on the walls of his study – past productions, holiday photographs, pinned crazily; he saw stacked papers on the floor, books everywhere, in mad confusion, with only the oldest of them in the book shelves: they had been there since they had moved in, and only occasionally taken out for reference. Covered in sticky dust now and grey with venerable age.

He saw the garden, which Harriet had rejected out of hand, and which he had only occasionally tackled, when he had needed relaxation. He saw the bird table, tipping drunkenly, that he had made for Ben, where they had excitedly recognized a nuthatch together, and concerning which Ben had spent so much of his time tearing down the stairs and out into the garden to chase Gertrude away from the hidden lair where she lay in wait for unsuspecting sparrows and blackbirds.

Sentiment or sentimentality? Whichever it was, Tom, like Alan, let restraint go, and sat down on the floor to cry his heart out. It was a glorious self-indulgence in the middle of all the cheerful assurance and strong-arm vibes he had been exuding for so long. Why not go home to Mother? he thought. *Why not?* Not for him the stresses and strains that Emma and Ben had had to go through with him and Harriet; his experience of childhood had been calm, placid, and uneventful. What bliss. Would Laura be able to care for him in the same way that he was now caring for her? Would she? Would she really?

He was startled out of his skin when he heard someone come in at the front door that he remembered he had left on the latch. The hairs on his body stood stiff and erect like the spines of a shocked hedgehog, and his scalp tingled with a thousand tiny electrical pulses.

The steps on the stairs were not heavy, and a small voice drifted upwards: 'Tom? Tom? Are you there?'

'RAJINI!' The relief was so great that he rolled over, leaped to his feet and almost fell down the stairs to engulf her completely in a vehement and breathless embrace.

It took several minutes for them to untangle themselves, to sit huddled together on the stairs and be able to speak coherently.

'I was passing and saw your bike . . .'

'I'm in the middle of an emotional crisis . . .'

'Your face is all wet . . .'

'You are exactly what I need at this moment . . .'

'Only at this moment?'

They made love there and then, on the stairs, in great discomfort and in the cold of a grey April day.

'Aaaa-ah . . .' said Rajini, 'I'm freezing, Tom,' and her teeth began to chatter, noisily. He wrapped her in his leather jacket and they stumbled together downstairs to shut the front door and light a fire.

Considering the circumstances, the Easter party was an unmitigated success. Everybody wanted to prove something and this seemed the obvious place to do so.

There were fourteen of them because Ben insisted thirteen was unlucky and suggested they should ask Grandma Cheevers to make up the numbers. There was a general sense of shock, but Ben pushed the case further: 'She is our grandmother, after all, and she'll be all alone because of Ma being in the Bahamas.' It was eventually agreed to ask her if Ben agreed to do the asking and the encouraging.

The only parents not invited were Laura's, that

distant, smiling prelate and his gentle wife who were for ever caught up in the mysteries of the see and the diocese at Easter and midnight masses at Christmas and so were usually only available in the summer.

'I haven't told them about Alan yet,' Laura said privately to Tom, 'or about me being ill. I wasn't sure that I could stand up to their forgiveness for my error in becoming Jewish in the first place, and their tolerance and their benevolence in never saying I told you so.'

Bernie and Esther came, loaded down with presents and Passover delicacies, and Esther and Millie spent most of the day in deep and animated conversation. 'Such a lovely boy he is,' Esther said, 'but that ex-daughter-in-law of yours, please God she gets punished for her wicked ways; to take my boy away and to wreck the life of your poor son the way she has, what a tragedy I tell you, what a tragedy.'

Millie had only to nod and murmur, but found a kindred spirit in Esther. 'We didn't even know till they asked us over, you know,' she said. 'Tom was always one to keep himself to himself. But how nice that he and Laura seem to be getting on so well; I couldn't ask for a nicer girl.'

'A good girl, a good girl,' Esther agreed, 'but the faith is not there; such a shame, but it's not really there. She would have been able to hold on to him if the faith had been there you know.'

Millie agreed, without knowing which faith Esther spoke of.

Leonie Cheevers had a little too much to drink, as did Bernie and George. The dread with which all three of them had anticipated the lunch party induced them to accept refills of the champagne cocktails Tom had mixed for them on their arrival. It was the best thing any of them could have done, since they relaxed immediately, and discovered that they had roses in common.

'I always use cow manure,' said Leonie. 'Marvellous stuff.'

'Ah, but have you ever tried blood, hoof and horn?' asked George. 'A bit pricey, mind, but good, oh yes, very good. Brings them on lovely.'

'It's the pruning that counts,' Bernie joined in. 'If you prune in December, you'll never go wrong. My Margaret Merills give me two perfect flowerings; big as cabbages they are.'

'Should have asked me for the Brussels,' George said to Laura. 'I've got plenty on the allotment. Tom should have told me. Much better than you get in the shops.'

The children basked in a plethora of presents, food and affection, and felt sick through eating too much chocolate. Hamish gave Emma a French kiss behind the bushes in the garden, which pleased them both. It was truly an enormous success.

'A new birth,' Laura said to Tom, after the grand-parents had gone home. She giggled rather sheepishly. 'I know it's corny, but my good old Christian upbringing means I do equate Easter with a rising from the dead and a new beginning. All something to do with spring and buds bursting and leaves burgeoning and everything. So hopeful somehow.'

Tom wondered whether he should attempt to join in with her expectations, but an uneasy anxiety that her recovery, and her certainty that everything was going to proceed smoothly from now on, might perhaps be premature, kept nagging at him. It was all too easy and happening too quickly, and he had no sense at all of being a born-again Christian.

'You've become very strong,' he told her. 'A quite incredible change from a few weeks ago.'

'Entirely thanks to you.'

251

'Oh come now.' He was truly embarrassed, and wished himself out of the position of being wonder faith healer. 'You have done as much for me.'

But then he wished he hadn't said that – she might ask him to explain, and what could he actually say? She had restored in him a sense of relaxation, hadn't she? And that had been what he wanted; at the time it had been exactly what he wanted. He pulled her towards him and kissed her cheeks and her hair and her mouth. She was such a thoroughly nice person.

'If I ever loved anybody,' he said, 'I should certainly love you Laura. You are entirely lovable.'

She screwed up her nose and pushed him away a little. 'Don't think I like the sound of that,' she said. 'It's all too cosy.'

So did she feel it too? This sense that a comfortable solution was settling down over them far too quickly, before anyone had had the time to consider what had happened to them all? Were they all clutching at straws? Pretending nothing much had happened so that they could all get on with their new lives in the smug satisfaction that they had dealt with their problems in a self-sufficient and entirely competent way? Tom felt himself go suddenly cold in the sure knowledge that they were all somehow heading for catastrophe.

He put his arms round her with a feeling of complete detachment. Because of the sensation of pending disaster, he felt as though he was not actually there at all, but sitting somewhere else and watching the play on a stage. Suppose she wanted him to make love to her tonight? He couldn't do it; there was no way he was going to be able to assist Laura through her trials and tribulations tonight. The sensation of helplessness was extremely frightening; he didn't remember ever having experienced it before.

She put her arms round him and held him tightly. 'I'm much too tired to talk to you tonight, or to make love to you, but I should very much like to go to sleep in your arms, if you don't mind.'

Tom melted with relief: 'That's exactly what I want to do,' he said. 'Happy Easter, Queen of the Cosies.'

Laugh it off, for God's sake; just need a good night's sleep to get back to normal.

31

The Passover party had not been a real success. Tom and Emma were only prevailed upon to go by Ben's insistence. 'It's a special occasion,' he said. 'They want to ask us back so we can see the other side of them. It would be rude not to go.'

Emma was not averse to encouraging Hamish's admiration, so the three of them attended in an awkward little bunch, which the enthusiasms of the other family never quite managed to overcome.

'You were impossible, Pa,' Emma said afterwards. 'Picking books out of the shelves and reading them.'

'But I always read at parties,' Tom said. 'Gives me something to talk about.'

'But you didn't talk,' Ben said, feeling that Emma had a point in her criticism.

'If we're going to get together,' Emma went on, 'then we're going to have to muck in with that side of them as well.'

Tom and Ben were both silent, considering their own attitudes to the situation. Tom was disturbed that the father-daughter role seemed to be becoming confused with daughter telling father how to behave, but he was certainly not willing to comment on the present circumstances at the moment. Any decision or resolution would have to be left teetering for now. In the meantime, the six children, Laura and Tom continued their shared existence from day to day.

'I think we're really beginning to get Mum through her breakdown,' Hamish said. Hamish and Emma admitted to a growing pleasure in each other's company.

'With Pa's help,' Emma said quickly. 'You could never have done it without Pa.'

Hamish paused for a fraction of a second; Tom had, of course, been a godsend when the disaster had first occurred, but Hamish was not sure whether the combined family arrangement was now helping to bring things back to normal or not. 'Of course,' he said. 'It was great your Pa helping us out like he did.' He looked sideways at Emma. 'Quite strange the way things have turned out too.' He gave a small laugh. 'What d'you think about him and her?'

Emma shrugged. 'Pa is so odd,' she said. 'I can never seem to rely on him somehow. Never know what he's going to do next.' Had Rajini given him up as a bad job? She supposed so; must have seen how things stood with Laura. Serve her right, the pushy little bitch. But how could Pa have been such an idiot to let her lead him on like that? Made him look so *dire*.

'He and Mum do seem quite keen though, don't they?' Hamish said. 'But I don't know how much she's missing Dad. She hasn't said anything to me.' There was a slight stir of hurt feelings; she surely could have confided in him – should have, in fact. 'Maybe it's just a rebound for both of them.'

'They're behaving as though they are about six,' Emma said. 'It's odd how one thinks of one's parents as grown up, and then find that they're not in the least.'

'I can't really imagine why Dad walked off like he did.' It was the first time Hamish had actually spoken of his sense of outrage with anyone; the first time he had allowed it to surface, in fact. He felt emotional and uncontrolled but made sure that it didn't show.

'Ma nagged Pa so much when they were together,' said Emma, 'that I always thought *he* might take off rather than her. It was a sort of continuous anxiety, really.' She smiled. 'I suppose he enjoyed it; a sort of masochism. Perhaps he thought it was sexy.'

They both laughed. 'Well, of course, it *can* be,' said Hamish. 'Not my choice, I'm afraid.'

'Don't be afraid,' said Emma, 'I'm no sadist.'

Hamish lapsed into silence, wondering if she meant that as a serious come-on to him. Should he take her up on it? But he'd left it too late anyhow; no way could he now turn the whole conversation into sex talk.

'Such a lovely party,' Millie Turtle said over the phone to Tom. 'I was glad to see you and Laura getting on so well; it must be a great comfort to both of you when that husband of hers is behaving so disgracefully with Harriet. Whatever came over the girl, Tom? Has it been brewing up for some time? Why didn't you tell us. Gave me ever such a shock when I heard. Dad just said good riddance, but then he's always a bit outspoken, and he never did like Harriet.'

Tom smiled at the simplicity of the reaction in hindsight: to them it was 'good riddance' because they 'never did like her', whereas to him, who had once adored Harriet's brilliance, her looks and her dominance, her fierce assurance and her certainty about everything, to him it was the admission that he had been hopelessly wrong in his assessment of an ideal partner.

So was he creeping back to mother in his lazy acceptance of the gentle, unfraught companionship of Laura? To his parents, and possibly to everyone else, it might seem better if he were to retire into the static comfort of the childhood he had escaped from. It probably would be far more understandable to them. Much more acceptable.

But then they would not know about the essential life-giving interludes with Rajini, which were also a retreat into childhood, and without which the quiet life would be unendurable. They would not have to know about that.

Emma tackled Ben: 'What do you want to do about Pa and Laura?' she asked him. 'Are you happy here? It seems Pa has got to move out of the old house and it looks highly likely that he's going to settle in here. Seems a good idea for both of them. Won't affect me because I shall be at university, so I'll only want an occasional bed, but you, will you be happy with that situation?'

'It's a bit neat and tidy,' Ben said. 'I don't think it'll really happen like that because it sounds too much like a story with a happy ending. "I don't like you and you don't like me so let's change partners with our friends." Things like that don't happen in real life.'

'But they have, haven't they? You can't always have shock and horror – that's what happens in books *these* days – happy endings are old fashioned.'

'And because we live now and not then, we shan't have a happy ending either, you see if I'm not right.'

'You're arguing back to front now – are we a story or are we real?' She was laughing at his silliness.

'I'm not sure,' Ben said, darkly; 'we shall have to wait and see.'

'You know,' Laura said to Tom when she got him alone, a few weeks after Easter, 'I have decided I'm strong enough to launch out again on my own. I don't think I need cosseting any more.'

'Is that a polite way of giving me my marching orders?' Was the feeling relief? Umbrage?

Laura seemed genuinely shocked by the idea. 'No, no, of course not. All I want is that you should feel free and not beholden to me because I'm an invalid – because I'm not.'

So the quiet, comfortable life was being withdrawn, leaving him with the stresses of an adolescent love life. His security felt minimally threatened.

'Of course you're not an invalid, I told you that.'

'Yes, you did, so now I'm absolutely agreeing with you.'

She smiled up at him with the sort of radiance that seemed to come naturally to her. It was a little off-putting, being so difficult to translate. What did she actually mean by all this radiance and veneration? Though flattering, it was disturbing to feel that you were some sort of god that could not have been done without. But was she actually now saying that she *could* do without him. It immediately brought up the question – could *he* do without *her*?

'I don't want to be a drag or hold up your life, Tom. I feel that you will be able to blossom now that there's no Harriet to cramp your style. I think there might be every possibility that life for you might well begin at forty.'

'Forty-five,' he corrected.

'You know what I *mean*.' She made her way round the room with a small watering can, feeling earth in pots and topping up with water; *loving* the plants, helping them to bloom again, Tom thought to himself as he watched her. They were like friends who were special to her, in very much the same way that he was special to her. He decided, rather sadly, that his own life didn't really seem likely to bloom again, whatever Laura said.

257

'I'm going to work full time on my course,' she said. 'This is the alimony I'm going to demand: sufficient space and money to allow me to get my degree and become competent to earn enough to keep myself and the children. And when I say children, I mean that I would love to give you and Ben and Emma houseroom until you find somewhere, if you wanted to, of course.'

Tom almost laughed out loud but controlled himself. Now that she had recovered, Laura was willing to add him to her family; another chicken to be gathered under the wing.

'Dear Laura,' he said, 'I promise I won't allow you to be a drag or to hold up my life. Though I'm not absolutely confident of blossoming in the immediate future, I am already starting to explore possibilities.'

They kissed each other, sex buried deep in the past; it was almost embarrassing to remember it.

Alan did his best to enjoy the Bahamas. He lay on the beach, he swam, he scuba dived, he fished and he drank iced drinks galore, but there was no relief and no meaning in any of it. The sun did not dispel the darkness that engulfed him, the heat did nothing to melt the ice that lodged inside his stomach. He couldn't bring himself to notice the bright life milling all round him, wrapped, as he was, in the despair that would not go away because of the conviction that the situation was not a real one.

Ever since the confrontation with Laura, there was a deadness in his mind that nothing seemed to shift. Even the turbulent sex that he and Harriet had enjoyed, waned distressingly almost as suddenly as it had appeared.

'I – I'm just a bit depressed,' he stammered. 'It won't last, darling. Please forgive me. It's – it's nothing to do with you.'

Harriet was devastated, but knew that depression could do strange things to people. If it hadn't cleared when the holiday ended, he'd have to get treatment. Plenty of wonder drugs about these days. Sure to be treatable.

Alan kept waiting for the mood to pass while being convinced that it never would. He took great care to hide his real despair from Harriet, as far as possible, and she gave no sign that he had not succeeded.

She lay in the sun and refused to consider any sort of problem that could not be solved. 'This is just what the doctor ordered,' she said, several times over. 'I really enjoy spending money in this way, where everything is done for you, and you can actually give thinking a rest. I don't even mind the inefficiencies of the staff; shows how relaxed I am! Stupid of our kids not to take us up on the offer.' She kept the twinge of resentment out of her voice, but then added: 'I worry sometimes, you know, whether your bloody wife and my bloody husband aren't going out of their way to influence our children against us with their smarmy, snide ways.'

Alan roused himself from emptiness to voice a small protest: 'I can't imagine either Laura or Tom troubling to attempt to influence anyone. Two more *laissez-faire* individuals would be hard to find. Children don't relish being told what to do.'

'That's one thing nobody could accuse me of doing.'

Alan felt a flicker of amusement at the falsity of this statement. 'It's not so much that you tell people what to do,' he said, 'it's more that you expect them to do it without being told.' He smiled suddenly. 'You're very like my mother in that way.'

Harriet felt deeply offended. '*Like your mother?* How can you say anything so outrageous? What an appalling thing to suggest.'

But the more he thought about the similarities, the

more they seemed apt: this whole holiday reminded him of the childhood holidays he spent with his parents in grand hotels, where he never felt comfortable, nor, when he thought back on it, did his parents. They always chose somewhere just that bit too grand, so that they were for ever at a disadvantage. There the analogy between Esther and Harriet diverged, because it was obvious that Harriet felt perfectly at home in the good life. The grander the surroundings, the more at home Harriet felt.

'It's just,' he said, 'that both you and my mother have this definite idea of how people should behave: you, because you have this crazy English upper-class tradition of what is, or what is not, the done thing, and my mother because she is steeped in the traditions and teaching of Judaism. You both have a total certainty of correct behaviour.'

Harriet turned her back on him and sulked for the rest of the day.

The high spirits and comforting warmth that had originally accompanied the relationship between Tom and Laura dissolved fairly quickly into the kind of even-tempered ordinariness apparent in many contented long-term marriages. And once Tom found himself again immersed in the task of clearing out his adult life and attempting to pack it into boxes and trunks without any clear idea where he was going to store it, he sank back into a slough of despondency. There seemed to be no time and no energy left to make decisions; time was mysteriously taken up again with everyday idiocies, like eating and sleeping and shopping and washing and lecturing and having his hair cut and dealing with students' problems. Laura was all right, Ben and Emma were all right, Harriet was as impossible as ever; he was the only one who seemed to be drifting on and on towards death.

Rajini was away, having been taken, protesting, to visit relatives by her parents. Tom found that her absence left an uncomfortable gap in his life, as though a light had been switched off. Though he never did the approaching where Rajini was concerned, not being able to expect the unexpected telephone call or visit made life seem very grey.

But then the world tipped and Rajini swept suddenly back, bringing turmoil, destruction and the means of life with her. On the day that she exploded into Tom and Harriet's sad and emptying house with its bare floors and packing cases, it was as though a flood had swept in, cold, cleansing, but of such force that it appeared nothing could stand against it.

'It's finished!' she shouted as she burst open the front door by pushing on it with her shoulder. Her hands and arms were stretched and clawing at falling parcels, boxes and suitcases that spilled over from her grasp. She was crying and not crying in a hysterical sort of way, stumbling over the things that fell, finally grovelling and then screaming into the pile of belongings she had dropped on the floor, beating her hands in rage among the jumble all round her.

Tom dragged her off the floor and held her close to him: 'What the hell is this all about? What's finished?'

But Rajini was still screaming in short, rasping bursts that pierced his eardrums, so he gave her a sharp slap in the time-honoured manner and was gratified to find that it worked.

'I've done – I've gone – I've run – I've run away. It got – he got – it was Appa – he said I – he said . . .'

Tom sat down in a soft chair and pulled her on to his lap. 'You'll have to start breathing if you're going to talk,' he said. 'Just breathe a little first, and then perhaps you'll be able to tell me what's happened.'

She began crying quietly after the storm had subsided. 'I've – run away,' she said eventually. 'I can't go home any more.'

'Want to tell me why?'

'It's impossible. They've decided I must get married now, immediately – because they won't hear of me going to drama school. *They've even found the man!*' Her voice started to rise, 'Can you imagine? They've actually found someone and they took me over there to meet him and his moronic parents and I was supposed to say hallo, yes I'll marry you tomorrow; and I won't I *won't*, no matter what they say.'

'And what do they say?'

'They just say that if I don't agree they'll send me back to India immediately, to live with my grandparents until I – become more amenable – that's what they call it: become more amenable. It's Amma's fault – Appa isn't so pig-headed – she has this absolute belief that the Hindu system is the right one for us, especially for me. And it's just not true, the whole thing is a disaster, and I'm not going to agree to it.'

'What's the young man like?'

Rajini rounded on him furiously. 'What does it *matter* what he's like? How could you ask such a fool question? Even if he was the most fascinating, handsome, intelligent man in the world, I wouldn't agree to anything that was forced on me.'

Tom struggled with an attempt to conceal the sense of superiority that welled up at the prospect of another country's unacceptable custom. 'Arranged marriages probably work on average better than love matches,' he said. 'Taking as our example the Turtle-Summerson set-up.'

She tried to get up off his lap, without success. He held her quite firmly.

'Let me go, you bastard,' she shouted at him. 'If I'd

thought you'd have the same, ghastly, back-sliding attitudes as my family, I'd never have come here. So let me go – I'll be able to share the flat of a friend in Shepherd's Bush. I thought perhaps you would put me up here for a bit, but it doesn't matter, I can go somewhere else.'

'Apart from the fact that this would probably be the first place your parents would look for you, seeing as it's just across the road, I have to clear out of the house myself this week.'

Rajini stared round at the desolation: 'Clear out? But where will you go?'

'No idea; just waiting for something to turn up.'

'It's fate, isn't it?' Rajini said, her eyes staring and her face tear-streaked. The only remnant of the hysteria was a violent trembling that Tom tried to contain by the firm restraint of his pinioning arms. 'Both of us adrift, with nowhere to go. It's fate.'

'That's crap, and you know it.' He began to feel as though he wanted to laugh; as though this whole drama of himself and the life he had led up till this moment was indeed crap and had to be revolutionized, exploded and metamorphosed.

'You have to go home,' he said, wondering just how he would enforce the suggestion: pick her up in his arms, carry her across the road and say 'Here is your daughter, Mrs Bhairavi. Will you please lock her up and see that she doesn't stray again?'

'I am NOT going home,' Rajini repeated. 'If you turn me out, I shall go to Piccadilly and sleep rough.'

'Why bother to go to Piccadilly? You could find a perfectly good cardboard box nearer home.'

'It's warmer in the centre and more anonymous. I could get myself lost there very quickly. But they won't look for me here. Please let me stay; it just wouldn't occur to them to look here.'

'It would be my duty to tell them where you were.'

'Now who's talking crap? I am eighteen years old and no longer their property. I can do what I like. If you do tell anybody, then I will run right away – from you too.' She moved away from him and stared out of the window, her arms wrapped round herself. 'You can't turn me out tonight, please Tom. If I go home they'll lock me in my room and get me on the first possible plane to India, and I can't stand the idea of a physical fight with them. Please Tom.' She turned round and clutched her arms right round him instead of herself. 'We can talk about it tomorrow and arrange something, and once I'm far enough away and sort of settled, then I'll let them know I'm all right. If you could lend me a little money, I'll pay you back when I have some. I can get a job until I get into drama school. Don't you see, Tom, it's just the opportunity we need. I have nowhere to go, you have nowhere to go, so we can look for a place together. It's only pushing things a bit further forward than we planned, that's all.'

'Planned?' said Tom. 'I don't remember planning anything.'

Rajini clutched him closer. 'But you never do plan anything, do you? You just sit back and let it happen.' Tears started to flow again. 'Well, this is happening, now. It's an emergency, and you're good in an emergency, you always know what to do.'

The telephone rang, and Tom released one of his arms to pick it up. Rajini's clutch became vice-like, and he could feel her stop breathing.

'Dr Bhairavi? Yes, Tom Turtle here . . . Rajini? . . . er . . . No, this is not one of her tutorial days. Ah . . . well, I don't know, but I thought I heard her say that she was going to stay with some friend out of London . . . no, she didn't mention a name, some school friend I thought. Oh, but I'm sure . . . yes of course . . . if she telephones . . . yes, I will. Goodbye.'

He replaced the telephone and broke out into a cold sweat. 'God,' he said, without attempting to extricate himself from the clinch. 'Now it actually is an emergency.'

32

'It's all too easy,' Ben said. 'Almost as if nothing has happened, and something *has* happened; a great upsetting thing has happened to all of us: we've all been turned upsidedown and yet we are sitting back and pretending nothing at all is wrong. It's unreal.' He looked as though he was about to cry, and Emma felt embarrassed for him and because of him.

She smiled at the rest of them, ranged round what had once been Alan's studio and amusing themselves in the various boring ways that were available in the hiatus when spring was turning into summer.

'Come *on*, you morose old freak,' Emma said. 'You can't go on wallowing in self-pity for the rest of your life. We've got to make the best of things, and it does seem that the parents have worked out a fairly adequate compromise between them.'

There were murmurs of assent and Daisy said: 'I like us all living together like this.'

Ben swung round on her: 'But we're NOT all living together, are we? I haven't got a mother, and you haven't got a father.'

There was a moment's shocked silence.

'You're being far too dramatic.' Hamish felt he

should take charge. 'Of course we've got mothers and fathers; it's just that the situation has changed for everybody. You can't expect things not to change, ever. We shall all be leaving home in a few years in any case. Our parents have just chosen to make the change a little earlier, that's all.'

'They should have waited,' said Ben. 'It wouldn't have killed them to wait a bit.'

'You're acting like a spoilt child,' Max said. 'Just being selfish and not thinking of anybody except yourself.'

Ben flushed red. 'That's what *they're* doing,' he said. 'They're doing just what they tell us not to, and if they're going to tell us not to, then they shouldn't themselves.'

'And it *is* like we haven't got a father,' Daisy added, 'because we never see him now; he never comes now that your mother's got him.'

Emma restrained a sharp response concerning the fact that Daisy's father had equally 'got' her mother, making life at home unacceptable, but realized the indignity of arguing with an eight-year-old. 'You've got *our* father,' she said in an ingratiatingly kind manner, realizing that this was not an adequate answer.

Why did Ben have to bring all this up now, just when everyone was trying to get used to the new arrangement? She felt suddenly as though she was in need of her own mother who would sort out the whole situation with one or two sharp remarks that would have made everything fall neatly into place. With Harriet around everything had seemed so safe because you were sure that she would be able to right all wrongs, and sail, triumphant, through all difficulties. There was a corresponding great desire in Emma, at that moment, to weep and wail and cry out 'I want my

Mummy', which would have been funny if it hadn't been so painful.

'We don't really want your father,' Louise said as politely as she was able. 'Though it's been very kind of him to help us out like this.'

'We'd really rather have our own,' Daisy agreed, 'because we do quite love him really.'

There was an awkward silence while everyone mulled over the word 'love' in their own minds: one of those uncomfortable words that on American TV children and adults alike seemed able to bandy about in a blatantly sentimental way, but which the British had not yet mastered. Love was obviously one of the big stumbling blocks that made the present family arrangement unsatisfactory, but it was not something you could discuss.

'Well,' Hamish made the effort to get the atmosphere back to normal, 'I think we really must try to make the best of things. I mean it's not that it's such an unusual happening, after all. At least half my friends have gone through it and they seem none the worse, so I don't see why we should be any different.'

'Just as long as we don't pretend nothing has happened,' Ben insisted. 'If we go on pretending that everything is normal and as good as before, then something really bad will happen just to pay us out for pretending or pay *them* out for making it happen.'

Hamish and Emma exchanged superior smiles. 'Don't worry, Bunsy,' Emma said, ruffling Ben's hair. 'I don't think God's likely to pick our parents out for any particular fire and brimstone; they're no worse than other people's parents, and I don't see why we should come in for punishment for making the best of things.'

'Just you wait and see,' Ben said, mortified at being ridiculed, but there was general laughter, and he stumped out of the room to find solace in Hamlet's unstinted approval of everything he did.

Laura wondered why Tom did not return to the house that night, and was anxious in case she had upset him. Had he taken offence because she had told him that the temporary arrangement *was* actually temporary? Various thoughts cropped up, some of them not altogether charitable. Had he just been making use of her? No more than she had made use of him – and where was the blame in that? There was no reason at all for him to feel upset that she wanted to live her own life, with him or without him; he probably felt exactly the same. Circumstances had thrown them together and circumstances were now allowing them to get on with their own lives.

But where was he tonight? The bed felt very empty and jealousy nagged at her: very dog-in-the-mangerish. She realized with shock that she no longer felt jealous at the thought of Alan and Harriet together, only angry resentment at their wickedness in setting this whole unhappy shambles in motion. Where could Tom be? It was puzzling.

He arrived back at lunch time. 'I was worried about you,' she said, trying to keep accusation out of her voice.

'Sorry, darling.' He felt accused. 'I was so completely bogged down and miserable, with all the clearing up and packing that had to be done, that I was too tired to do anything other than go flat out on the bed; lost consciousness till the morning.'

So now we were the guilty husband inventing lies for the wronged wife, were we? What an absurd situation. But there was no way he wanted to explain what had happened last night: the stark panic, over-taken quickly by unrepressed and exciting lust that had set in after Dr Bhairavi's telephone call. It had something to do with the intense apprehension he had felt after ranging himself inalienably against convention by denying that he was hiding Rajini from her parents. All very laudable if he was rescuing her from a father who beat her – but was an arranged marriage a form of abuse? Did he have the right? The blue funk remained with him now. Had he really bundled Rajini, helmeted and disguised with enveloping scarves, out of the back gate this morning? Had he actually wheeled his bike, silently, into the small unobserved lane behind the garage in order to avoid being overlooked? Had they both roared away together, fleeing justice, into the anonymity of west London and the Shepherd's Bush area, in order to find a safe hiding place? Was he completely mad? The anxieties continued to race through his head, and he found great difficulty in bringing himself down to earth.

'You poor thing,' Laura was saying. 'What are you going to do with everything? Do you want to store something here? We have the attic and I'm sure we could find room.'

But that was not what he wanted, not at all what he wanted. What he wanted was to get away, by himself; all by himself. To find somewhere quite isolated where he could shut himself up, hide himself, and sort himself out. That was what he wanted.

Ben came blundering down the stairs with Hamlet, barking and full of joy at the idea of being taken out for a walk. Noise, activity and enthusiastic hullabaloo filled the downstairs rooms as Hamlet and Ben greeted Tom rumbustiously.

'Hallo Pa. Where were you yesterday? I wanted to show you a great computer game I borrowed off my friend; it's really brilliant – have you got a minute? We could play it now, I've got it set up. Oh, come on, please Pa, it's much better to play with someone rather than just on your own.'

He took hold of Tom's arm and pulled him through the door and Hamlet's tail, ears and expression drooped into deep depression. No walkies, then. Tom experienced almost exactly the same reaction, but he followed his son without demur.

Harriet made the excuse of her mother having flu to escape Alan's gloom for a few days. 'Probably politic to show care and concern,' she explained. 'She *is* seventy-five, after all; could pop off any time, and then I'd kick myself for not being dutiful.'

She was experiencing, for probably the first time in her life, a feeling of unease that had begun to worm its way into her existence. She had done what she could: a holiday in the sun; an understanding, patient attitude towards his lethargy; but still Alan did not respond, not even to sex. It was discouraging, to say the least, when things had every possibility of being so good between them. A few days away might help to clear the mind, and would make Alan realize the discomfort of life without her. There was really no time to be lost if they were to make a go of the notably successful start to their combined business effort.

'He's such a fabulous designer,' she told her mother, 'but he seems to have developed this almighty block; it's a real bugger.'

'That sort of language is so unnecessary, Harriet,' said Leonie. 'I suppose he's suffering remorse.' She lay back in bed with an expression of disapproval which Harriet found extremely irksome. 'There's really no need for you to stay if you want to get back to him,' Leonie added. 'I'm perfectly well looked after by Mrs Mann. And I don't intend to die just yet.'

'Really Mother, you talk like some turn-of-the-century cleric. When marriages don't work these days, you don't suffer remorse, you do something about it; you don't just stay together and nag each other into the grave like you and Father did. Our marriages weren't working, so we moved out of them, for the benefit of all.'

Leonie laughed and coughed and laughed again. 'Damn this cough, it'll be the death of me. Your generation is such a naive lot. Are you really any better off, plunging yourselves and everyone else into pain and confusion in search of satisfaction? You spend your lives trying to escape suffering and only succeed in coming up against it somewhere else.'

'You are sounding untypically old world.' Harriet was embarrassed by Leonie's unexpected dissertation. They never spoke of anything that actually mattered; one did not expose one's feelings: just stated facts and commented on the behaviour of others. But this could not go unanswered. 'Personally,' she said, 'I consider it a sin to sit back and let life go crawling over you. One has to grab at things as they crop up and make the best possible use of them. No-one has the right to waste their lives in non-achievement.'

Leonie collapsed into a fit of coughing again. 'I'm much too ill to argue,' she gasped, 'but it does depend on what you grab. Are you sure you've grabbed the right thing in Alan?'

'As sure as anyone can be – but if it doesn't work, then we'll both have to look elsewhere. If he can pull himself together and get back to what he is really capable of, then there should be no stopping us – we're a fantastic team: he's the creator and I'm the producer. It's an exciting combination. We neither of us could achieve our potential before because we hadn't got the right partners.'

'From what you say,' Leonie looked at her daughter rather sadly, 'it doesn't look as though either of you can achieve much on your own.'

'Not true,' Harriet felt irritation and a slight waver of uncertainty. 'Not as far as I'm concerned, anyway. I'm pretty competent in my own right, though I say it myself. If I wasn't teamed with Alan, then I could go back to doing the sort of thing I was doing before. Or start something new. I've got quite a yen to plunge into politics rather than busy myself with local council matters. I might get myself into Parliament if I tried hard enough.' She contemplated the idea with interest. It was the first time she had thought of it.

She felt much refreshed by the discussion, and squeezed Leonie's hand appreciatively. 'You give me fresh heart,' she said. 'I was really a bit depressed before I came. Alan is so gloomy at the moment that I thought I'd give him a bit of breathing space.'

'I shouldn't give him too much; he might run home to mother. Have you, by any chance, bitten off more than you can chew with this Alan escapade?'

Harriet smiled: 'I rather think he's done the biting. As I said, we're capable of great things together; it's up to him to come up to scratch, don't you think?'

'I suppose it is,' Leonie held on to her daughter's hand, 'with a little help from his friends.'

But Alan found that he really had no friends at all and, when Harriet informed him that she was going home to mother, he understood it in the old-fashioned final sense. Life on his own was unbearable; life without Harriet was unliveable. The only thing he could consider doing in the circumstances was to take his fairly new and very smart Porsche out on to the M25, and to run it, at a hundred and ten miles an hour, into the central reservation. No-one else was killed in the accident.

33

'I told you,' said Ben, when the first wail of grief from the mustered family had ebbed to muffled sobbing from Daisy and Louise and the shocked stillness of Hamish, Max and Emma.

Laura turned to look at Ben, with her arms round as many of her children as she could enclose. The object of all her death and destruction wishes such a few months ago had now fulfilled those desires, and she was devastated, convinced that it was somehow all her fault. There was no way she could escape responsibility for the tragedy: she must have been so inadequate that he had escaped from her into Harriet's grasp. If only she had tried a bit harder, made more effort to know what sort of a life he had needed. If only she had had the wit to realize that he was suicidal; fancy not knowing that, after living with him all those years. She should have foreseen; she could have prevented it. Because of course it *was* suicide. It was being called an accident, but she knew better, didn't she?

'What did you tell them Ben?'

Ben jumped, because he somehow had not expected to penetrate their grief with his voice. He had really been pointing out the fact to himself, rather than to them. Laura sounded as though she was accusing him of having caused Alan's death. A wave of fear swept through him as he wondered whether his previous warnings had actually been prophecies; had he brought about a curse on everyone by just uttering warnings? That sort of thing did happen in stories; even in the Bible it happened.

'I just said that things like this don't usually have happy endings.'

'Things like what?'

He shrivelled up in an agony of discomfort and guilt. What if he had caused it all? 'Like . . . like families going through divorces and things. I mean people – people often say it's for the best, but I don't think it is, and I just said so the other day, that's all. I said I thought something bad would happen if we went on pretending everyone was happy and cheerful and that we could all be pleased with the way things turned out. And now something bad has happened, but I didn't mean . . . I didn't know . . .' He started crying noisily. 'It's not my fault,' he said, 'really it isn't.'

'Of *course* it isn't your fault, Ben.' Laura let go of her own children and hugged Ben to her. 'It's nobody's fault. It's just something that has happened and you are absolutely right to say that we shouldn't try to pretend bad things don't happen, because they do however hard we try to avoid them. We just have to try to deal with them in our own way, that's all.'

Ben thought suddenly – with fresh horror – supposing it had been Pa. Pa on his motor bike, flying over the handle bars and landing in the road, all mangled and bleeding. His throat constricted, and he turned to the weeping Daisy and put his arms round her. 'It's nobody's fault,' he repeated in her ear, but he kept thinking over and over to himself: they should have dealt with it better than they did, grown ups are supposed to know how to deal with things. How could they have got it so wrong?

The police phoned Leonie's house from Harriet's flat, where they had gone with Alan's keys and wallet. Harriet answered and, after determining she was who she was, they explained what had happened, quite nicely and kindly, and asked if she could return home as soon as possible.

It was the very first time Harriet had ever been dealt a blow of this magnitude, and she found that her mind became totally blank for what seemed far longer than a few seconds. The first thought that thudded back along with a deafeningly noisy heartbeat was that it could not possibly be true; out of the question. Why should he have got involved in a car accident when she had left him crying at a table much too drunk to walk straight, let alone get into a car and drive?

'No,' she said loudly, then 'NO!' and a great red rage engulfed her. 'Alan,' she said, looking round at her mother from the desk where she had answered the phone, 'Alan's dead. There must be some mistake.'

There was a second or two of silent shock before Leonie was able to say anything at all. 'Dear God,' she said at last, full of deep concern for her daughter. 'What an appalling tragedy. But not entirely surprising.'

'But I don't believe it,' Harriet said. 'What do you mean, not entirely surprising? It can't possibly be true. He was there the day before yesterday, sitting at the table. He just sat there all day long, not doing anything. There was no reason for him to go out in the car. He wouldn't have just gone out in the car like that; there was no reason for him to go out in the car.'

Leonie was downstairs in her padded satin dressing gown, sitting by the fireplace with a blanket over her knees. She put the blanket aside, guided Harriet to the chair, and poured out a brandy from the drinks table. 'Did he ever mention suicide?' she asked, handing the drink to Harriet.

'Suicide? No, of course he didn't. *Suicide?* Alan would never have killed himself, that's ridiculous. Jewish people don't commit suicide – he told me that

275

once. It was an accident, they said. He must have been drunk.'

She paused, staring at the brandy and wondering why she had a glass in her hand. She had a sudden memory of racing through the Rome streets, missing death by inches from hurtling cars, in the rush to get back to blissful bed, and she dropped the glass on to the floor and broke out into a tempest of weeping as she realized that the new beginning to her life had now closed for ever. She was back where she started.

'What a selfish bastard,' she said. 'How could he do such a thing?'

Laura telephoned Tom at the now almost completely empty house where he had spent the night in his sleeping bag after making a final search among the sad remains of emptiness and finding many small lost treasures that had fallen behind furniture and into the backs of cupboards: the beloved Parker pen he had mislaid six years ago; the first edition Penguin, *Ariel*, by Maurois; the tie Emma had knitted for him at primary school; children's drawings that had been pinned to his wall.

The telephone blasted such a harsh shrillness through all the echoes that Tom practically leaped off the floor with shock.

'Tom dear – ghastly tragedy . . .'

Tom brought his mind back, and attempted to organize it into talking to Laura about a tragedy. His body seemed to shrink into some small shrivelled thing, full of sharp needles of anxiety. What further distress lay in store?

There was a sharp intake of breath at the other end of the phone. 'It's Alan . . . Alan's been killed . . . in a crash. He could have done it on purpose.' She was crying into the phone.

'*Alan – dead?*'

The jolt of this news shattered the silence of the near-empty house with an almost physical force. Tom was left gasping and trembling. *All those kids*. What had that bloody woman set in motion? But as quick as the thought came its addenda – but if I hadn't . . . And then again – if only I had . . .

'Oh Laura, darling – what a bloody mess.'

'I don't know what to do, Tom,' Laura wailed. 'I mean, he's still my husband; the police are coming to question *me*. What do *I* know about it? Perhaps it was an accident, but I can't help feeling . . . well you know Alan . . . such a sense of duty. Oh God – I don't know what to think. I don't know what to do . . . and his parents . . . all the special customs . . . and the funeral – who arranges the funeral? Do I? Does Harriet? What happens?'

Tom heard the hysteria building up, and cold, down-to-earth calm immediately surged into his own momentarily vacuumed mind. She was expecting him to arrange the funeral, wasn't she? He was going to be expected to wade right back into the middle of this wretched mess in an attempt to restore order. Who did they think he was? God or something?

He owed it to Laura; he owed it to Emma and Ben. He owed it above all to Alan, who had been snatched, used and hounded to death by Harriet; and Harriet had originally been his responsibility. Thus Alan's death became his responsibility as well. He owed all round, it seemed.

'Give me time, Laura. I have to take it in. I will ring you back. Can't talk now.'

There was a shocked silence that hung heavily over the telephone: a non-sound that gave Tom the impression he had actually been cut off; made him feel the necessity of saying Are you still there? which he resisted doing. It was her turn to speak. It seemed a long time until she did.

'But Tom,' she said, 'I don't know what to do. Will you phone me soon? Couldn't you come over?'

'Yes, yes I will; of course. Are Emma and Ben being helpful?'

But why should they be expected to be helpful? It wasn't their fault; it was nothing to do with them, and they would need his support as well, surrounded, as they were, by a bereaved family. 'I'll come over soon,' he said and put the phone down. Shouldn't have done that; much too abrupt; didn't even say goodbye or sorry or I love you or any of the things one should say when someone dies.

He sat on, staring at the telephone and trying to keep his mind on this new ghastly situation. But it was impossible; try as he might, his thoughts kept sliding away from the present into those exquisite moments of escape he had shared with Rajini. How horribly unfeeling that he should only be able to dwell on his own pleasure at such a time.

He had made a point of not contacting Rajini since the day he had helped her to escape to friends in Shepherd's Bush; had deliberately and shamefully avoided her because he had been afraid of the consequences. No matter what the special gifts different age groups could give to each other, you weren't supposed to run off with someone who was 'young enough to be your daughter'. What a load of rubbish.

He had just worked himself up into a satisfactory rage which blocked out the idea of Alan smashing himself up in his car, when the telephone rang again:

'YES?' He shouted his anger down the line.

It was Emma.

'Pa? Why are you shouting? Where have you been? I've been trying to get you for ages. Have you heard?

Isn't it frightful? We don't really know what's happened yet, they just said it was an accident on the M25.' She started to cry. It was a long time since Tom had heard Emma cry. 'Oh Pa, it's awful to be in the middle of so much sadness. I keep thinking, suppose it had been you. I didn't like Alan and Ma being together – I don't really know why I didn't because Alan was all right. I liked him when he was with Laura; I just can't believe he's dead. And what do you say to them all? What do you do? I couldn't stand it, so I ran out on them and I'm staying with a friend. Laura knows. But couldn't you come home? I mean can't you come back to Laura's and be with us all? It was fine when you were there too – at least it was better, even if it wasn't exactly *home*, it was better.'

Tom's anger softened because he felt sorry for Emma. Was it altogether fair to imagine that she wasn't really feeling the deep and real things of life? Just because she gave the impression of being like a child still, was that any reason to suppose she felt less deeply?

'I'll see what I can do,' he said, and went on sitting in the desolate house because all the enthusiasm and the pleasure he had felt in knowing how to help people through their difficulties had faded suddenly away. He was like a spent balloon, sitting there, cold, sad and lifeless.

The phone rang again, shrilling through the house. It was Rajini.

'Tom, you bum, what happened to you? Why haven't you rung? You knew I couldn't ring Laura's and yet you never phoned me. I've been trying this number for days but never got you.' Her voice rose several semi-tones and quivered dangerously.

Should he tell her that he might lose control if she started to cry? Should he warn her that his present hold over himself was tenuous, to say the least? That he might well explode, and become some frenzied, violent fireball? All these paranoid changes of mood frightened him; how could he deal with them while presenting the calm, strong front that was expected of him?

'Alan has been killed,' he said, realizing that attack was his only defence at this particular moment. The ploy was successful.

'WHAT?'

The quaver had vanished; they were now on equal grounds: no tears, no melting lamentation; no weeping and wailing; just complete shock.

'How? Why? Did she go berserk again and do him in?'

Now it was his turn to be jerked out of the melancholy in which he was wallowing. Here was an outside view of the situation: someone who looked on the whole thing as a story you might read in the papers. *Did she go berserk and do him in?* What a deplorable way to describe a tragedy concerning people you love. But to Rajini they were just ordinary people, no reason for her to feel involved or responsible.

'Car crash,' he said.

'Oh God, how horrible.' She was silent for a moment, then she said: 'Can I talk to you about something else? Or are you too caught up in their problems to listen to mine? Not that mine are problems at all, but this dismal news has probably spoilt the atmosphere for talking about us.'

'As it happens,' he said, 'I've been having very passionate thoughts about you this morning.'

'You have? Then why didn't you phone me? Why didn't you come and see me? You didn't even ring to find out how I was getting on or anything. I've rung the parents by the way.'

'Well, thank God for that, I was expecting to be arrested any minute. What was the outcome?'

'They're seething, of course; threatened all sorts of things and they won't give me any money because they think I won't be able to exist without it. But they don't know this friend I'm staying with so they'll never find me . . .'

So she's now my responsibility, Tom thought. He realized Rajini was continuing to talk:

'. . . and Tom, I've found something, I've found something for us; it's perfect; can you come over and see it now? Because I do need some more money as well, I can borrow a bit from my friend, but I shall need some more . . .'

Tom had a vision of life with Rajini in a furnished flat in Shepherd's Bush and it struck him as comic relief in the midst of tragedy.

'Are you still there?' The silence had been too long. 'Why don't you answer?'

Tom's thoughts jumbled themselves together with a jolt. 'I'll bring you some money,' he said, 'as soon as I can sort things out a little. I have to make some arrangements. I can't come immediately.'

Rajini made an explosively impatient sound. 'I knew it. All these wretched people demanding things of you, and you'll respond the same as you always do and not have any time to satisfy any of them properly. You may be a saint, but you're a *very* ineffectual one.' And she slammed the phone down.

Good title for a play, Tom thought: The Ineffectual Saint. And he replaced the phone slowly and carefully, daring it to ring again before he had recovered his composure.

It did.

'Tom Turtle? Claude Columbo here.'

Columbo thought the rather prolonged silence was

probably due to the usual time-lapse hesitation. 'Speaking from Montreal,' he added helpfully.

'Good God,' said Tom, trying to adjust his mind to what might have happened six or eight weeks ago. It was difficult to imagine that there was any time other than the present moment. He could think of nothing whatever to say to someone from the ordinary world out there, who knew nothing of the tragedies and disasters of the small Tom Turtle world in here.

'I've been talking to the powers that be,' Columbo continued, now slightly nonplussed by the lack of response, 'and they're interested.' He felt as though he was talking into silence. 'That is – if you still are?'

Tom returned to earth. 'Oh God – oh yes – absolutely. Of course—'

But Claude Columbo and the production happened centuries ago; everything had changed since then; that was the time of certainties and successes and euphoria. Now was the recession.

'I wondered,' Columbo went on, 'if you could come over to discuss possibilities with us over here. It might be useful to strike while the iron's hot, so the sooner the better. You could come and stay with me and we could probably persuade the faculty to pay your passage as a visiting lecturer. Rajini might like to come too perhaps.' He added that a little too diffidently, Tom thought. Was that the real reason behind the invitation?

But quite suddenly, and for no good reason that he could think of at the time, all hesitation and doubt were swept straight out of Tom's mind. 'Strangely enough,' he said, without giving the suggestion a moment's real consideration but feeling an oppressive weight lift itself from him, 'I have just been contemplating the idea of taking a holiday in Canada.' What was he saying? Nothing had been further from his thoughts. 'I could indeed be interested.'

'You could? Oh superb! You have my address? Let me know when you're coming and I'll meet you.'

Tom felt choked. 'I think it might be uncommonly soon,' he said. 'I believe standy-by tickets are not hard to come by. I'll phone you when I get there.' And he sat back to collapse, after a few stark moments, into a hysterical burst of laughter and tears which, though embarrassing, was a blessed relief.

34

Tom did not respond to any of the pleas or demands made to him over the telephone that evening. Instead, he took the phone plug out of the socket, went out and bought himself a bottle of whisky and proceeded to drink himself into insensibility. He knew that it was the only way to stop himself doing what he did not want to do, and with its help he would also be able to blot out life for a few hours.

Whether things would be more, or less, clear when he woke up was uncertain, but he knew, before he took the first drink, exactly what he wanted to do and half-way through the session he built up sufficient courage to make a list.

Money, he wrote; passport: tickets: change of clothes: driving licence. Then he wrote LETTERS, and underlined it. Under this heading went: the Dean: Laura: the parents: the students' group. A slight pause, then: Emma, and a much longer pause and then, written very small and very slowly – Ben. Underneath, he wrote: Telephone Rajini.

He left the list on the floor where he had been sitting,

and stared at it while he set about inducing uncon-
sciousness. It didn't take all that long, really, and was
probably helped by the exhausted condition he was in
before he started.

The hangover was not as bad as it should have been,
but it was bad enough to wipe out most other thought.
The immediate task was to get oneself into a sufficiently
lucid condition to get round to doing everything on the
list. Not the letters, of course, they would be written on
the plane and posted on landing.

Passport – yes; tickets – should be no problem:
change of clothes – pick up some pants and socks at
Heathrow: driving licence – yes: so what else? He
stumbled into the bathroom to wash and shave and
take Alka-Seltzer. Teeth, hair, cleanish shirt, money;
all correct – now, phone Rajini. He felt a distinct chill
at the idea of connecting himself up with the outside
world again, but started to search through his pockets
for the telephone number which he had written down
somewhere. Where, for God's sake? He spent a good
five minutes looking, without success. Swearing softly,
he decided he would have to call in on the way,
couldn't delay any longer; just get there on the bike.

He hoped against hope he might be able to take the
bike with him, otherwise long-park it and perhaps
arrange to sell it later. Get to the airport, that was the
most important, before anything or anyone stopped
him. No thinking, no looking back, just get to the
airport for God's sake. He did up the straps on his
rucksack and put on the old leather jacket and boots:
leave them in left luggage at Heathrow. Get to the
airport.

In the hall he paused. Last time? He felt quite badly
sick but thought he could contain it and resolutely
opened the front door.

Ben was sitting on the step with a bag full of belongings beside him; he was leaning against the door, and fell backwards into the hall as it opened.

'I thought you weren't in,' he said. 'I rang the bell but you didn't come, so I thought you weren't there and I didn't know what to do.'

He got up and put his arms round Tom. 'I can't stay there any more,' he said. 'It's all so horribly sad, and they think it's Ma's fault and so they hate us. It wasn't her fault was it?'

'No, of course it wasn't.' They sat down on the step together. 'It's nobody's fault. I didn't hear the bell; it's probably out of order.'

There was a very long silence between them, and then Ben said: 'I was hoping I could stay with you. Even if you haven't found anywhere to stay yet, we could use the tent and set it up in the garden here for the time being. I've got my scout camping stuff still.'

Tom found that answers did not spring to mind easily. 'I was going away for a bit,' he said.

Another long silence, broken finally by Ben.

'Can I come?'

'I was going for rather a long time.'

Ben turned to look at him. 'A long time? How long? Were you running away from us?'

'For a bit I was; I thought perhaps people's lives would be less complicated if I was out of the way for a time.'

'Mine wouldn't be, please let me come. Where are you going?'

'Canada.'

'You're *joking*! Oh go on, please let me come, I'd really like to go to Canada.'

'What about Hamlet?'

'Well, I asked Daisy if she would look after Hamlet for me if I went and stayed with you because she really

285

loves him and looks after him properly so I wouldn't mind so much.' Tom noticed that he still minded considerably.

'We could run away together,' Ben went on, 'that would be brilliant – and we could send them a post card when we got there.'

'Does Laura know where you are?'

'I told Daisy to tell her I'd gone to see you. She's been trying to telephone you but she couldn't get through, so I thought I'd just come.' He paused a moment and then added, 'She might come over in the car to find you; she said something about doing that.'

They looked at each other and smiled.

'So immediate flight is indicated,' said Tom. 'Mind you, as far as you're concerned, it's just a short break, a week's holiday while we sort out our future.'

'But if we *like* it there . . .' Ben glanced sideways to watch his reaction, 'we might want to stay, mightn't we?'

Tom laughed out loud. 'Future plans will be discussed in the future. You're lucky I kept you on my passport, otherwise we might have ended up on the Isle of Wight.'

Ben jumped up and flung himself at Tom. 'Oh *mega*,' he said. 'Come on then, let's go, let's go now before they catch us. Oh excellent, what a brill adventure.'

So they roared away together on the bike and, in his mind, Tom added Rajini's name to the list of letters to be written on the plane.

THE END

Playing For Real
by Patricia Angadi

'A new book from novelist Patricia Angadi is always a delicious surprise. Each one is entirely different from the last: you never know quite what to expect . . . but you do know it will be good. *Playing For Real* is quite delightful . . . an imaginative story superbly told'
Sue Dobson, *Woman and Home*

There were two of them, both lonely and withdrawn misfits. Four-year-old Joanne had been dumped on her Cornish grandparents by an irresponsible and unmarried mother who promptly vanished back into the London Blitz. Peter Petherick, son of the Big House at Zennor, had grown up adored by two eccentric parents, and hated by five elder sisters.

They both had problems – Joanne wanted to rid herself of her grandmother who was a witch, and Peter wanted to run away from school. And on the wild and isolated Cornish headland they formed a disjointed friendship, made more weird and uneasy by the private worlds in which they both lived.

The friendship lasted, survived Joanne's loneliness and Peter's battle against his domineering and overwhelmingly jolly sisters. When the time came for them to assess the past – for Joanne to track down her mother, for Peter to take charge of his inheritance, their tenuous childhood bond was just strong enough to hold them together.

0 552 99464 2

BLACK SWAN

A SELECTION OF FINE WRITING FROM BLACK SWAN

THE PRICES SHOWN BELOW WERE CORRECT AT THE TIME OF GOING TO PRESS. HOWEVER TRANSWORLD PUBLISHERS RESERVE THE RIGHT TO SHOW NEW RETAIL PRICES ON COVERS WHICH MAY DIFFER FROM THOSE PREVIOUSLY ADVERTISED IN THE TEXT OR ELSEWHERE.

All Black Swan Books are available at your bookshop or newsagent, or can be ordered from the following address:

Corgi/Bantam Books,
Cash Sales Department
P.O. Box 11, Falmouth, Cornwall TR10 9EN

UK and B.F.P.O. customers please send a cheque or postal order (no currency) and allow £1.00 for postage and packing for the first book plus 50p for the second book and 30p for each additional book to a maximum charge of £3.00 (7 books plus).

Overseas customers, including Eire, please allow £2.00 for postage and packing for the first book plus £1.00 for the second book and 50p for each subsequent title ordered.

NAME (Block Letters) ....

ADDRESS ....

....